A Spirited Refusal

"Dear God, Gillian," Cord whispered. "I don't know what is happening to me. I've never felt this way about anyone. . . . I've spoken many pretty words to many pretty women, but you are unique—and so are my feelings for you."

All the while he spoke, his hands caressed her hair, her cheeks, the tender nape of her neck until she thought she would simply dissolve in a puddle of mindless desire.

"Gillian, I have never said this before—but I think I'm fall—"

"Falling under my spell?" Gillian asked brightly. "Goodness. For a man of your charm and experience, you are being dismally trite."

Cord stepped back as though she had struck him.

"I am, of course, flattered by the attention, but I fear that if I do not take care, I shall become another in a long line of conquests. I shall therefore bid you good night, sir."

With these words, still spoken in that light, brittle voice, she whirled from him and darted into the house. Cord was left staring at the closed door, his eyes dark pools against the whiteness of his face.

Praise for Anne Barbour's
A Man of Affairs

"Sparkling dialogue and great characterizations make this Regency stand out."—*Rendezvous*

Coming next month

SAVED BY SCANDAL
by Barbara Metzger
"One of the genre's wittiest pens."–*Romantic Times*
Abandoned at the altar, Lord Galen Woodbridge decides to stir up a scandal–by wedding the London songstress Margot Montclaire. But in saving his pride, he never planned on losing his heart....
0-451-20038-1/$4.99

MISS TIBBLES INVESTIGATES
by April Kihlstrom
Pamela Kendall is in love with her childhood friend Julian, who pines for an altogether different girl. But as luck would have it, her mother's former governess, Miss Tibbles, is visiting–and she knows the best way to avert a disaster of the heart....
0-451-20040-3/$4.99

CASSANDRA'S DECEPTION
by Gayle Buck
While pretending to be her twin sister, Cassandra Weatherstone finds passion in the arms of a refined young suitor. But being true to her heart means being exposed as an imposter. And is any love strong enough to survive such a scandal?
0-451-20037-3/$4.99

Buried Secrets

———◈———

Anne Barbour

A SIGNET BOOK

SIGNET
Published by New American Library, a division of
Penguin Putnam Inc., 375 Hudson Street,
New York, New York 10014, U.S.A.
Penguin Books Ltd, 27 Wrights Lane,
London W8 5TZ, England
Penguin Books Australia Ltd, Ringwood,
Victoria, Australia
Penguin Books Canada Ltd, 10 Alcorn Avenue,
Toronto, Ontario, Canada M4V 3B2
Penguin Books (N.Z.) Ltd, 182–190 Wairau Road,
Auckland 10, New Zealand

Penguin Books Ltd, Registered Offices:
Harmondsworth, Middlesex, England

First published by Signet, an imprint of New American Library,
a division of Penguin Putnam Inc.

First Printing, May 2000
10   9   8   7   6   5   4   3   2   1

REGISTERED TRADEMARK—MARCA REGISTRADA

Printed in the United States of America

PUBLISHER'S NOTE
This is a work of fiction. Names, characters, places, and incidents either are
the product of the author's imagination or are used fictitiously, and any resem-
blance to actual persons, living or dead, business establishments, events, or
locales is entirely coincidental.

To Mary Jo Putney, whom I am proud to call friend. She has served as mentor and general booster to countless aspiring authors, myself very much included, and she is a writer of awesome talent.

ACKNOWLEDGMENTS

I wish to thank Aude Fitzimmons, Assistant Curator of the Pepys Library, Magdalene College, Cambridge University. Her kindness on my visit there was much appreciated, as was her invaluable assistance in my pursuit of the history of Samuel Pepys and his fascinating diary.

Chapter One

"Gone!" Lady Binsted bristled, her fine eyes afire. "What do you mean, gone?"

"I meant just what I said, Elizabeth." George, the Marquess of Binsted, ran plump fingers around his collar and retreated to a corner near the fireplace. "Gone. Disappeared. The fellow has evaporated, apparently, into thin air."

The couple stood in the drawing room of Binsted House, which nestled sedately in a row of fashionable town houses in Mayfair's Mount Street. The chamber appeared even more elegant than usual. Great bouquets of hothouse flowers stood in vases about the room and each lustre on every chandelier had been washed and polished to diamondlike radiance.

"But the dinner party is only two hours away." Lady Binsted all but wailed. "Our guests will be arriving soon. The Rantrays will be here any moment! Where *is* he?"

If her husband harbored any thoughts on the subject, he kept them to himself, merely shrugging his shoulders. He turned swiftly when a tap on the door heralded the entrance of Blevins, the butler, with the intelligence that Mr. Wilfred Culver had just arrived at the house.

"Well, show him up," snapped Lady Binsted. "Perhaps he can tell us something."

"Doubt it," interposed Lord Binsted. "You know how Wilf and Cord feel about each other."

"I know," her ladyship agreed with a sigh. "One would never know they were brothers." A few moments later, the door opened again to admit a tall, slender gentleman in his late twenties. Every line of his person declared him the dandy in full flower. His mouse-colored hair was painstakingly arranged in the Brutus style af-

fected by the Prince Regent. His coat of lavender super-
fine was carefully fashioned to make the most of a rather
meager chest and narrow shoulders. Pale yellow inex-
pressibles clung lovingly to carefully padded calves, and
his tasseled Hessians were polished to blinding perfection.

"Gone?" he declared blankly in response to Lady
Binsted's dramatic declaration. "What do you mean
gone?"

"I should think my meaning is quite clear," Lady
Binsted replied impatiently. "Cordray knows very well
that the party is tonight. I spoke to him about it just
yesterday. You remember, do you not, Binsted? We
made a special trip to Curzon Street to speak to him
about it."

"Mm, yes." The marquess rubbed his nose dubiously.
"And do you remember, m'dear? He told you right
then—the same as he did last week—that he had no
intention of coming tonight—or of asking—"

"Tchah!" In anyone less exquisitely refined, the expletive might have been called a snort. "He inevitably re-
fuses the slightest request on my part, but I cannot
believe he would behave so shabbily on such an important occasion. As I recall, last week he said he would
think about it."

"Mpf. As if that meant anything. If you ask me, he
was in a strange mood."

"Cordray is always in a mood. Lord, how could my
brother and dear Calista have produced such an
aberration?"

"Come, now, Bessie," said the marquess, absently using
an appellation that invariably set his wife's teeth on
edge. "Cord ain't a bad fellow. He just has an aversion
to marriage."

"Aversion!" Her ladyship sighed. "I just don't know
what is the matter with the boy. Ever since he inherited
the title, he has proved to be a lazy degenerate with no
regard for his family obligations. Do you know how
many years it took to bring him up to scratch—to actually promise to propose to Corisande? Well, of course,
you do."

Lord Binsted acknowledged this last with a grimace.

Mr. Culver, examining a vase of pink chrysanthemums through his quizzing glass, murmured absently, "Don't know why you went to all the bother, Aunt. Corisande and Cord are completely unsuited to each other."

Lady Binsted gaped at her nephew. "Well, of all the unmitigated nonsense. Their union has been planned since they were in infancy."

Mr. Culver merely grunted.

"And now," continued Lady Binsted, "when the stage is set, so to speak, he is nowhere to be found. I suppose he is in one of those unspeakable hells he patronizes and will stroll into the room an hour after everyone is seated at table without so much as—" She halted abruptly, an expression of horror on her patrician features. "Dear heaven! You don't suppose he's bolted!"

Lord Binsted cleared his throat noisily. "Well, now, m'dear, it did occur to me that he was balking at the bit when we saw him yesterday. You know, I've told you more than once, you can't force a man, especially one like Cordray, into matrimony when he don't want to cooperate. However, I expect you're right," he concluded placatingly. "He simply found himself engaged in, er, other pursuits, and will show up . . . if not on time, at least to do the pretty."

A discreet knock was followed by another appearance by Blevins, this time carrying a folded note on a small silver salver. He glided across the floor, coming to a halt before Lady Binsted. He proffered the salver.

"This was just delivered, my lady. It was brought by one of Lord Cordray's footmen." The marchioness snatched the missive and perused it, before crumpling it in her hand with an audible gasp.

"He *is* gone!" she shrieked, handing the note to her husband. "Binsted, he *has* bolted! I simply do not believe it!" She tottered to a cherry-striped satin wing chair and dropped into it, limp and red-faced.

" 'My dear Aunt,' " read the marquess aloud, "I find it necessary to leave Town for a few days on business. I hope my departure will not cause you any inconvenience, and I hope your dinner party will be a success.' "

"I cannot believe it. The wretch *knew* we were expecting him. He *knew* how important his presence was tonight."

"By God, he ought to be horsewhipped!"

At the sound of the angry voice, Lord and Lady Binsted whirled to stare at Wilfred. The young man reddened, shuffling his feet against the carpet.

"I just meant . . . well, it is extremely uncivil of him to serve Corrie such a turn. She has her heart set on marrying Cord, after all."

"Ah, well, m'dear." Lord Binsted waved an expansive hand. "We must carry on. P'raps he'll turn up after all. You never know with Cord. He changes his mind as often as his cravat, y'know."

As time plodded inexorably forward, however, the marquess's words echoed hollowly in his wife's ears. The guests arrived, dinner was served, eaten and the covers removed, all without the desired arrival of the man with a duty to perform that evening.

At about the time when the Marchioness of Binsted was making yet another apology, by now bordering on the frantic, to her guests, a solitary rider made his way over the rolling landscape of East Anglia. The skies were clear and starry, and he was grateful that the moon shone full as well.

Why in God's name, wondered Christopher Culver, the Earl of Cordray, had he chosen to make his journey in the dead of night on horseback? A sensible man would have embarked in broad daylight, in his eminently serviceable—to say nothing of dashing—curricle, complete with valet and tiger. The answer, of course, was obvious, he reflected with a grimace. He was in full flight, haring off from London in the dead of night like a thief with the family silver in his pockets. Cord sighed. And it was all because he simply could not face the prospect of marriage, particularly not marriage to the Honorable Corisande Brant.

"Corisande," he muttered. Was his aversion to the wedded state in general, or Corisande in particular? He knew the answer to that one, too. It was Corisande, oldest daughter of the Viscount Rantray. A perfectly decent female, he supposed, but she'd been a tedious little girl, and now possessed the capability of boring him to paralysis after five minutes in her company. She was intelligent enough, for a woman, but her thoughts rarely strayed beyond her wardrobe, her relatives, the latest *on dits*—and, of course, the thinly veiled references to her plans for him after they were wed.

For their future union had been considered a confirmed fact. Since their estates marched together, the two had been constant companions all during their formative years. He liked the chit well enough, he supposed, but . . . well, actually, no, he didn't. She was a tad too grasping, a bit too set up in her own estimation, and a great deal too smug in her expectations, which centered on her future position as the Countess of Cordray.

This evening was to have been the culmination of their lifelong understanding. Corisande and her parents had been invited to a dinner party at his aunt's house. Corisande's older brother and younger sister, Lionel and Hyacinth respectively, were also to have been on board. After dinner, despite Cord's best efforts over the past several years to avert disaster, he was scheduled to ask formally for Corisande's hand.

He'd told his Aunt Binsted that he had no intention of proposing to Corisande, indeed, that he would not put in an appearance at the dinner party. As usual, of course, she hadn't believed him—and as usual, he nearly capitulated. This time, however, the noose was too visibly in place above him, and in the end, he just couldn't do it.

He'd awakened this morning with a bit of a head. All right, to be honest, after a night at the Beefsteak Club and the revels that had followed, the little men with pickaxes inside his skull were in full form, threatening to burst through his eyeballs. He'd forgone breakfast, electing instead to take himself off for a meditative ride in the park. The coming festivities at his aunt's home and their unpleasant results had weighed heavily on him, and on his return home he'd ordered Hopkins, his man, to pack a portmanteau and sent him off. A few hours later, knowing his aunt would soon be on site to chivy him further into attending the proposed dinner party, he dashed off a note to her. He knew this was an act of sniveling cowardice, but he'd then crept stealthily from Cordray House. Now, here he was, well on his way to sanctuary.

Sanctuary, in this case, was a pleasant estate outside the village of Great Shelford, which, in turn, was only a few miles from Cambridge. The estate, Wildehaven, had been a bequest from a fond uncle several years ago. Cord had visited the place upon being notified of the gift, but had never returned, content to leave it in the hands of its competent manager. The Earl of Cordray was an urban creature and had never experienced the slightest desire to "let the countryside and the gliding valley streams content him."

Until now, that is.

When he had begun searching for a bolt-hole, an image of Wildehaven had appeared in his mind like a line thrown to a drowning man. All the time he'd been aware that he was going completely beyond the pale, that Corisande would never forgive him and that her father would no doubt come after him with a horsewhip. Indeed, Rantray would no doubt be obliged to stand in line behind his Aunt Binsted. But, dear God, he had to do something before he made the betrothal official by a formal proposal. When the engagement was announced, papers sighed, and settlements arranged, it would be too late. He would be trapped forever in a union he knew to be doomed at the start.

He could not avoid the unpleasant consideration that his flight was an exercise in futility. He must return to London sometime, and when he did, Corisande would still be waiting for him to appear on bended knee. His family would still be at his back, wedding gifts in hand. All he was doing, he reflected gloomily as he picked his way along the rocky path that led to Wildehaven's formal parkland, was postponing the inevitable. All he would have accomplished was to make a great many people furious with him. Not that this bothered him a great deal. He was accustomed to carrying on his life at his own pace and pleasure, and had been the object of his family's schemes on many previous occasions. This was different. He knew very well that his position behooved him to marry. He must preserve the line. This fact had been drilled into him with great thoroughness by his father—and grandfather before him. God forbid the title should go to Wilfie was the general consensus among his relatives, and Cord could not but agree. Wilf was a nice chap, but had the judgment of an infant. He had some years ago formed a connection with Lord Brinhaven, a close associate of the Regent, and had drifted into the Regent's set. Wilf had apparently somehow made himself indispensable to the Regent. He had told Cord once of tactfully retrieving a packet of indiscreet letters for the Prince. However, keeping up with this rackety conglomeration of elderly roués was rapidly bringing him to *point non plus.*

A flood of guilt washed over Cord. The thing was, that through all this, he had conceded long ago, in his own mind, that he would marry Corisande. Not just because she was the choice of his family, but he had come to accept the notion that if he must marry, he might as well marry Corisande. He knew her well, and would no doubt become accustomed to her presence in his life. She had been bred to fill just this position, and she would be a credit to his house. She knew the mores that guided life in the *ton* and would make no attempt to interfere in the pleasurable tenor of his life. She would make no unpleasant scenes over his *cher amées,* nor, as long as his expenses did not impinge on her own comfort, would she object to his gambling losses—or the time spent away from home in these amiable pursuits. There was certainly no other female to whom he'd ever had the slightest inclination to become leg-shackled. Lord knew he wasn't stupid enough to look for love. Love was for fools and poets and the writers of those god-awful novels. But, was it too much to ask that the woman with whom he must spend the rest of his life, would be someone whose company he could enjoy?

Cord sighed and turned his reflections to his present predicament. On the bright side, it would be some weeks before the madding crowd would track him down. The only person to whom he had confided his plan was his man of affairs, Geoffrey Tomlinson, and good old Geoff could be relied upon to keep his mouth shut. Perhaps in that space of time, mused Cord hopefully, he could

come up with something—perhaps even a plain statement to Corisande that they simply would not suit. He
should have said this long ago, of course, instead of putting it off while Corisande's expectations swelled to unig-
norable proportions. If he had only—

His dubious reflections were interrupted by a flash of
movement caught from the corner of his eye. He observed a horse and rider emerge from a small spinney
crowning a nearby hill. Silently, they slid through the
shadows into the moonlight before disappearing into a
winding dale. The horseman was slender, seeming too
small for his mount, a huge, long-tailed gray. What the
devil . . . ? thought Cord bemusedly. He was sure he
was now on Wildehaven property. What was this fellow
doing, crossing it in the middle of the night? A tres-
passer? A thief? Cord hastened after the figure, bringing
both the rider and the Wildehaven manor house into
sight at the same time as he rounded the curve of the
hill. To his surprise, the rider swung away from the
house, taking a path that led far to the right and over
another knoll. Anxious to remain unseen, Cord followed
more slowly this time, with the result that when he
crested the rise, the rider was nowhere to be seen.

Pursuit, of course, was impossible. Even if he were to
catch sight of the stranger again, he would make his
presence known in doing so. Thoughtfully, Cord retraced
his path. He had almost come into view of the manor
house when he spotted something glittering on the
ground ahead of him. Dismounting, he scooped up the
small object.

To his surprise, it appeared to be an ornamental comb,
such as a woman would use to catch up her hair. The
sparkle had been a shaft of moonlight reflecting from
one of the tiny gems that adorned it. On closer inspec-
tion, it was apparent that the comb had not lain long in
its present position. It was smooth and bore no traces
of dirt. In fact, Cord could swear a trace of warmth from
its wearer lingered in his fingers.

Could it belong to the rider who had passed by here
just a few moments ago? The rider was a woman? Well,
well, he mused, his little mystery was becoming more
fascinating by the minute. He would certainly lose no

time in ascertaining the identity of the female who rode the contours of his estate in such an unseemly fashion.

Clambering atop his mount once more, he came soon to the yew alley that led to the manor's great front door. He wielded the knocker absently, and the door swung open at once to reveal two figures, apparently awaiting him in some dudgeon.

"Hopkins!" exclaimed Cord. "When did you assume butler duties? At any rate, I'm glad you arrived in such a timely fashion. Hullo, Moresby," he said to the butler, who was engaged in wresting the door handle from his valet.

"Yes, sir," replied Hopkins, releasing the handle to usher Cord ceremoniously into the house. "I arrived several hours ago, and I have made everything ready for you to assume residence here. You will find your bed made up and a nice fire burning in your chambers."

"Actually, sir," Moresby said in a testy voice, "the staff has maintained the house in accordance with your direction since you became its owner. When we were apprised of your imminent arrival, it was necessary merely to remove the covers from the furniture. Mrs. Moresby, of course, has placed flowers in all the rooms and has prepared a small nuncheon for you—in the library, also with a nice fire burning. We had no need"— he paused to cast an austere glance in Hopkins's direction—"of further direction."

Cord smiled placatingly. "Thank you, Moresby, I knew you would manage everything." He turned to Hopkins with another, equally ingratiating grin. "And thank you, Hopkins. If you will return upstairs, I'll be up presently."

With a lofty bow, Hopkins turned and moved up the staircase, the picture of complacent dignity. Cord glanced around the manor's main hall. The house was, perhaps, not what he would have chosen for himself, had he decided to take up permanent residence in the country, for it was heavily baronial in style. The hall was hung with weighty tapestries and strewn with the requisite suits of armor and the occasional halberd on the walls. It was a pleasant abode, however, comfortable and spacious, and Cord found himself looking forward to a brief stay. The operative word, he supposed, was "brief." His thoughts returned to the inescapable knowledge that he was mad to have come. Still, he was resolved not to be caught in parson's mousetrap—at least, not yet—and particularly if Corisande Brant was to be his trap mate.

His reflections continued in this vein, even as he consumed the cold collation provided for him by Mrs. Moresby. The library was warm and comfortable, furnished with upholstered chairs so large one could take up housekeeping in them. Even so, the silence, to a dedicated city dweller, was oppressive. The only sounds to be heard were the clink of silver on china and the crackling of a brisk blaze in the hearth.

Cord sighed. He was not given to ruralizing. He agreed with Dr. Johnson's famous sentiment that he who tired of London was tired of life. He enjoyed the companionship of friends, the entertainment to be found in Town, even the endless, frivolous round of socializing that comprised life in the *ton*. On the other hand, he mused, a little rustication might do him good. He had discovered within him recently a certain disenchantment with his routine. Too many late nights, he supposed. Too much wine, women and song—though not necessarily in that order. He frowned. Perhaps it was wrong of him to leave the management of his affairs in the very competent hands of his agents and stewards, but he had done so for years. Why should he bother with such mundane affairs when there was a world of gratification to be explored? The frown deepened. When had it all begun to pall? he wondered—and what was he to do now to fill his time?

He wondered idly if there were neighbors in the area with whom he might strike up a convivial acquaintance. Surely, being so near to Cambridge, there must be more than a few choice spirits ripe for any spree with whom he could liven the tranquility of quiet country evenings.

This train of thought led him to his near-encounter earlier with the mysterious rider. He removed the comb from his pocket and subjected it to a meditative examination. The gems were faux, as he had expected, but he was more than ever convinced that the comb had been dropped recently.

"Tell me, Moresby," he inquired of the butler, who had just entered to remove his tray. "Who are our nearest neighbors?"

"That would be Squire Trent, my lord. His estate marches with yours in an easterly—or no, strictly speaking, your very nearest neighbor would be Sir Henry Folsome. He lives right on your property."

"Indeed?" asked Cord in some surprise.

"Yes, my lord. He and his sister and niece live in Rose Cottage, about three miles from here—not far from the river. Sir Henry," continued Moresby chattily, "is a fellow of Magdalene College. He and Sir Frederick were great friends, and upon Sir Henry's retirement, Sir Frederick offered the use of the cottage to him on a lifetime basis. In other words, he will be living there until both he and his sister pass on."

Cord's pulse quickened. "Indeed. I remember the agent—what's his name?—Jilbert, telling me about them. Yes, I agreed to let the commitment stand. But I don't remember a niece."

"Yes, my lord—or rather, no, my lord. Her name is Miss Gillian Tate, and she's the daughter of yet another sister, I believe. Mrs. Ferris—Mrs. Louisa Ferris, that is—Sir Henry's sister—kept house for her brother for years, but, the frailties of age having caught up with them, Miss Tate came to stay. She will, of course, be obliged to leave when both the Folsomes are gone. However, they are still in reasonably good health, so—"

"Yes, I understand, Moresby," said Cord, his thoughts on the unknown niece. "But, tell me," he continued, determined to cover all the possibilities, "might there be a family living—say, in a westerly direction—who number in their household a young man, possibly in his twenties, or younger?"

Moresby fingered his chin dubiously. "N-no, my lord. There's the Winslows. Their son, Tom, is two and twenty, but they live at some distance. Might I inquire, my lord, why you ask? Perhaps, I—"

Cord waved a hand. "Never mind, Moresby. Just an idle question." He gestured to the tray and the remains of his meal. "Do thank Mrs. Moresby for an excellent repast. And now, I believe I will seek my bed."

With great ceremony, Moresby conducted Cord to the master's suite and deposited him tenderly into the keeping of a waiting Hopkins. Thereupon, with due reverence, the valet prepared his master for his night's repose. Cord's last thought before sliding into sleep was that on the morrow one of his first priorities would be to visit Rose Cottage to make the acquaintance of Sir Henry and his little family. To be sure, the presence of a lithe stranger, possibly—or even likely—a female, on his property in the dead of night did not present a problem of earth-shaking proportions, but solving the puzzle might provide a bit of piquancy to the tedium of his sojourn in the wilds of Cambridgeshire. The presence of a young female, apparently unbound by social convention, almost guaranteed a fascinating mystery to explore.

Not far away, in Rose Cottage, Miss Gillian Tate was also making herself ready for bed. The knot she had so carefully crafted to keep her thick mane of brown hair concealed under a bulky hat had come loose and had been hanging below the hat brim for the last half hour. The reason for this defection became immediately apparent. Drat! She had lost one of her favorite combs. Not that she used it much, since it was suitable only for evening dress, but it was sturdy and serviceable—just the thing for binding up one's hair for unauthorized activity.

She discovered that her hands were still trembling slightly. Who the devil, she wondered, had been on her trail? No, no. Surely, it was purely by accident that another rider had happened along the same path as she. There was no doubt that having seen her, the man had attempted to follow, but she had successfully eluded him. Had he recognized her? Dear Lord, if anyone so much as suspected that she was given to . . . to midnight excursions, she would be ruined—to say nothing of Uncle Henry. But, no, the rider could not possibly have so much as determined she was not a man, let alone make out her features. She certainly had seen nothing of his.

Who could he have been? The staff at Wildehaven consisted of Mr. Moresby and his wife, plus Mr.

Standish, who tended the garden. Standish was seventy if he was a day, and she'd absorbed the distinct impression of a tall, muscular stranger who was, if not precisely youthful, certainly a strapping figure.

Bundling her hair into a plait, Gillian climbed into bed. Tomorrow she would have another chat with Uncle Henry on the unwisdom of his current activities. She would no doubt be wasting her breath, as she had on all the other occasions she had expostulated with her uncle. He was a dear soul, but sure as she sat here fretting, one day he would cause a scandal that would get them all tossed out of the university on their ears, and the cottage, as well.

They were fortunate, Aunt Louisa had told her, to have a roof over their heads. Aunt Louisa had never met the new owner of Wildehaven personally, although she had heard that he was a titled gentleman. Mr. Jilbert, the estate agent, had told her that since he had no real obligation to honor Sir Frederick's gift of tenancy, it was only out of the goodness of his heart that he had done so. Uncle Henry, of course, had experienced not a twinge of concern, but Aunt Louisa had breathed a sigh of relief.

"I mean, where would we have gone, child?" she had asked with a sniff. "We could certainly afford our own domicile, but we are comfortable here, and removing to another location at our age would be such a strain. Lord Cordray must be a good Christian gentleman, and so I told Sir Henry. Not that he paid me any heed."

Of course, he would not have, reflected Gillian ruefully. Uncle Henry's thoughts, scattered as they were, rarely strayed from his studies these days. And his studies, of course, rarely strayed from that wretched diary. Dear Heaven, she wished the poor old soul had never heard of Samuel Pepys.

Gillian breathed one last hope before closing her eyes for sleep that she would never again encounter the tall rider who had nearly been the ruination of her and her two elderly charges.

Chapter Two

Despite the lateness of his arrival at Wildehaven, Cord rose early the next morning. Declining to ring for Hopkins, he dressed for a ride before breakfast.

Arriving at the stable yard, he glanced approvingly about him. It was a spacious complex, apparently well maintained.

"Good morning, me lord." Cord turned at the sound of a hearty voice to behold a sturdy personage, red of face and beaming of expression. The man touched a respectful forelock.

"Ephraim Giddings at yer service, me lord. I be the head groom, and I'm pleased t'tell ye yer mount is ready for ye, tail high and eyes bright. We gave him a good rub and brush when he were brought in last night—as well as the carriage hacks, o'course, and he's had a handful of oats t'iss morning. Sure, and he's a prime 'un, me lord. Oy! Rafferty!" he called to a waiting minion. "Saddle up his lordship's bay."

"Thank you, Giddings, and I'm sure Zeus thanks you as well."

During the few minutes it took for his mount to be readied, Giddings escorted Cord on a prideful tour of the stable complex. Cord's first opinion of the excellent management prevailing at Wildehaven was confirmed as he viewed the stable itself, the loafing barns, the exercise yards and other accoutrements.

Once astride Zeus, he returned Giddings's vigorous wave and cantered briskly from the yard. Recalling his promise to himself the night before, he turned Zeus toward the west, and, following this direction for some minutes, eventually approached a sturdy brick house, whose rosy color explained the cottage's name. The house appeared to have been kept in good shape, its mullioned windows sparkling in the morning sun. Chimneys and stone work were neat and trim. Even from a distance, it could be seen that the brass knocker on the front door was blindingly polished, and pots of early blooming flowers were set about the entry.

He would not avail himself of that knocker, of course. At least, not yet. It was much too early in the day for a formal call. He would come back later that afternoon to introduce himself to Sir Henry Folsome and his sister, as well as the person who might prove to be his tantalizing mystery woman.

Cord swerved around the cottage, choosing a path that took him farther away from the manor house. His gaze swept the gently rolling country that was Cambridgeshire, absorbing the scent of the fresh breeze and the sounds of birds going about their busy routine. Perhaps, he mused once again, there was something to be said for a spot of ruralizing.

At that moment, his attention was abruptly diverted by the sight of a riderless horse pounding toward him. It was a large, dappled gray, long-tailed gelding, still possessed of bridle and halter, but missing his saddle.

At the speed at which the horse was traveling, Cord realized it was impossible to catch him. Surely, however, the beast would return to its stable in its own good time. He twisted in his saddle to watch the horse vanish into the distance. For a moment he felt a twinge of envy for the unfettered exhilaration apparent in the gray's fluid stride and the arrogant toss of its head. He had assiduously pursued this kind of liberty for himself, but despite his efforts, his freedom had left him unsatisfied. Sometimes freedom bore its own shackles, he mused sourly.

With a sigh, he swung about again, only to note a figure walking along the road toward him. The owner of the gray, he assumed. To his surprise, for the gelding was one of the largest he'd ever seen, the unseated rider was a woman—and, he observed as she neared, an altogether toothsome specimen of the gender.

She was tall, although the trim waist displayed in her modest riding habit could be spanned by his two hands. She looked far too slender to manage a mount the size of the gray. Her stride was purposeful, however, and she lifted a slim hand in greeting as she neared.

He lifted his own, and in that second he realized that the horse that had just galloped past him could easily have been the same one he had seen the night before between the legs of the unknown rider.

Was it possible . . . ? He slowed and gazed intently at the woman. My God, he thought, she was beautiful! Long, thick hair, the color of firelight on polished mahogany, was swept under a small hat trimmed with a single feather. Her eyes were wide-spaced, and, from this distance, appeared to be a light gray. The spare lines of her habit clearly delineated lush curves that made his mouth go dry. What was such a goddess doing in the backwaters of Cambridgeshire? He was forced to the obvious conclusion that, since she was riding on Wildehaven land, she must be the Folsomes's niece.

And, possibly, the rider whom he had seen the night before on a mysterious foray.

Cord nudged Zeus to a quicker pace.

Gillian Tate watched his approach warily. She supposed it had been unwise to lift her hand in greeting to a stranger, but her predicament had reduced this civilized nicety to an absurdity.

She drew in a sharp breath. There was something vaguely familiar about the rider. Tall and muscular, he displayed a loose-limbed strength in the saddle. Good Lord, he might well be the man who had followed her last night! She knew an urge to turn on her heel and run in the opposite direction. Instead, she affixed a rueful smile to her face as the stranger pulled up before her and dismounted.

"I'm sorry," he said with an engaging grin. "We have not been introduced, but I'm assuming you're a damsel in distress, and certainly that particular nicety is not a requirement in such a situation. Allow me to present myself. I'm Cordray, and very much at your service, ma'am."

Gillian laughed. "How very lowering to appear in such a light, but alas, I am, indeed, in distress. I am Gillian Tate, and I live in Rose Cottage on your estate," she finished with lifted brows. "For, if I am not mistaken, my lord, you are our new landlord."

She was somewhat taken aback when he swept off his hat and bowed low over her hand. His hair, dark and thick, reminded her of a sable pelt, and his eyes, for heaven's sake, were green—the purest emerald she had ever seen. Under his curiously intent scrutiny, she felt as though she were being washed in a tropical rain.

"I believe I encountered your mount just a few moments ago. A fine, ribbed-up gray."

Gillian sighed. "Yes, that was Falstaff. So-called because all he thinks about is his stomach. When my cinch broke a few minutes ago, the saddle fell off. I could not grasp his halter, and despite my desperate entreaties, he turned about and careened off toward his stable, where he is not doubt this very minute cajoling Simms for a bowlful of oats."

"You have no one attending you?"

Reading a note of appreciative interest in his tone, Gillian stiffened slightly, but returned laughingly, "No— and that will be a good lesson to me to come out without a groom. I do so enjoy a few moments of solitude before the day begins, and I invariably head out alone on my early morning forays. I feel perfectly secure, of course, when I am on Wildehaven land."

"Most understandable." The gentleman smiled once more, leaving Gillian to wonder why this should leave her with a profound feeling that he was somehow a threat to her well-being. And not just because she strongly suspected he was the rider she had come so close to encountering the night before. No, her uneasiness sprang from the man himself, for it ever Gillian had felt she was meeting a predator on two feet, it was now. Despite his seeming indolence, he bore an unmistakable air of command. More important, he fairly exuded that dangerous self-possession she had encountered too often. This was a man accustomed to having whatever took his fancy, whether it be a fine wine, an exquisite painting or an attractive woman.

Her mirror told her she belonged in the latter category, to say nothing of the attempts over the years on her virtue by various enterprising males of her acquaintance. She whispered inwardly, *Ah, my lad, you may smile and smile with your green-fire eyes, but you may look elsewhere for your next conquest.*

"I am sure," the gentleman said smoothly, "Zeus would deem it an honor to offer himself as replacement to Falstaff, who, if I may say so, hardly seems a fit mount for a lady. That is, he looks a bit much to handle."

"Perhaps he might be for some," Gillian replied tartly. "However, he is much attached to me and would not dream of treating me discourteously. At least," she amended with a blush, "most of the time."

"To be sure." Lord Cordray cupped his hands and tossed Gillian lightly into the saddle. Grasping Zeus's halter, he started back along the path to Rose Cottage. "I cannot say I am the *new* owner of Wildehaven, since the estate has been in my possession for two years and more. I am that most reviled personage, an absentee landlord. In my defense, I can only say that having examined my new demesne and found it in good order, I felt comfortable in leaving it in the hands of that most excellent agent, Silas Jilbert."

"Oh, yes." Gillian nodded in vigorous agreement. "Mr. Jilbert is highly regarded in the area. He is most conscientious in his duties and empathetic in his dealings with the estate staff. Uncle Henry and Aunt Louisa consider him a good friend. Sir Henry Folsome, that is, and Mrs. Ferris. I am their niece and they—"

"Yes, Jilbert told me of the arrangement made between my uncle and Sir Henry. It was my pleasure, of course, to maintain his status of honored guest in Rose Cottage."

"That was very good of you," said Gillian impulsively. "My uncle and aunt are getting on in years and are grateful for such a comfortable place to spend their declining years."

Cord bent an overt glance of admiration on her. "As I said, it was my pleasure," he returned smoothly. "I understand your uncle is affiliated with the university?"

"Yes. Uncle Henry graduated from Trinity, then became first a don and then a fellow of Magdalene College. He lives and breathes academics—even more so now that he has retired from his duties."

Her expression grew troubled, and Cord's brows lifted. She uttered a brittle laugh. "He has of late become absorbed in the seventeenth century, particularly the reign of Charles II. He spends every waking minute in his study amidst a welter of papers and charts and—but I am babbling. Tell me, sir, what brings you to the wilds of Cambridgeshire? I understand you reside in London."

For an instant, gazing into eyes that he realized were not just gray, but were wide and changeable as a cloudy sky, Cord felt an urge to confide the tale of his flight from London and the reasons thereof. He stifled the impulse immediately, of course. He was not in the habit of discussing his personal affairs with good friends, let alone a lithe sylph he had met only moments before. His laugh, however, was a trifle strained. "Yes, I admit to being the complete city creature. I am merely looking for a spot of rustication."

Miss Tate cast him a sardonic glance. "Creditors on your heels, my lord?" At his expression of affront, she laughed. "I'm sorry, but is that not why a peer usually ruralizes?"

Cord relaxed. "I suppose so, but no, no, it's nothing like that. My finances are in order and my conscience clear." Well, mostly, he thought with a grimace. "I simply found that the duties expected of me have become burdensome for the moment," he concluded with the most limpid smile at his disposal.

"I see." Miss Tate cast him a noncommittal glance. "Do you—?"

She paused abruptly, as a man, apparently a groom, approached on horseback along the path to Rose Cottage. He was leading the big gray, newly saddled.

"Miss Gillian!" he called. "Are you all right? Falstaff came into the stable yard just a few minutes ago and we—"

"Yes, Simms, I'm fine, but I'm afraid you're going to have to retrieve my saddle. The cinch broke, and it came off just abreast of the bridge. Despite all my entreaties, the wretched beast hared off as fast as four feet would take him for home and a handout."

Simms expressed dismay. "Cinch broke?" he exclaimed. "Well, I never! I know a certain lad who's goin' to wish he'd been more careful with his tack chores. I'll retrieve the saddle right now, miss."

Touching a respectful finger to his forelock, he proceeded along the path.

Gillian swung back to the earl, and the two resumed their journey.

"Do you reside in London all year, then, my lord?" asked Gillian, dimly aware that she was, perhaps, being a bit presumptuous. It was none of her concern, after all, where the earl whiled away his life.

"Yes." The warmth of his gaze told her he had taken no offense. "I've made my residence in Town since I sold out, and—"

"Sold out?" Gillian's voice lifted.

"Yes," the earl said again. "I was in the army for several years after I came down from Oxford." He lifted his brows, and now there was a certain stiffness in his tone. "You seem surprised."

Gillian laughed self-consciously. "Oh, no! That is . . . you don't have the look of a military man."

At this, a definite flash leapt into his lordship's eyes. "Really?" he asked coolly. "Not enough swagger, do you think? Or, perhaps I should sport a set of mustachios."

Gillian put her hand to her mouth. "Oh, I am sorry! My wretched tongue. I only meant that . . ." She trailed off in embarrassment.

Lord Cordray laughed. "Never mind. Even during the thick of the fracas with the Corsican Monster, I never considered myself a military man, so I suppose it's not surprising that I don't look like one."

Gillian returned his smile tentatively and changed the conversation to a lighter subject. They rode companionably, and it was not long before the outlines of Rose Cottage could be seen. They turned toward the stable yard, where a young man ran out to greet them. Cord was somewhat surprised. Did the Folsome family coffers extend to more than one groom? Sir Henry was obviously not the impoverished academic he had envisioned. Once Gillian had been assisted to the ground, Cord prepared to remount.

"I am pleased to have made your acquaintance, Miss Tate. I hope—"

"But are you not coming in?" Gillian bit her lip. Why in the world had she said that? She had the feeling that the less she had to do with this man the better for her well-being. In addition, though he had come to her rescue, she certainly did not want him to think she wished to push the acquaintance to something more.

Indeed, Cord felt some surprise at the invitation, but answered immediately. "It is certainly my intention to pay a call on your aunt and uncle—and you, of course—but it's very early, and I thought . . . If it would not be an inconvenience, however," he continued hastily, observing her obvious discomfiture, "I am most anxious to meet Sir Henry and his sister. Will they mind receiving a visitor at this hour?"

"Oh, no. Both are early risers, and they will no doubt have been apprised of the ominous circumstances of Falstaff's riderless return. They fret so over me, you see, and are no doubt watching for my safe return."

As though in answer to her words, a window in an upper story at the back of the house was thrown open. From it a head protruded, covered with thinning gray hair. A pair of spectacles clung to the tip of the man's rather bulbous nose, and his plump jowls were quivering under a strong emotion.

"Gillian! Gillian, what the devil do you mean by it? It's gone, by God, and I well know who is responsible! You will come to my study immediately!"

Chapter Three

Miss Tate swung about to face Cord. He noted with interest that she blushed very becomingly. He also observed that she was breathing very rapidly, an activity that did interesting things to her upper body.

"On the other hand," she said after a moment, "I do

not wish to importune you. I'm sure you have much to do right now. Perhaps, as you said, later in the day would be more convenient. I'm sure . . .''

A spurt of unholy amusement surged through Cord. If he had an ounce of conscience—or social sense—he reflected briefly, he would exit this intriguing scene. On the other hand, if he were possessed of either, how many times would he be forced to leave his admittedly overactive curiosity unassauged?

"My dear Miss Tate," he replied smoothly. "I'm most pleased to accept your invitation. I would very much enjoy meeting your uncle and his sister, and, since he appears to be awake and about, I feel there is no time like the present."

Gillian made a strangled sound in her throat. Good Lord! Here was a disaster in the making. She could not allow Lord Cordray and Uncle Henry to come face-to-face. At least, not until she had an opportunity to confront Uncle Henry herself. She could not help but observe that the wretched earl was hugely enjoying the situation. Had he no more sense of propriety than to stride into a family contretemps—particularly when he had not even met most of the family?

After staring at him for a moment in such a manner to leave him in no doubt of her disapproval—and meeting with a marked lack of success in this tactic—Gillian nodded stiffly and ushered him into the house.

Here they were greeted by an elderly gentleman whom Miss Tate introduced as Widdings, the general factotum at Rose Cottage. Cord wondered if Miss Tate was responsible for the atmosphere of warmth that seemed to envelop him like a friendly embrace as he stepped into the modest entry hall. The décor was not fashionable, being structured toward comfort rather than elegance. A table in the center of the hall bore several periodicals, a riding crop, a few books and what looked like letters from a recently opened post. A scattering of paintings, sentimental of subject and some of such amateurish quality that they might have been created by a favorite relative, were hung in casual arrangement.

Removing her hat, Miss Tate led Cord into a small salon just off the hall.

"If you will wait here for a moment, my lord," she said, again a little breathlessly, "I shall notify my aunt and uncle that you are here."

She turned to send Widdings off for tea, but paused. "Have you breakfasted, my lord?" When he shook his head, she said, "Perhaps you would care to join us. The repast will not be lavish, but I believe we can provide you with a satisfactory meal."

In some bemusement, Cord replied, "Thank you, I would like that very much."

"I shall be just a moment," Gillian said again before whirling to run up the stairs. She hurried down a long corridor, and was intercepted by a plump figure carrying a jug of water.

"Why, Gillian," said the lady, peering over her spectacles. White hair curled from under the rim of her ruffled cap, feathering about her placid features like a halo. "We have been so worried!" she continued. "Simms told us that Falstaff had returned without you. I'm glad to see you met with no harm."

Without offering an explanation for her predicament, Gillian laid a hand on the lady's arm.

"Aunt Louisa! We must do something about Uncle Henry. He can't find the diary, and he's in a terrible state. I was in the stable yard with Lord Cordray, for heaven's sake—you know—our landlord—I encountered him on my ride," she added to forestall the question she could see forming on her aunt's lips. "When Uncle Henry fairly bellowed at me from his study window, Lord Cordray insisted on coming in the house, despite my efforts to discourage him. He wants to meet you and Uncle Henry. I . . . I invited him for breakfast. That may not have been a good idea, but as long as he is here, I think it would be a good idea to . . . to get his measure."

Aunt Louisa stared at her for a moment in incomprehension before her expression cleared. "Oh, I see," she replied. "As in, how will he feel about the presence of a certified eccentric on his property?"

Gillian nodded, and the two hurried along the corridor, stopping at a heavily paneled door. Gillian knocked sharply, and without waiting for a response, opened the

door. The stout gentleman whose face had so recently
protruded from the upstairs window looked up at their
entrance.

"There you are!" were his first words. "Gillian, you've
been at it again. I cannot find the diary, and I must
assume you've been up to your tricks. I demand—"

"Uncle Henry," Gillian interrupted, "we cannot discuss that now. Lord Cordray is downstairs waiting to
meet you and Aunt."

"You must compose yourself, dearest," interposed her
aunt. "It would not do for his lordship to suspect what
you've been up to."

"Up to!" exclaimed Uncle Henry, pounding a meaty
fist on his desk. This structure was piled high with books
and stacks of assorted papers, notes and general detritus,
all of which stirred fretfully in the draft created by the
open door. "I have merely taken appropriate steps to
defeat the small-minded, pettyfogging—"

"Yes, Uncle, but the fact remains that what you have
been doing is illegal, and of all the persons whom we do
not wish to know about it, I'd say Lord Cordray ranks
high on the list. So, please compose yourself, slip into
your most charming academic persona and come down
to meet him."

For a moment, it appeared that Sir Henry was not to
be swayed from his battle position, but glancing first at
his sister and then at his niece and back again, he sighed
and deflated visibly.

"Very well," he said, with only a trace of belligerence
remaining in his tone. He fixed his niece with a basilisk
stare. "However, I am not through with you, young
lady." He smoothed his hair with both hands and accompanied his ladies from the room.

By the time the little group entered the small salon
where Lord Cordray awaited them, Sir Henry had
straightened his skewed cravat and affixed a benign
smile to his lips. Gillian performed the introductions and
Aunt Louisa beamed delightedly.

"We are so very pleased," she said, "to make your
acquaintance at long last. Do let us go in to breakfast,
for it has been awaiting us since Simms returned with
his unpleasant news."

Mrs. Ferris led the way to a small, sunny chamber toward the rear of the house. "May I ask what brought you to Wildehaven?" she asked, then indicated the sideboard, laden with eggs, toast, kippers and all the other accoutrements of a hearty country breakfast.

Under her direction, Cord helped himself to a generous portion of each, and sitting at the table, he accepted coffee from the young maid who circled the room anxiously. From the awed glances she sent in his direction, he assumed the news of the arrival of a certified peer had already spread around the household. He took a dignified sip. "As I explained to your niece, I merely wished to escape the bustle of city life for a while. One can take such solace in the country, do you not agree?"

"Oh, indeed, my lord," Aunt Louisa agreed solemnly. "Was it not Virgil who said, 'May the countryside and the gliding valley streams content me'?"

"Precisely, dear lady."

Good Lord, thought Cord. I sound like a park saunterer. He turned to his host. "I understand, Sir Henry, that you are affiliated with the university."

"Mm, yes," replied that gentleman with an offhanded gesture that served only to indicate his pride in the words. "I graduated with a degree in arts from Trinity in 1770, became a don at Magdalene in '75, and I've been a fellow for over forty-five years. My particular field of study is the Restoration period."

"Ah, yes," chimed in Cord, feeling himself on firm ground. "Charles the Second. An engaging rascal, I've heard."

Sir Henry bent an austere glance on him. "I have little knowledge of His Majesty's moral behavior. It is the men of letters who thrived under his reign in whom I am interested. Dryden, Bunyan, Congreve, Rochester and Samuel Butler among many others."

"Ah," murmured Cord, after which an awkward silence fell on the little group.

"Indeed," added his sister pridefully after a moment, "Sir Henry held the Chair of Restoration Literature for a number of years before his retirement and is still in demand for lectures . . . at least . . . An expression of dismay crossed her amiable features for a moment.

"That is . . . well, the many essays and books he has published over the years are still much in demand."

Sir Henry's hand jerked a little, and a splash of tea joined one or two other stains on his cravat. He cleared his throat.

"Of course, strictly speaking, I have not truly retired."

Miss Tate and Mrs. Ferris exchanged agonized glances.

"No, indeed," continued Sir Henry importantly. "I am currently engaged in a project, which, if I may say, will produce a significant—nay, profound—effect on English letters."

"No!" exclaimed Cord, entering into the spirit of this declaration. "Do tell me about it, sir."

"Mm, no, I'm afraid I can't do that."

Cord noted with some puzzlement the simultaneous sigh of relief uttered by the two ladies.

"No," continued Sir Henry. "I cannot discuss the matter, at least not until my thesis is brought to fruition. There are many who would sabotage my efforts. Not," he added expansively, "that I number you among their pernicious number, but it is too easy to drop information in all innocence." He sighed heavily. "Mine is a lonely task, one which requires all the knowledge and skills I have acquired during a long, and may I say, productive career in the Groves of Academe."

"I understand completely, sir," said Cord, who for the life of him could not fathom what the old duffer was talking about. "I honor your dedication. May I assume the, er, kernel of your project deals with some facet of the Restoration?"

Sir Henry glanced at him suspiciously, but answered with courtesy. "Of course. In fact"—he bent forward with an air of confidentiality—"it concerns one of the great mysteries of the period."

He sat back quickly, as though afraid he had said too much. Portentously, he laid a finger alongside his nose. "I'm sorry, my dear fellow, I simply cannot say more. I wonder, though, are you familiar with the works of Samuel Butler?"

"Ah," replied Cord, searching frantically in his mind. "One of the more obscure Restoration poets, I believe. Um, let me see . . . did he not write a satire called *Hubris*?

Or no, *Hudibras*. Mm—'Such as do build their faith up the holy test of Pike and Gun; call fire and sword and desolation, a godly-thorough-Reformation. . . .' "

"Yes!" cried Sir Henry delightedly. He swiveled to face his sister. "Can it be that Wildehaven is to be inhabited by someone literate?" To Cord, he said, "You must visit us often, sir—or, that is, my lord." This in response to a barely perceptible nudge from his sister. "I cannot tell you how much I look forward to discussing Butler and all the others with you." His smile was beatific.

Cord cleared his throat. "I thank you for the invitation, Sir Henry, but my sojourn at Wildehaven will be short. As I said before, I am merely rusticating for a brief period—probably not more than a few days."

Sir Henry's eyes grew wide. "But that is absurd. How could you wish to return to London when you have the opportunity to partake in some meaningful conversation? You can't tell me you get much of that among the fribbles who inhabit the Polite World?"

"Dearest!" gasped Mrs. Ferris, "you do not have the ordering of Lord Cordray's life. If he wishes—"

Cord laughed. "You are quite right, Sir Henry, but I must say I do number among my friends gentlemen who can discourse on topics other than the set of their coats or the latest news from the turf. However, with your kind permission, I shall avail myself of your hospitality on a frequent basis while I am here."

Sir Henry's expression softened.

"Of course, my lord. You are welcome in my home at any time."

The conversation turned to generalities. Cord gleaned a few facts about his neighbors, those living on nearby estates and others who dwelled in the village of Great Shelford. All the while, Cord surreptitiously watched Miss Tate. The affection she bore for her aunt and uncle was obvious. Her care of them was revealed in the manner in which she quietly gestured to the maidservant to attend to their every need as they ate. Plates were replenished and cups filled unobtrusively—as was his own, of course. He found to his surprise that he had eaten a great deal more than was his wont in London. Fresh air, he mused, did wonderful things for a man's appetite. Once more he covertly surveyed the lissome Miss Tate—and not just for eggs and kippers.

After a discreet interval, Cord took his leave. He promised to visit Rose Cottage again soon, and garnered a promise from Miss Tate to go riding with him on the morrow.

After seeing his lordship to the door, Gillian closed it behind him with a sigh of relief, and from the drawing room window watched him canter easily down the drive. She released the breath she felt she'd been holding ever since she'd encountered the earl some two hours ago. The Earl of Cordray, she reflected uneasily, was as charming as he could hold together, but she could not escape the impression that he posed some sort of threat. Her main concern was Uncle Henry, of course, and what he might blurt out, but in some corner of her consciousness, she knew the earl carried the power to upset the peace of mind she had worked so hard to acquire. A poor job she had done of that, too, she thought unhappily as she hastened back to the breakfast room.

Her aunt and uncle were just rising from the table, Aunt Louisa brushing off any stray crumbs that might have fallen to her ample lap, and Uncle Henry to wander abstractedly from the room. Gillian lost no time in corralling both of them into Uncle Henry's study.

"My dears," she began, "we must talk."

Settling herself comfortably on a worn leather settee, Aunt Louisa replied, "Yes, indeed. What a very nice young man, don't you think?"

"What young man?" replied Sir Henry, his attention already buried in one of the volumes on his desk. "Oh, the earl. Yes, seems a decent sort. At least, he knows a bit about things that matter. I doubt, of course, that he's so much as heard of Samuel Pepys."

"That's what I wish to talk to you about, Uncle," Gillian said in some exasperation. "And you, too, Aunt."

The two merely looked at her inquiringly.

"I'm pleased, of course, that both of you like our landlord. I beg of you to remember that that's exactly what he is. He has the power to cast us all out into the road if he wishes. He—"

"Oh, for God's sake, Gillian, don't be so dramatic. Why would the fellow evict us?"

"I'm glad you asked that, Uncle, because if he ever got wind of what you've been doing, he would undoubtedly do just that."

"Bah!"

"Oh, but Gillian is right, dearest!" interposed Aunt Louisa. "And just think of all the other unpleasant things that could happen, all because of this . . . well, I don't know what to call it but an obsession."

At this, Sir Henry reddened alarmingly. He rose and pounded his fist on the desk, causing the assorted papers and notes to leap like startled chickens. "Obsession?" he roared. "This from my own sister? Louisa, I thought you understood what I am trying to accomplish here!" The flush faded, but the injured tone remained. "I tell you now, Louisa—*and* Gillian—despite your efforts to undermine my project, I shall continue on my unalterable course in the pursuit of knowledge. Now, if you will excuse me, I must be on my way."

Both ladies paled, and Mrs. Ferris spoke falteringly, "G-going? Where on earth are you going, Henry?"

"Why, to the college, of course." He fixed his niece with a significant gaze. "I have work to do there." With which pronouncement he ushered his ladies from the room, ignoring their faint protests.

Outside the study Gillian and her aunt stared at each other. At last, Mrs. Ferris asked despairingly, "Do you suppose—?"

"Yes, I do," Gillian replied in an equally bleak tone. She sighed heavily. "I only hope this will not mean another midnight excursion for me." After a moment, she said firmly. "We shall have to take steps, Aunt. This cannot continue." She turned to stride down the corridor.

Her aunt echoed the sigh and, shrugging despondently, plodded after her.

"And," Gillian tossed over her shoulder, "we must hope that the Earl of Cordray will not adhere to his promise to visit us on a regular basis."

Chapter Four

Meanwhile, in London, stirring events were brewing over the hapless head of the Earl of Cordray. In Binsted House, a council of war was in session. Present were Lord and Lady Binsted, the Honorable Wilfred Culver, and, seated stiffly on a brocade settee, the Honorable Miss Corisande Brant. Miss Brant's parents, the Viscount and Viscountess Rantray had chosen to absent themselves from the assemblage, which was probably just as well, since it was felt that the presence of the infuriated viscount would contribute nothing to the discussion at hand.

Wilfred, lounging in a padded window seat, declared at large, "Well, I popped over to Curzon Street this morning, and he never came home last night at all. 'Course, he might still be out somewhere, dossed down at a friend's house, or . . ." He coughed delicately, sending a glance toward Corisande, who stiffened into an even more rigid position. "At any rate, it looks as though he was serious about leaving Town."

"Good Lord, Wilfred," snapped the marchioness, "It's almost five o'clock in the afternoon. Surely, he would have returned to his abode by now if he were in Town. It's just coming up on the Promenade. You know he scarcely ever misses an opportunity to strut about on that bay of his."

Lord Binsted rubbed his nose. "I agree with you m'dear." He, too, glanced at Corisande, who so far had contributed nothing to the discussion. It was agreed in all of Polite Society that Corisande Brant, though not an accredited Beauty, was nevertheless an attractive young woman. She was slender. Her skin was very white, her features regular and she carried herself with an elegance that was the envy of her peers. If her blue eyes were more the color of an ice floe than an azure sky, or her expression cool and composed even on occasions when others might have broken into a laugh or a sob, such observations were not taken into account by her admirers.

She spoke for the first time. "You need not take my feelings into consideration." Though her tone was slightly peevish, it could now be perceived that Corisande's voice was as highly bred as the rest of her.

"Lord Binsted, I am old enough to know the habits of a gentleman, and I do not complain." She hesitated before continuing. "There is nothing formal between us, after all," she concluded, her tone still faintly aggrieved

"Nonsense." Lady Binsted paced the floor restlessly. "It is time for some plain speaking. There has been an understanding between our families for years. Please do not think, my dear, that Cordray is not fully prepared to do his duty—at last. If I thought that, I should never have requested your presence at this little, er, conference. It is my fear that"—she paused for dramatic effect—"something has happened to him!"

Her glance rested directly on Corisande, but if she had expected an outburst of maidenly concern, she was doomed to disappointment. Corisande merely raised her eyes in an expectant, if skeptical, gaze and made no reply.

"What are you saying, Bess, that Cord was abducted by Mohawks?" Lord Binsted completed his question with a guffaw, causing his wife to bend a stare on him that might have felled a water buffalo.

"Of course not," she sniffed. "But there are any number of circumstances that might have occurred. I cannot believe that he was so lost to duty to have actually left London for any duration. However, he might have taken a ride and met with an accident."

"Surely he carries his cardcase with him," responded Corisande colorlessly. "You would have been notified if anything untoward had taken place."

"Not necessarily," interposed Wilfred. The marchioness cast him a grateful glance. "He might have fallen in a ditch and nobody's found him yet."

The grateful glance was extinguished, to be replaced

by one of exasperation. "That hardly seems likely. He would not have set out on his own, certainly."

"Mmm." Lord Binsted again entered the conversation. "Told you he was in a strange mood. Seems to me he might well have hared off by himself."

Wilfred glanced at Corisande and cleared his throat. "I don't see that he would have done that," he said tentatively. "He was scheduled to ask for Corrie's hand. How could he have got up to something that would jeopardize that?"

Corisande cast him a grateful glance, and Wilfred's thin cheeks reddened momentarily.

Lady Binsted drew a sharp breath. "In any event," she said bracingly, "the thing to do is find him. We'll assume for the moment that he actually did leave Town suddenly, and something prevented him from returning in time for the dinner party."

She gazed around at the group as though waiting for argument. When none was forthcoming, she continued. "I think we might assume that he went to the Park."

"Cordray Park," expostulated her husband. "What the devil would he go up there for?"

"It is the family seat, after all. He did say he had business to attend to. He might have received word that he was needed for . . . for . . . something."

Lord Binsted eyed his lady dubiously. "Mmp."

The marchioness, apparently accepting this less than enthusiastic response as acquiescence, moved to the bell-pull. "Good. We shall send to Cordray Park to see if he is there, or at any rate to see if a message was sent to him—and I think we might try Rushmead and Cotsburn, as well. They are lesser estates, but they are closer to London than the Park, and Cord might very well have simply dashed down to one of them for reasons of his own."

Lord Binsted pulled on his upper lip. "It shall be as you say, m'dear, although I must say, I don't think we'll be any the wiser. If you want my opinion—"

"Yes, dear," interposed his wife hastily. "I may be very wrong, but I want to get something in motion. We cannot remain just sitting on our hands when Cord may be in dire straits."

At this, Miss Brant rose with a sibilant hiss of skirts. "Now that that is settled, Lady Binsted, I really must be going. I have an appointment for which I am already late." She pulled on her gloves, which she had removed and replaced and then removed several times during the course of the discussion. Smoothing them over her hands, she moved to Lady Binsted. Wilfred stood as well.

"I'll take care of sending out the bloodhounds, if you wish," he said. Ignoring Lady Binsted's frown at this remark, he strolled across the room and took Corisande's arm. "May I escort you home, Corrie?"

"That would be very nice, Wilfred," she replied coolly. She kissed Lady Binsted on the cheek and bowed slightly to the marquess. Then she looked up into Wilfred's face and proceeded with him from the room, gliding over the carpet like a swan moving over a tranquil lagoon.

"Whew!" The marquess pulled a voluminous kerchief from his coat pocket and mopped his face. "What a piece of work she is! No more emotion than if she'd just been asked directions to the Tower. You'd think she'd show a little concern."

"Nonsense," replied his wife sharply. "Corisande is always all that is proper. It would be most unbecoming of her to wail and wring her hands, after all."

Again, Lord Binsted's guffaw sounded about the room. "O' course. No sense in broadcasting her humiliation to the world."

Lady Binsted's brows rose. "Humiliation?"

"Good God, Bess, if the gel didn't tell everyone of her acquaintance that she was expecting a proposal on bended knee last night, I'll eat that arrangement of what-ever-they-are." He waved a hand toward a vase of hothouse cyclamen.

"Nonsense. I'm sure Corisande is much too well bred to have done any such thing. At any rate, her actions are not the issue here. Our concern is Cord's whereabouts. *Where* could the wretched boy have gone?"

At that moment, the wretched boy was en route from Wildehaven to Cambridge. Upon crossing the River

Cam on the outskirts of town, he set a course along King's Parade Toward Magdelene College. He crossed the river once more just before reaching the gates of the college, and entered the Porter's Lodge as the clock in the ancient bell tower tolled five of the afternoon.

His inquiry to the porter elicited the information that Mr. Edward Maltby was indeed in his lodgings. He was given directions, and a few minutes later, after a climb of three stories in the first quadrangle, approached a heavily paneled door. His knock produced a cheery, "Enter at your peril, you foul, empty-headed little leech!"

Cord opened the door onto a sitting room of generous proportions, whose every available space—tables, chairs, desk, cabinets and even a footstool—overflowed with books and papers. The chamber exuded an oddly pleasant odor of must, mice and pipe smoke, the last of which emanated from the person seated at the desk.

He and Cord shared the same number of years, but Professor Maltby had already settled into the aspect of middle age. Slightly balding, his light brown hair was touched with gray and fell untidily over a pair of spectacles perched over an impressive nose. His wide mouth seemed created for smiles, but was now folded in an expression of irritation that lightened immediately on catching sight of his guest.

"Cord! By all that's holy, what the devil are you doing in the profane precincts of Academe?" He leaped up from his desk, scattering papers in his wake, to envelop Cord in a rib-crushing embrace.

Laughing, Cord returned the salutation. "Ned!" he exclaimed a little breathlessly. "It's good to see you, as well." He glanced about the room. "So this is where England's primary expert on practically everything maintains his ivory tower?"

"Well, yes and no. I do my work here, and my tutoring—actually, I thought you were one of my students who is presently late for his appointment with me—the little toad is not going to put in an appearance, of course—but, I live in a little place just off the Trumpington Road."

"Ah, the perquisites of dedicated scholarship."

At Ned's invitation, Cord shifted a pile of papers from a wing chair to the already laden table beside it. Seating himself, he accepted the glass of wine held out to him by his friend. He smiled affectionately at Ned. Although different in mien and personality as chalk from cheese, the two had been inseparable friends during Cord's undergraduate days at Cambridge. As residents of Magdalene College, they had soon become the scourge of that institution. After graduation, their paths had diverged widely, Cord's to take him into the army and then into the exalted heights of the *haut ton*, while Ned had pursued a comfortable academic career, engaging in scientific research. The two seldom saw each other, but corresponded frequently, and the last Cord had heard, Ned was engaged in some sort of meteorological study, mapping clouds and wind currents throughout the country.

"So, what brings you to the wilds of Cambridgeshire?" asked Ned, settling his lanky frame into a badly sprung armchair.

Briefly, Cord explained his recent acquisition of Wildehaven.

"Really?" asked Ned in surprise. "Sir Frederick Deddington was your uncle? I did not know that. Then you must have made Sir Henry Folsome's acquaintance by now."

Cord crossed his legs. "Indeed I have, and his sister and niece as well. Do you know them?"

"Mm, yes," replied Ned noncommittally. "Not nearly as well as I'd like to know the niece, however." He upended his pipe to tap the dottle into a nearby bowl.

Cord's eyes lit in amusement. "Ah, Miss Tate. Are you smitten, then, Ned, with the lovely spinster?"

Ned shifted in his chair. "Oh, no. Not smitten, precisely. At any rate, you know me. I'm more the sort to worship from afar. Besides, I wouldn't care to further my association with her uncle."

"Sir Henry? He seems a affable chap."

"Oh, yes, a completely decent sort—he's simply mad as a March hare."

"What?"

Ned shrugged again. "Well, perhaps that's coming it

too strong, but the old fellow definitely has a rat or two in his attic.''

"I must admit he gave me that impression.''

Ned, after fishing in the pocket of his dilapidated coat for some moments, came up with a tobacco pouch, from which he began filling his pipe. "Wasn't always that way, of course. He's been a fellow here at Magdalene since before God created rain, I think, and for almost as long was one of the college's shining ornaments. Held the Chair of Restoration Literature, or some such.'' He waved negligently. "Don't keep up on that sort of thing much. At any rate, it wasn't until a few years ago that he began turning at bit balmy. That was when he got a bug up his arse about Samuel Pepys.''

"Pepys?'' asked Cord, his interest truly caught. "And who might he be?''

Ned, having completed the pipe-filling ritual, drew a straw from a container near the dottle bowl and rose to light it from the fire. Returning, he plunged once more into his chair. "Well you may ask,'' he muttered, beginning the next ritual, that of creating the perfect draw. "Samuel Pepys graduated from Magdalene some time in the early 1600s. He took up residence in London, married, and obtained a position with the navy—became a procurement official, I believe. In any event, he did very well for himself and by the time he died, he was living quite comfortably. In addition, he'd amassed an impressive collection of books, all leather-bound. However, his main claim to fame at the present is that for a number of years he kept a diary.''

"Oh?'' So far, reflected Cord, he could see no reason for Sir Henry's reverence for Mr. Pepys.

"Yes, 'oh'. Nearly a hundred years after his death— in 1725 or thereabouts, his nephew bequeathed the diary, along with the rest of Pepys's library to Magdalene, where it was housed in the building directly behind this quadrangle. It's called the New Building, though it must have been built over a hundred years ago.''

Cord was puzzled. "Did the diary contain anything of import?''

"Aha!'' Ned drew manfully on his pipe, producing the

desired glow in its bowl. "That's just it. No one knows—
for he wrote the thing in some sort of code!"

"Code! You mean it's been sitting there all this time,
and no one can read it?"

"Precisely. There have been one or two efforts, because according to tradition, Pepys brushed elbows with
some fairly influential people—up to and including King
Charles—the Second, that would be.

"Now, of course, interest has increased in the work
because of the publication of John Evelyn's diary last
year. I think it is not too much to say that its popularity
swept the country. A new edition is coming out shortly."

"Yes, indeed. I read it when it first came out. A fascinating glimpse into Charles's court. Mmm," Cord added
speculatively. "I think I see where this is going."

"You always were a perspicacious chap, Chris. Yes,
the powers that be at the college are now most anxious
to garner a coup of their own by publishing Pepys's
work. However—"

"No one can read it," finished Cord with a chuckle.

"Precisely," said Ned again. "The efforts have increased tenfold, with every runny-nosed undergraduate
in the university having a crack at it. With absolutely
no success."

"And I suppose Sir Henry is leading the pack of
would-be code-breakers."

"Yes. It was thought that with his background in letters, it would be Sir Henry who would carry off the
prize, but he hasn't translated so much as a single word.
He keeps saying he's on the right track, and it's only a
matter of time before he reaches his goal, but he's become such a fanatic on the subject that his credibility
has sunk to zero."

"Surely a little eccentricity is permissible in a man of
his years and background."

"It's gone beyond mere vagary. The fellow's obsessed.
He will talk of nothing but the diary and has blown its
importance as an historical document all out of propor-
tion. He hints mysteriously at revelations that will rock
the entire conception of Restoration England. He's even
suggested that the real author of the diary is old Char-
lie himself."

"I see." Cord rubbed his chin thoughtfully. "He is still working on the translation, I take it?"

"Lord, yes." Ned paused to relight the pipe, which had unaccountably gone out. "He's here almost every day, driving the library staff wild with his demands. He requires dictionaries of every sort be brought to him, as well as texts on every code known to the government and the military."

"I wonder why he doesn't work on the manuscript at home. Surely, he has plenty of reference works there."

"Ah, there's another point of friction. He began taking it home with him and keeping it there for days on end. At last, after complaints from the staff, as well as from others having a stab at the translation themselves, young Neville, the master of the college intervened. That would be George Neville. He was appointed three or four years ago. He was only four-and-twenty at the time. He has some influential relatives—needless to say, I suppose. His uncle, Thomas Grenville, a well-known bibliophile, is also interested in the diary. He and Folsome now have some sort of blood feud going, I hear. At any rate, young Neville has prohibited Sir Henry from taking the diary out of the library. The old man has even been limited in the amount of time he can keep possession of it in the building. He was rabid at first, and he's still pretty miffed, but he seems to have cooled down some now."

Cord stared meditatively into the fire. "He said nothing of all this to me when we met. Of course, he was hardly likely to confide in a stranger, but, though he seemed determined to create an atmosphere of portent and mystery, he did not seem unduly frustrated."

"Believe me, Cord, the man is to be avoided. I shall say no more on the subject. You still have not told me, by the by, why you suddenly decided to visit a property you've owned for what is it, two years?—without evincing the slightest interest in it. The tipstaffs after you, old friend?"

Laughing, Cord rolled out his tale of a desire for rustication, and the conversation turned to recollections of past misdeeds when they had been hey-go-mad undergraduates themselves. After catching up on the present lives of other of their friends, and having got through the better part of Ned's wine supply, the two rolled out of the lodgings in search of dinner.

It was late when Cord returned to Wildehaven. As he crested the hill that brought him into its precincts, he paused and stared into the starlit blackness surrounding him. Would the midnight rider be abroad tonight? Was the intruder, as he surmised, the lovely Miss Gillian Tate, and if so, what was her purpose in these clandestine excursions? Ned had mentioned Sir Henry's obsession with the Pepys diary. Would the man stoop to stealing the papers that were otherwise denied him? Could his niece be a participant, willing or otherwise, in his nefarious activities?

The night returned no answers save for the whispering of a scented breeze and the rustlings and soft twitterings of nocturnal creatures engaged in their various pursuits. After remaining motionless for several minutes in expectation of he knew not what, Cord slowly made his way to the manor house and thence to his bed.

Chapter Five

The next day dawned fine, and Gillian woke with an undefined sense of anticipation. It was not until she had risen to throw back the window hangings that she remembered yesterday's encounter with the Earl of Cordray. The recollection, along with the brilliance of the morning sun, flooded her mind, bringing with it the reminder that she was to go riding with him this afternoon. To her annoyance, her pulse quickened.

She breakfasted hastily and returned to her bedchamber for a ruthless surveillance of her person in the looking glass. She supposed a certain maidenly fluttering was not to be wondered at, for it had been a very long time since she'd spent any length of time alone in a man's company. And there seemed little doubt that this man was a cut above the others of her acquaintance. However, that was no reason for her to spend the day dreaming through her busy routine. She was even more annoyed with herself when, after luncheon with her aunt and uncle, she spent an hour dressing in her most becoming habit, twisting this way and that before her mirror, and teasing at one curl until it lay just there between the rakishly tilted hat brim and her left eyebrow.

She was ready and waiting long before the designated hour of his lordship's arrival, but, naturally, when he was announced, she let ten minutes pass before she made her way down the stairs to the front parlor.

She entered the room to find the earl pacing before the hearth. Goodness, she thought, startled, Lord Cordray seemed to fill the room with his presence. He was not overly large, but there was that about him that commanded attention and shrank his surroundings to insignificance. He moved as though he were constructed of Toledo steel. When he turned to greet her, an internal light seemed to spring to life behind his emerald eyes and she found the effect extremely unsettling.

"Good afternoon, my lord," she replied, aware of the slight breathlessness in her voice. "I'm sorry my aunt and uncle are not on hand to greet you, but they usually nap after luncheon."

The earl moved to take her hand, holding it just a fraction of a second longer than might have been considered proper. "Perhaps I shall see them when we return." Lord Cordray bent to retrieve the riding crop he had laid along the back of a settee. "I need not ask," he continued, smiling, "if you are ready for our outing. Your habit, if I may say so, is exceptionally becoming. That color suits you."

Since this was precisely the reason Gillian had chosen the ensemble of a deep cherry that brought out the tint in her cheeks and lent a richness to her brown locks, there was no reason why she should feel a tide of heat rise to her cheeks. Indeed, she was surprised to note that the earl himself looked slightly taken aback at his own words.

Gillian managed a simple "Thank you, my lord" before turning to lead the earl from the house. Falstaff, in the care of Simms's minion, awaited her just outside the front door. He greeted his mistress with courteous enthusiasm.

"He looks as though he's trying to make amends for his disgraceful behavior yesterday," remarked Lord Cordray.

"I fear he's merely trying to cozzen me into giving him the sugar lump he knows I have tucked in my pocket," Gillian replied with a laugh. "Here you are then, you shameless rascal."

The earl moved forward, precipitating the groom, to toss Gillian into the saddle, and the two cantered off companionably down the gravel.

Well, thought Cord, who would have guessed that so soon after his flight into obscurity, he'd find himself on an outing with a beautiful woman? Yes, indeed, there was much to be said for a repairing lease in the country. He turned to Miss Tate.

"Since you are far more familiar with the terrain, hereabouts, perhaps you will choose our itinerary."

"Certainly, my lord. Would you—"

"Please, Miss Tate, I am called Cordray by most of my acquaintances, and my friends call me Cord. I hope I can count you among the latter."

Gillian laughed. "But we hardly know each other."

"Yes," replied Cord gravely, "however, one can sense these things. I feel myself in the presence of a kindred spirit."

Miss Tate laughed again, but Cord realized with some surprise that the words he had just spoken were true. He always responded to the presence of an attractive female, but Miss Tate, with her speaking gray eyes and her engaging smile was something quite special. From their first encounter, he had felt a rapport that he seldom experienced with a woman. To be sure, he liked women. He *enjoyed* women—in every sense of the word—but one did not ordinarily make friends with one of that sex whose minds rarely rose above the state of her wardrobe or the latest *on dits*. One engaged in frivolous chatter, or perhaps a judicious bit of dalliance. Might Miss Tate, he wondered, be interested in the latter? Judicious or otherwise? Undoubtedly, it would be interesting to find out, but he rather thought such a plan would have to be contrived with extraordinary finesse.

"Very well . . . Cord . . . would you like a tour of your own estate, or would you prefer to travel farther afield—to Cambridge, perhaps?"

Cord noted that she had omitted an invitation to make use of her first name as well. *Finesse, indeed.*

"Well, Madame Guide, I should like to start out with a short jaunt over the immediate grounds, with perhaps a foray through Great Shelford. I'm reasonably familiar with Cambridge, so perhaps we could save that for another day—with luncheon at the Pelican?

"Yes," Miss Tate replied somewhat distantly, "perhaps."

Mmm, mused Cord, mentally discarding the finesse concept. A full-blown siege now appeared in order.

Gillian smiled inwardly. The predator in Lord Cordray that she had sensed on their first meeting was definitely on the prowl. If the man were possessed of a tail, it would be twitching in anticipation. Ah well, she liked the earl, and she was always up to a challenge. It should prove amusing to match wits with him.

An hour or so later, they had ridden to the limits of the Wildehaven Home Farm. Gillian pointed out the various tenantries as they moved past fields of freshly tilled earth.

"The ground is still too wet for sowing, but some plowing has been done. As you no doubt know, these fields will be producing oats and barley and those over there hops." She gestured toward a cluster of distant groves. "Most of the fruit trees have budded and soon will be in full bloom."

Cord smiled. "You seem remarkably knowledgeable about my estate's crop production."

"Ah, well, I have lived in the Cottage for three years now, and have become well acquainted with most of your tenants, as well as Mr. Jilbert, of course, who frequently stops in to chat with Uncle Henry." She cast a glance at him from beneath her lashes. "Of course, all your activities are of extreme interest around here."

Cord's brows lifted. "Really!"

"Why, yes, the doings of the lord of the manor must

be the primary topic of conversation at the greengrocer's and the local ale shop—and now that the lord has descended from the lofty heights of the London social scene for a visit to this, the most minor of his establishments, the village is absolutely abuzz."

"I see."

The earl's tone was so colorless that Gillian was unable to ascertain the effect on him of this information. She proceeded cautiously.

"For example, there has been much conjecture at your arriving alone, without a party of guests. Of course, there is little to offer in the way of entertainment at this time of year. So, the question is, why would his lordship want to visit at all in early April, when there's no fishing to speak of, or hunting or shooting?"

"I have told you, Miss Tate," began the earl in some irritation, "I wish merely to escape the confines of the city—for a breath of fresh, country air. I do not see—"

Gillian flung up a hand. "Please, my lord, you owe me no explanations. I was only expressing the gist of the local gossip since your arrival—without prior notice," she could not help adding. She continued hastily, suppressing a grin. "Now, here, where the ground begins to rise, are the beginnings of the Gog Magog Hills."

"That much I know," said Cord, bending a severe glance on his tutor. "I cannot think where they got their name, however. Is there some reason for supposing that the famous mythical pair dwelled hereabouts?" He glanced about as though expecting two fur-clad giants to appear over the horizon.

"Not that I know of. Perhaps they merely stopped by to wreak a spot of havoc before heading on to terrorize London. In any event, it's a lovely area."

"Yes, it is. That little inn over there looks even lovelier at the moment. Shall we refresh ourselves?"

"Mm, yes," replied Gillian, stretching in her saddle. "A cup of tea would be wonderful right now."

Once settled in the coffee room by the inn's equally comfortable owner, Cord gazed across the table at Miss Tate. What, he wondered, had been her purpose in excavating so crudely into his personal life? Was it simple, vulgar curiosity? She scarcely seemed the type to indulge in mindless gossip simply for the sake of acquiring a few tidbits to drop in the villagers' avaricious ears. No, rather she seemed to be playing a game with him—nudging him to irritation with her ingenious questions. Well, m'dear, he concluded, it's time for the gander to spoon a little sauce over a particularly tasty goose.

"How long have you lived with your aunt and uncle, Miss Tate?" he began innocuously.

"I came to Rose Cottage three years ago."

Cord said nothing, but arranged his features into an expression of courteous expectancy. After a slight pause, Miss Tate continued. "Uncle Henry and Aunt Louisa are in good health for their ages, but they have come to a point in their lives where they need help with their ordinary routine."

"But, how is it they came to ask you? And why did you agree to leave your home in . . . ?" Cord lifted his voice questioningly. He had meant merely to discomfit her, but found himself awaiting her answer in some anticipation.

She paused again, and Cord thought he detected an expression of chagrin on her delicate features.

"My home is in a village called Netheringham. It's some distance north of here, not far from Lincoln."

"Mm, a long way indeed. You lived there all your life?"

By now, Miss Tate was looking decidedly uncomfortable under Cord's questioning, and Cord could not help but wonder why. His interrogation had been rather persistent, to be sure, but he had surely said nothing untoward. Nothing that any interested person would not have asked of a new-met friend.

"Yes," replied Miss Tate, a hint of exasperation in her tone. "My father is a squire, with a fairly large holding near the village. He is the local justice of the peace. Is there anything else you would like to know, my lord?"

"N-no, I guess not," returned Cord blandly. "But, I must say, I cannot help but wonder why an exceptionally attractive young woman like yourself has chosen to immure herself here in this small village."

Really, thought Gillian, this was the outside of enough. How dare this arrogant peacock importune her for an-

swers to questions that were none of his business? She
supposed she had opened herself up to such treatment
with her own impertinent delving into his personal business but . . . *really*!

"If you are asking me why I am not married, my
lord," she replied tartly, "I take leave to tell you. Did
you serve in the Peninsula when you were in the army?"
she asked dismissively, as though sure he would not have
taken part in action of any significance. "Were you at
Waterloo? I was betrothed to a young man who was
killed there." As Gillian absorbed the earl's expression
of shock, she reflected wildly. *Good God,* what had possessed her to divulge this information? She had not discussed Kenneth's death to anyone since her arrival at
the cottage.

"I . . . I'm sorry, Miss Tate." Lord Cordray had paled,
and Gillian knew she had said enough. However, she
was further appalled to hear herself continue. "Such
were my feelings for the gentleman that I have no desire
to so much as think about marriage. Now, my lord, is
your curiosity satisfied?"

Cord was shamed. He had entered into this little game
of cat and mouse with the sole object of discomfiting the
tantalizing Miss Tate. She had started the whole thing
with her probing questions about his reasons for coming
to Wildehaven. Whatever her motivation in doing so—
and he strongly suspected they involved retaliation for
his blatant gallantry—he had presumed unforgivably on
the situation, resulting in humiliation for Miss Tate and
much-deserved embarrassment for himself.

"Please forgive me, Miss Tate," he began again. "I
cannot say that I did not mean to pry, for I fear there
can be no other explanation of my words. However, I
intended you no pain. And no," he added quietly, "I
was not at Waterloo. I sold out just after the Battle of
Toulouse, when we thought we had Napoleon safely
caged."

At this, Gillian experienced her own moment of morti-
fication. She could have escaped Lord Cordray's probing
with a few light words. Instead, she had chosen to inflict
on him a measure of the pain that had washed over her
at his question. *Good Lord,* it had been four years since

Kenneth's death. Surely, her spirit should have begun to heal by this time. She grimaced inwardly. She supposed it might have if it were not for the burden of guilt that surfaced along with the pain every time she thought of him.

She faced the earl squarely.

"No, my lord . . . that is, Cord . . . it is I who must apologize. There was no need to inflict my private grief on you." She forced a smile. "I suggest we cease this, um, mutual interrogation on which we seem to have launched ourselves."

"Cry friends then?" asked Cord, extending a hand across the table.

Gillian hesitated a moment before reaching forth to accept the grasp of his fingers. They were very warm, she reflected absently—and strong, for all their slenderness.

"Friends," she answered, feeling oddly shy. "And to cement my good intentions, I shall offer gratis the information that I am the youngest of two sons and four daughters, all of whom *are* married. Two of my sisters live near Metheringham, while my other siblings have taken up residence farther afield. My brothers are both in Lincoln, and my other sister resides in York. And that, surely," she concluded with a laugh, "is more than anyone would want to know about *anybody*—even a friend."

Not by half, thought Cord, releasing her hand with some reluctance. He poured what he hoped was a gaze of pure sincerity into Miss Tate's brandy-colored eyes, experiencing a peculiar dizziness as he did so.

"I shall reciprocate," he said solemnly, "by informing you that I am one of only two offspring of my late father—who passed away several years ago, by the by. My mother predeceased him by a year. My brother, the Honorable Wilfred Culver, lives in London, where, I take leave to tell you, he has winkled his way into the Prince Regent's set and cuts quite a swath there."

"I am duly impressed, my lord," returned Gillian with equal gravity. "May one assume he is also a member of the dandy set?" She stopped short, putting her fingers to her lips. "Oh, dear, another question. Please forget I spoke."

"Nonsense." Cord smiled. "The answer is an emphatic yes. To behold Wilf in all his tailored glory is to experience the personification of the most exquisite elegance. In fact, I suspect it is through his sartorial magnificence that he has endeared himself to the Prince. Wilf tells me His Royal Highness seeks his advice on every aspect of his wardrobe. As you might imagine, Wilf on the strut in Bond Street is a sight to behold. Do you get to London often, Miss Tate?" he asked innocently.

If Miss Tate noticed the insertion of yet another question, she made no dispute. She merely laughed and replied, "Goodness, no. Every once in a great while Aunt Louisa persuades Uncle Henry to make the trip. On these occasions—usually in coincidence with some museum exhibition or other in which Uncle Henry is interested—she and I make flying visits to the shops and drapery merchants, and then Aunt Louisa pesters Uncle Henry into attending the theater. I daresay, however, we have not set foot there for over a year."

"I hope," remarked Cord, in what he admitted to himself was a slightly oily tone of voice, "that you will notify me the next time you plan an excursion to the metropolis. I should like the opportunity to escort you—and your aunt and uncle as well, of course—to the theater, or perhaps to dinner."

Miss Tate smiled faintly. "That would be very nice," she responded in the tone of one who sees little chance of her words coming to pass.

Having finished their repast, the earl and his guest took their leave of the inn, to the accompaniment of the landlord's earnest good wishes for the rest of their day and the hope of their return to his hostelry at an early date.

"Where to now, Miss Tate?" asked Cord as they trotted leisurely from the inn yard.

Glancing at the little timepiece pinned to her lapel, Gillian uttered a small cry. "My goodness! I had no idea the hour was so advanced. Dinner is less than an hour away. Aunt Louisa will be sure we have been set upon by brigands."

She wheeled her horse about, and Cord, sighing, turned to follow her.

"But we haven't covered half my estate," he said plaintively.

"It is not my fault that Wildehaven is such an extensive property, my lord." Gillian's tone was tart, but Cord had no difficulty in discerning the smile beneath her words.

"Of course, not. Perhaps on another day we could set out in a different direction."

Again, Miss Tate's response was not encouraging. "Perhaps," she returned, noncommittally.

Good Heavens, thought Gillian. What was the matter with her? The gentleman had issued an invitation for a pleasant outing—a repeat of the one today, in fact—and she had reacted as though he'd suggested an assignation. Not in the coffee room of the quaint inn they had just departed, but in one of its bedrooms!

To be sure, she could not help but feel that such was the earl's ultimate goal, but he appeared to be willing to play the game according to the rules. That is, first some flirtation, hours spent in agreeable pursuits, perhaps at some point an innocuous gift, such as a posy or a book. All this, she felt she could handle. She had done so many times. The problem was, she admitted to herself, she was strongly attracted to this particular game player. Why this fact so unnerved her, she was unwilling to fathom at the moment. She knew only that she would be much better off at this point by drawing back.

She spurred her horse, and the two rode in relative silence for several moments until Cord, looking up, clicked his tongue in annoyance. Following his gaze, she beheld the figure of Silas Jilbert riding toward them. He was still some distance away, but he raised his hand to hail them.

"*Now* what does the fellow want?" Cord muttered in displeasure.

Gillian lifted her brows inquiringly, and Cord continued, "He came to see me yesterday, carrying a briefcase stuffed with matters that 'required my immediate attention.' I sent him on his way, of course, telling him that's what he's paid for—to spare my immediate attention, but he keeps turning up, usually with some project in mind that will improve the estate and create prosperity for one and all."

"But he would be remiss in his duty if he did not seek ways to increase the estate's productivity."

Cord found the expression of mild disapproval on Gillian's face irritating. "Good God!" he exclaimed. "I pay the fellow well, and he seems to know what he's doing. Why can't he just go off and do what he does without bothering me?"

Gillian's eyes widened, but before she could respond, Mr. Jilbert was upon them.

"My lord!" he said rather breathlessly, "I am glad I caught you."

Mr. Jilbert was a small man in his early fifties. When he removed his hat, a thatch of thinning brown hair was revealed. His eyes were an unremarkable brown and partially obscured by a pair of large, thick spectacles that he wore pressed firmly against the bridge of a long, thin nose. He passed his hand over his hair as he nodded respectfully to Cord and Gillian.

Cord sighed. "What is it, Jilbert?"

"It's about the tenants' cottages. I believe I mentioned this to your lordship before, but now the matter has become critical. As you have probably observed, the ground is very damp."

"Yes?" Cord replied unencouragingly.

"That's because, though today is fine, we've had a lot of rainfall this spring. As you know, the tenants' cottages were built in a low spot. This should have been remedied years ago," he added somewhat severely, then continued hastily, noting the earl's growing signs of impatience. "Now the road between the cottages and the fields has become almost impassable. In addition, the river flows close to the cottages, and it has become swollen. I am fearful of flooding. I have instructed the men to erect a barrier of sandbags."

"Well—that should take care of the problem, shouldn't it?" Lord, thought Cord, why did the man keep nattering on? This encounter was coming close to spoiling his idyllic afternoon with the lovely Miss Tate.

"Temporarily, my lord," said Mr. Jilbert, stolidly persevering. "However, it has become necessary to create a more permanent barrier."

"Then do it, man." Cord could hear his voice rising

irascibly, but he didn't care. He hated this sort of thing, and the sooner Jilbert became aware of that fact the better.

"But it will mean a great deal of expense, my lord."

"Surely not beyond my means, however?" He raised his riding stick to tap his boot.

"N-no, my lord, but a project of this magnitude is surely something that should be discussed—"

"No, it should not," snapped Cord. "I hereby give you carte blanche to do whatever the devil is necessary for your little 'project.' If you cannot manage without consulting me at every turn, Jilbert, perhaps you should seek employment elsewhere."

Jilbert paled. "No, my lord! That is . . . yes, my lord. I did not mean—" His glance darted to Gillian and back to Cord. "I shall, er, take my leave, my lord."

Cord merely nodded as Mr. Jilbert clapped his hat to his head and, wheeling his horse about, clattered off.

At his side, Gillian simply stared at him. Good Lord, even for an idle peer of the realm, Cord's behavior had been quite rude. And, even from her short acquaintance with him, seemed completely out of character. Why, he had nearly bitten poor Mr. Jilbert's head off, when the man had only been doing his job. Was Cord so addicted to a life of idleness that he could not bear the slightest interference in his pleasures?

Cord glanced at her, and, as though aware of the character flaw he had revealed, he flushed.

"I'm afraid I was rather harsh with the fellow."

Gillian could not but agree. She nodded gravely. "Yes, you were."

Cord smiled disarmingly. "I shall apologize the next time we meet. I shall freely admit that it was ill-done of me to vent my spleen on Jilbert just for attempting to ruin our enjoyment of this lovely afternoon."

Gillian was far from satisfied by this disingenuous little speech, but she smiled dutifully. She remarked again on the lateness of the hour, and the two continued their ride in more pleasant conversation.

"I was hoping," remarked Cord as they approached Rose Cottage, "to further my acquaintance with your uncle."

Gillian's lips curled derisively. This new ploy was surprisingly obvious in a man of Lord Cordray's seeming skill in the art of dalliance.

"I'm sure he would enjoy more conversation with you, my . . . Cordray," she replied serenely, sure that Cord had no more intention of sequestering himself with an elderly academic for a serious discussion of the works of the poet Dryden than he had of embarking on a voyage to the Tasmin. "Since his retirement from his academic duties he has few contacts with the outside world. I'm sure a visit or two from you would do him a world of good."

"Excellent."

Gillian opened her mouth to point out a particularly ancient oak tree just to the left of their path, but Cord forestalled her by adding casually, "I heard from an old friend at Magdalene the other day that your uncle has developed an interest in a diary written by someone called Pepper or some such."

Gillian turned to gape at the earl, her blood seeming to congeal into great clumps in her veins.

Chapter Six

"Wh-what?" blurted Gillian haltingly.

"Pepper . . . or, no—" Cord snapped his fingers. "Pepys! That's it. Samuel Pepys." He watched Miss Tate's discomfiture with what he knew was unbecoming glee. "You know," he continued, feigning a wholly innocent interest, "in view of Evelyn's recently published diary, this—"

"Where—" Miss Tate moistened her lips. "Where did you hear of my uncle's interest . . . ?" She trailed off with a dismal flutter of her fingers.

"Why, I thought I just said—I have a friend—a don

at Magdalene. Perhaps you know him. His name is Edward Maltby."

Miss Tate merely nodded convulsively.

"He said your uncle is working on a translation of the manuscript. How odd of the fellow to write in code, don't you think?"

Cord toyed delicately with this theme for a few moments, noting the color that flooded her cheeks and the agitation stirring her magnificent bosom. Good Lord, he had surely hit a nerve. She looked as though he had just proposed swimming naked in the Cam. To his disappointment, they arrived at their destination just as Miss Tate seemed to recover her composure. However, if he'd expected an invitation to dinner, or even so much as a cup of tea, he was doomed to disappointment. When he assisted the lady in dismounting from her horse, she merely gave him two fingers, thanked him for a most pleasant afternoon and whirled away into the house.

Inside, Gillian leaned against the front door, her breath coming in great, gulping gasps as though she had just escaped a band of highwaymen. She struggled for composure as Widdings crossed the hall toward her at a stately pace.

"I was just about to open the door for you, Miss Tate," he said reproachfully. "I came as soon as I heard the stir of your arrival. His lordship did not see you inside?" His voice contained the barest hint of disapproval.

"Yes, Widdings." Gillian fought to speak calmly. "That is, no. No. Lord Cordray was obliged to leave."

To this, Widdings made no response, and, contenting himself with an austere bow, turned and retraced his steps into the nether regions of the house.

Gillian wearily climbed the stairs. She was vaguely pleased to note that she had, after all, arrived home in time for dinner, thus escaping an interrogation by her aunt. In her bedchamber, she tossed her hat on the bed and began fumbling with the fastenings of her riding habit. By now, her emotions had been buttoned into their usual neat bundle of control, but she forbore to ring for assistance. Instead, she flung herself on the bed beside the hat to give herself up to a torrent of cautionary reflections.

There was no reason for her to have flown into the boughs at Cord's mention of the diary. He had no doubt spoken in all innocence. Why had she taken it as a direct accusation of her part in her uncle's recent flurry of chicanery? She knew the answer to that well enough! It was her own guilty conscience that had pointed to her like an avenging sword poised to thrust into her very core.

How had she ever been caught up in this impossible situation? How could she ever have been mad enough to involve herself in Uncle Henry's ludicrous pursuits? Aunt Louisa had tried to dissuade her—but the poor old soul had offered no alternative solution to the problem.

Gillian had warned Uncle Henry of the probable consequences of his obsession. She had listened in growing despair to his cavalier dismissals of her concerns and to his unrepentant declarations of future transgressions. She tried to take comfort in the fact that he had not visited the little library in Magdalene's New Building for some days. Perhaps his interest in Mr. Pepys's diary was waning—not likely.

Or, perhaps he felt he had gleaned enough information from the original text so that he need not refer to it on a continual basis. *Yes.* Now, there seemed a more plausible concept. Lord knew her uncle had transcribed enough notes from Mr. Pepys's six leather-bound volumes to caulk a sinking ship.

Gillian cast her thoughts back to her conversation earlier with Lord Cordray. If Uncle Henry's name had come up—as it might well have, since the two had met only the day before—in a chat between the earl and an old friend, it would have been odd, indeed, if said old friend had not mentioned Sir Henry Folsome's fascination with the Pepys diary. After all, tales of her uncle's skirmishes with the college authorities had been widely circulated through the academic population of Cambridge for months.

Yes. Certainly. There could be no doubt Cord's question had been prompted by the most casual interest. He had merely been making conversation.

Why, then, had she discerned a gleam of pure mischief in the depths of those jeweled eyes? Dear God, did the earl know something?

Aware that she was indulging in the wildest speculation, Gillian sat up abruptly. There was simply no point in conjecturing about the earl, either his motives or the extent of his knowledge of her clandestine activities. She had no reason to suppose he was actively seeking proof of wrongdoing on her part. Nor did his queries into Uncle Henry's work with the diary indicate more than the most casual interest.

Clutching this thought firmly to her bosom, she rang for her maid to assist her in making her ablutions for dinner.

The following two weeks passed in relative calm. To Gillian's dismay, the earl visited Rose Cottage on several occasions, but after the merest greeting to her, he sought the company of Uncle Henry. The two fell into the habit of closeting themselves in Uncle Henry's study for an hour or two, to emerge on the best of terms, still disputing a point in some obscure passage of Restoration poetry.

Twice Lord Cordray accepted Sir Henry's invitation to stay to dinner, but the conversation during the meal was unexceptionable.

"Do you mean to say, my lord," asked Aunt Louisa on one of these occasions, "that Lady Harriet allowed the Earl of Sindwick to kiss her on the lips in pubic?"

"Indeed, Mrs. Ferris, I saw it with my own eyes—and right in front of the Regent!"

"Well, I never!" exclaimed Aunt Louisa. "Things must be coming to a pretty pass in the *ton,* when such behavior is accepted in the highest circles."

"Yes," replied the earl languidly, reflecting on the tales told him by Wilfred of the doings of the Regent's set, "but, one wonders just who inhabits the highest circles these days."

Gillian pressed her napkin to her lips to stifle an inadvertent giggle. She raised her eyes to intercept a sparkling glance from Cord, and before she knew what she

was about, she returned it with one of laughing
appreciation.

"You are never saying," she remarked demurely,
"that the Prince Regent is not considered a good *ton*!"

"I would never say anything so treasonous," Cord replied promptly. "However, there is a school of thought
that asserts it does one's reputation no good to be seen
in his company."

"My lord!" gasped Aunt Louisa, much rattled. "You
speak of the First Gentleman of our country—nay, all
of Europe."

"Mm, yes, so I'm told," Cord responded irrepressibly.
Gazing at Mrs. Ferris's shocked countenance, he re-
lented. "Of course, some may fault the Prince for
allowing his friends too much latitude in their behavior,
but others contend, with good reason, one might say,
that this trait is one of his finer attributes."

"Oh, yes." Aunt Louisa beamed once more in innocent agreement. "I've heard that the Regent is extraordinarily condescending to those in his circle."

Shortly after dinner was concluded that night, Cord
made his departure. He never stayed late at these visits
to the Folsome menage. Not that he wasn't tempted. An
evening spent by the fire with the enticing Miss Tate
would have been much to his liking. Unfortunately, such
an evening would also have included the presence of her
aunt and uncle. Sir Henry Folsome and his sister were
sterling individuals, but Cord's idea of companionship
for an evening did not generally run to sterling
individuals.

In addition, Miss Tate never indicated by the slightest
nuance of behavior that she would have welcomed an
additional few hours of his company.

In fact, reflected Cord as he wended his way back to his
own domicile, Miss Tate showed no inclination to en-
courage his attentions at all. Charm he might ever so
diligently, she seemed immune to his efforts to separate
her from her virtue.

Once more, his thoughts turned to the rider he had
encountered on the night of his arrival at Wildehaven.
The more he knew of the proper Miss Tate, the less
likely a candidate she seemed for his midnight marauder.

It was all but impossible to imagine this beautiful but eminently proper spinster, donning breeches and tucking her hair under a cap for an excursion in the small hours of the night.

Was it possible she crept out to meet a lover? Highly unlikely, he thought. Even if she were so inclined, there were easier ways to contrive an assignation. At this time of year, there were innumerable leafy bowers available in which to while away an afternoon in illicit pleasure.

No, if his mysterious visitor was indeed Miss Tate, the most logical explanation involved her uncle's preoccupation with the writings of Samuel Pepys. Impossible as it seemed, was she stealing volumes of the diary for Sir Henry's perusal? Had her ride over the starry hills of Cambridgeshire been a one-time occurrence, or had she been out since then, booted and capped? More interesting, was she likely to venture forth again? And how would he know of such an outing? He did not fancy patroling the grounds of Wildehaven in the dead of night on the off chance he might see her.

The answer to his unproductive musings was provided one afternoon a week hence. Cord had just emerged from Sir Henry's study, laughing dutifully at one of the old gentleman's more ancient jests. To his pleasure, when they entered the parlor, Miss Tate was seated in a cherry-striped wing chair near the window. She rose at their approach, gathering up a handful of embroidery silks and the handkerchiefs she had been monogramming. Even before she spoke, Cord sensed an unusual tension fairly vibrating through her slender form. She greeted him distractedly, her gaze swiveling between Cord and her uncle.

"Did you two have an, er, interesting discussion?" she asked at last.

Cord sensed that she held her breath until her uncle replied heartily, "Of course, we did, my dear. I am still trying to tell this young whelp that he's absolutely wrong in his interpretation of Dryden's *Annus Mirabilis*."

The old man swung to his guest, but not before Cord observed Gillian sag in noticeable relief. Sir Henry continued, "You see, my boy, it portends to relate to the

Anglo–Dutch Naval War, but in reality— By Jove, now, who's that?"

The question was prompted by a knocking at the door, followed a few moments later by the entrance of Widdings, who was in turn followed by a tall young man. He could not have been more than nineteen or twenty years of age, and, though he was shabbily dressed, his demeanor was dignified and open.

"John!" cried Sir Henry delightedly. "Do come in, my boy."

Gillian's smile was almost as bright as that of her uncle, and Cord knew a wholly unwelcome stab of jealousy. Could this unprepossessing sprout be the object of Gillian's theoretical yearnings? He pulled himself up short a moment later. What was the matter with him? The boy was scarcely of an age to shave his chin. Not that it mattered to him where Miss Tate's maidenly affections might be engaged.

In any event, despite the brilliant smile, Gillian did not seem pleased to see the young man. She had stiffened perceptibly at his entrance, and her face was pale. Her hands trembled as she requested Widdings to see to refreshments. With a nervous gesture, she led the young man to a comfortable chair.

Cord thrust out his hand as Sir Henry made introductions. "My lord, may I present John Smith? He is an undergraduate at St. John's College. John, meet our landlord, the Earl of Cordray."

The young man blushed furiously, then turned pale. His mouth opened and closed several times before he murmured almost inaudibly, "My lord . . . honored, I'm sure."

"John and I have been working on a translation of a certain diary." He glanced significantly at John before continuing. "I mention no names, of course, but"—he transferred his gaze sharply to Cord—"it is the one of which I spoke some days ago."

He put a finger aside his nose and nodded portentously. He continued, "Enough said about that." He turned again to Mr. Smith. "Have you made any progress since our last meeting?"

"N-no," replied the young man, his awed gaze still on

the earl. "I have found Lord Grenville's guide to be completely unhelpful, and—"

"I'm sure Lord Cordray has no interest in your work with John, Uncle." Gillian's tone was so sharp that Cord swung to her in surprise. Lord, she was strung like a fiddle! What was going on here? What was this innocuous-looking young fellow to her that she could behave in manner he would have sworn was quite foreign to her.

Sir Henry, too, displayed astonishment at Gillian's demeanor. At that moment, Mrs. Ferris entered the room, and by the time greetings had flown about the room once more, Miss Tate had regained her composure—at least to some extent. Her distress was still evident in the rigidity of her posture as she returned to perch on the edge of the cherry-striped wing chair. Absently, she plucked at the fringe of her shawl.

Much as Cord would have liked to assuage his curiosity, he could not help but be struck by Gillian's obvious distress. Since he was also sure that his presence in the house was the prime cause of her unease, he did not take a seat. Bowing to both Miss Tate and her aunt, he shook hands with Sir Henry and John Smith and declared his intention to depart.

"No, thank you, dear lady," he replied in response to Mrs. Ferris's inevitable invitation to stay for dinner. "I can see Sir Henry is champing at the bit to confer with Mr. Smith on his pet project. Another day, perhaps."

Gillian, a trace of color at last returning to her cheeks, rose again to see Cord from the house.

"He seems very young," he commented idly as they left the room. "Mr. Smith, that is. What does he bring to the study of Mr. Pepys's diary?"

"Oh!" Miss Tate started visibly. "Yes, well he is the son of an old friend of Uncle Henry's. He took John under his wing when the boy came to Cambridge with his wife and son."

"Wife and son?" Cord's brows lifted. "Good Lord, he scarcely seems old enough to—"

"Um," continued Miss Tate hurriedly. "He is barely nineteen. We heard there were compelling reasons . . . In any event, it was at Uncle Henry's instigation that

Mr. Neville, the college master, who is a mere four-and-twenty himself, asked John to take over the translation of the diary,"

"But, I thought Sir Henry—"

"Yes, he, too, is working on a translation, of course. I think if it were anyone else, Uncle Henry would not be so generous with his assistance, but he is very fond of the boy."

By this time, they had reached the front hall, and, accepting his hat and gloves from Widdings, Cord bowed a graceful farewell.

Having arrived at an informal footing with the household, he declined to wait for a groom to bring Zeus around from the stable. He proceeded to the back of the house. On passing the kitchen garden, he observed several chickens meandering among the newly seeded plot, selecting from the buffet with gustatory and wholly unauthorized enthusiasm. Cord glanced about uncertainly. Apparently no one had noticed the chickens' escape. If left undetained, they would no doubt consume the season's entire vegetable supply. Shrugging, Cord turned toward the kitchen entrance to the house. As he approached the door, he was halted by the sound of feminine voices drifting from an open window. Edging close, he positioned himself nearby.

". . . I don't believe he's told John." The voice belonged to Mrs. Ferris. "But, that's not to say—"

"We can only hope," interrupted Miss Tate. "Do you know, he's picked out two volumes this time."

Mrs. Ferris groaned. "Two!"

There was a moment of silence before Miss Tate continued. "You know what this means, don't you?"

Mrs. Ferris sighed deeply. "Oh, my. Must you, my dear?"

"You know I must. I feel I have an obligation to Uncle Henry, after all. And wouldn't you know?" she continued despairingly. "The moon is dark tonight. I'll have to bring the large lantern—with a reflector—and even then it will take me forever to make the trip."

Mrs. Ferris sighed again. "Very well. I'll make sure we can find . . ."

Cord strained to hear the rest, but apparently Gillian

and her aunt had left the room. After a moment's startled thought, he turned and hurried toward the stable, the feathered marauders forgotten.

Inside the house, Gillian continued her conversation with her aunt as they moved into the kitchen.

"Honestly, Aunt, the situation is becoming completely untenable."

"I know, dearest. I feel so bad that—after all you've done for us—why, you're giving up the best years of your life caring for a couple of doddering old people. And now Henry is putting you in an impossible position. I've never known him to so unfeeling in his demands."

"Or so criminal, I'll warrant," Gillian said tartly. "Well, there's no help for it, I suppose. However—and I know I've said this before, but this time I mean it—this is the last time. I care nothing abut 'the best years of my life,' but I draw the line at going to prison. The next time he speaks of taking any part of the diary from the college, I'll . . . I'll bind and gag him."

"And I'll help you," averred her aunt stoutly.

Thus it was that as the clock in the front hall of Rose Cottage struck midnight, a slender figure clad in dark breeches and a bulky coat crept down the stairs. Gillian, making sure she was unobserved, turned toward the back of the house and thence to the stables. Lighting a lantern from the candle she carried, she silently saddled Falstaff. A few moments later, she walked the gelding slowly from the yard. The journey to Magdalene, accomplished in utter darkness, took over two hours, but at last she drew Falstaff to a halt outside the college wall, where it sloped down to the bank of the Cam.

Scaling the low wall was the work of a moment, even with the encumbrance of the satchel she carried inside her coat. Once having gained the precincts of the college, she blended with the shadowed landscape as she made her way to the rear of the New Building. Here, without a sound, she raised the window whose lock she knew to be broken. Inside, she hurried to accomplish her mission, and fifteen minutes later she was up and over the wall again, smoothly and noiselessly.

Her feet had no sooner touched the ground when an arm snaked around her waist and a voice whispered in her ear, "A bit late for swanning about the countryside, doncher think?"

Chapter Seven

Gillian's terrified squeal was silenced by the strong, warm hand clamped over her mouth. Her heart seemed to leap into her brain, where it banged crazily as though seeking escape. Her knees gave way beneath her, but she struggled against the figure whose arms pinioned her to his breast.

"It's all right, Miss Tate," the man said. "It is only I, Cord."

Well, of course it is, you idiot, thought Gillian wildly. She'd known who it was the moment he'd caught her swinging down from the wall. Only Cord. *Only* Cord? The man who had the power to bring her and Uncle Henry to ruin. The man who could turn Uncle Henry and Aunt Louisa out of their home. Dear God, every disaster she had imagined on these interminable midnight jaunts was now taking place.

She stopped struggling. She took several long, deep breaths until her heart had returned to its normal location and rate—more or less.

"Good evening, my lord," she said, managing to speak the words with remarkable calm. "I suppose you're wondering what I am doing here at this time of night."

Good Lord, what a stupid thing to say! The thin smile revealed in the narrow ray of light from the lantern he carried gave evidence of the earl's agreement with this assessment.

"On the contrary, Miss Tate, I have a very good idea

why you're here, but I suggest we postpone our discussion until we are away from the town.''

Gillian would rather have ridden into the jaws of hell than accompany Lord Cordray anywhere at this moment, but she knew the futility of argument. She followed as he led her to where Falstaff was tethered and remained silent as he assisted her into the saddle. He said nothing further as they walked the horses through the silent streets of Cambridge, and it was not until they were well on their way along the Shelford Road that he drew up into a little spinney beside the thoroughfare. A few paces more brought them to a small clearing, where the earl dismounted.

He put up his arms to assist Gillian, and after a moment's hesitation, she allowed him to lower her to the ground. Leading her to a conveniently placed fallen log, he settled himself and patted the space next to him.

"I prefer to stand, my lord," she said stiffly.

"As you will," he replied agreeably. "Miss Tate, I should very much like to hear the explanation you have no doubt concocted by now."

A wholly irrational urge to strike Lord Cordray across his bland smile swept over Gillian. How dare he! He had jauntered up to her in the middle of the night, making mice feet of her plans to save her uncle from ruination. He had forced her to accompany him away from the college, and now, here he was demanding explanations! She knew her fury stemmed from fear and the knowledge that she had brought her troubles upon herself, but she let the fire of her wrath spread its tendrils of warmth and a fine, if completely unwarranted, moral outrage.

"I owe you no explanation for my behavior, my lord." She fairly spat the words.

"Perhaps not, but I think you are going to give me one. One hates to mention this, Miss Tate, but you are rather in my power at the moment. There is no question, I think you will agree, that I could make life extremely unpleasant for you. I have no intention of doing so at this point, but . . . well, you have been caught red-handed, stealing from Magdalene College."

"Stealing!" Gillian's jaw dropped in shock. "*Stealing!*

I was doing nothing of the kind! How could you even think such a thing? I have never—"

"Please, Miss Tate." Cordray glanced at the satchel protruding from beneath her coat. "How could I come to any other conclusion? I saw you creeping in and out of the college in the dead of night. You're carrying a bulging satchel that is . . . or, well, no it's not bulging," he admitted as Gillian jerked the satchel from its hiding place and thrust it at him.

"I have never stolen anything in my life," Gillian gasped, pushing the case at him until he nearly fell off the log. "Please—do examine it, my lord, you will find it empty."

Cord did so, after which he looked up in puzzlement. "Are you concealing the volumes someplace else? I don't understand . . ." He gazed at her wrathful countenance for a long moment.

"Please do sit down, Miss Tate. And forgive me if I have offended you. Perhaps I have jumped to an unwarranted conclusion, but—"

Gillian plumped down beside him, expelling a sigh that seemed to come from the soles of her feet. "But," she finished, "what else could you think? Did you realize it was I whom you saw the night you arrived at Wildehaven?"

Cord chuckled. "Not right away, but the list of neighborhood suspects was woefully short. And then I found your comb." He turned to face her. Taking her hand, he spoke softly. "I know I have no claim to your confidence, but would you please tell me what is going on?"

Gillian returned his gaze. Even in the dim lantern light, his green eyes had taken on a fire of their own, and she felt her pulse quicken.

"You are right, of course," she said as prosaically as she could manage. "My trek to the college tonight did involve the Pepys Diary. But I did not come to steal it— I came to replace it."

"Replace it!" Cord's amazed stare was slowly replaced by one of dawning comprehension. "Are you telling me Sir Henry has been—"

"Yes," said Gillian miserably. "Oh, Cord, he is such a good man, but he seems to have become utterly unhinged over the diary. He has always relished a challenge—the opportunity to demonstrate his skill and ingenuity. Sometimes, I think that's the whole point of this absurd start. For the past year or so he has thrown himself completely into its translation, and when the volumes were denied him, he believed the only way open to him was to take them from the library. To . . . to steal them, as it were."

"And you have been returning them," Cord murmured in fascination. "Good God, Gillian, do you realize the risk you have been taking?"

"Yes, of course, I do, but what was my alternative? If the thefts had been discovered, Uncle Henry would have been the prime suspect—and if anyone were to ask him if he was the culprit, such was his outrage that he would have owned to it immediately—and castigated the college authorities for forcing him into thievery."

"Yes, but—Lord, Gillian, how many of these little excursions have you made?"

Gillian noted the use of her first name, but could not bring herself to remonstrate. For one thing, she was in no position to preach propriety at the moment, and for another, the sound of her name on his lips was somehow comforting, as though he thought of himself as her friend. Was it possible Lord Cordray did not mean to turn her over to the constable, or to evict her and her little family from the cottage? She turned her thoughts from these roseate concepts.

"How many times? Oh, six or seven, I suppose. Apparently, Uncle Henry had no difficulty in purloining the volumes. The manner of their keeping is quite lax. He would wait until the staff had left the building in the afternoon. Then he would simply bundle them up with the rest of the books he had been using and walk out with them. At first, he would leave them openly on his desk, but when I began returning them, he took to locking them away. Fortunately, there is no place in the house with which Aunt Louisa is unfamiliar. She was able to rescue them from under his mattress and behind cupboards and from various cabinets. She has keys to everything, of course."

A low laugh escaped Cord. "No wonder your uncle

was in such a taking the morning after one of your forays—the day on which we met."

"Yes, he cannot understand why I am undermining his efforts in such an undutiful manner."

Cord sobered. "Yes, but you cannot keep this up. One of these times, either you or your uncle will be caught at your nefarious activities, and then you'll truly be in the suds."

Gillian, too, grew grave. "Am I not in the suds right now? That is, I have been caught, haven't I?"

Cord started. "Good Lord, you don't think that I— well, I know what I said, but I would certainly never—" He blew an exasperated sigh. "I thought you knew me for your friend, Gillian, and Sir Henry's and his sister's as well. Your uncle's motives in this fiasco must be highly suspect—even though I'm sure he feels he is merely borrowing the volumes. And you certainly have done nothing wrong. That is, you are returning the college's property."

"Yes, that's true, but a purist might consider that in not preventing Uncle Henry from committing his, as you say, nefarious activities, or in not reporting him, I am . . . well, an aider and abettor."

"How fortunate, then, that I am not a purist. I have no intention of seeing you—any of you—come to harm over this."

If Gillian had not been seated already, she would surely have fallen to the ground, so great was her relief. She expelled a shuddering sigh and said simply, "Thank you, Cord."

Cord placed his hand over hers and clasped her fingers lightly. "Now then," he said briskly, "the next matter up for discussion is, what do we do next?"

"Next?" Gillian echoed stupidly.

"Yes. Having agreed that this situation cannot continue, what are we going to do to prevent an occurrence—either of Sir Henry's thievery or of your, er, antithievery procedures."

"I don't know," said Gillian slowly. "I plan to talk to Uncle Henry again, but I doubt it will do much good."

"I agree. From my short acquaintance with the gentleman, I have no difficulty in believing that, once he has his mind set on something, one can't change it with blasting powder."

Gillian smiled faintly. "Your assessment is eminently correct, sir."

Cord remained silent for several moments, and Gillian became aware of the wholly improper intimacy of the scene. The shuttered rays of the lantern created a pool of light over the little log upon which they sat. Outside that circle, the rest of the world lay dark and silent except for the sounds of the night that surrounded them. She and Cord huddled so close together, she was sure he could feel her heartbeat. His fingers on hers created a warmth that permeated her body down to her toes, which curled deliciously inside her boots.

As unobtrusively as possible, she slid her hand out from under his.

At length, Cord uttered a small laugh. "You know, I think I may have a solution—at least a temporary one—to the problem."

Gillian turned to him, taking care as she did so, to place several inches between them.

"I am not," he continued, apparently not noticing her move to safety, "acquainted with the new master of the college, Neville, I believe his name is. However, in the past, I have donated copiously to Magdalene for various projects. It is my opinion, that if I were to introduce myself to Mr. Neville and express my recently developed interest in the writings of Mr. Pepys, he would not be averse to letting me borrow them—on a temporary basis, of course."

"Mm. I've met the master on occasion, but I do not know him well. However, I daresay you're right. The wishes of a titled gentleman with such deep and open pockets would certainly work strongly on his sensibilities."

If there was a hint of irony in Gillian's tone, Cord ignored it.

"Splendid. I shall visit the gentleman on the morrow, and when I return home victorious, with one or more volumes of the diary in my possession, I shall drop them into your uncle's greedy hands—with the firm proviso, of course, that they be returned to *my* hands in a few days. Do you think this arrangement will suit him?"

"Not nearly so well as keeping them permanently, but I think he can be talked around. But . . ." Gillian hesitated. "You are willing to do this? I feel we should not ask you to become a part of Uncle Henry's . . . obsession. We have no right— That is, it is very kind of you to make such an effort on our behalf, but—"

"Nonsense." The word was spoken sharply, acting as a dash of cold water on Gillian's heated incoherences. "It will be my pleasure. I must do something to avoid the boredom of my forced rustication. And, I must say, I have become somewhat interested in this mysterious diary myself. I should not at all mind having a look at it—perhaps I shall be the one to crack the code, thereby covering myself with glory."

"Then, I can only thank you from the bottom of my heart, my lord—that is, Cord." She rose. "And now, if we have reached a solution to our situation, it is very late, and I must be getting home."

Cord stood as well and followed her as she hurried back to the horses. As he bent to lift her into the saddle, however, he paused and gripped her shoulders lightly.

"You know," he said huskily, "I would do a great deal more for you, Gillian." He bent and brushed her lips lightly with his. A tingle jolted through her, but so angered was she at this practiced attempt at seduction that she swung way from him to grasp her saddle horn. She lifted her foot and waited, allowing nothing to show on her face but mild distaste.

Cord stepped back abruptly. In the darkness, she could not read his expression, but after a moment, he cupped her boot in his hand and tossed her into the saddle.

They rode in silence for several moments before Cord said flatly, "I'm sorry, Gillian, that was ill-done of me. Although," he added in a more natural tone of voice with just a hint of self-deprecating humor, "I can't say I'm sorry for the kiss—such as it was."

"Then for what are you apologizing?" Gillian strove to keep her tone cool, albeit friendly.

Now he did laugh. "You wretch! For the smarmy little speech that accompanied it. I don't know what made me speak so."

It was Gillian's turn to chuckle. Her anger had dissolved at his words, and she felt oddly pleased. "Perhaps you can blame the situation. An enterprising gentleman, finding himself secluded with a lady in the dead of night in such a romantically sylvan setting might be considered backward indeed if he failed to pursue the advantage."

"I think," said Cord meditatively, "that anything I might say in response to that statement would get me into even more trouble, so I shall pass, groping all the while for a suitably innocuous topic with which to turn the conversation."

"How about this one? I'm not sure it's innocuous, and may get *me* into trouble, but what was that you said about 'forced rustication?' I thought your descent into the countryside was due to a sudden desire for a breath of fresh air and a dollop or two of sunshine."

Cord was silent for so long that Gillian feared he had taken grave offense. At last, however, he sighed. "No, of course, it was not that. The truth is it was a craven scuttling out of town to avoid a . . . a certain situation."

When Gillian said nothing, Cord continued awkwardly. "You see, my family has had an understanding with another family . . ." The dismal little tale was not long in the telling, and at its end, Cord gazed hopefully at Gillian. "It was contemptible of me, but—"

"This, er, young woman," said Gillian severely. "Had you spoken to her of your forthcoming formal proposal?"

"No!" exclaimed Cord in a startled tone. "At least— well, I suppose I gave her to believe—in an oblique fashion that I would—" He sighed. "In our formative years, I always looked on her as a pestilential younger sister, and when we grew older, we . . . well, I guess you could say we barely tolerated each other. She's a decent enough sort, I suppose, but I can't see myself married to her."

"And how does she feel about you?" Gillian, repressing an altogether irrational pleasure at his words, maintained the ice in her voice.

Cord smiled thinly. "I don't think she cares tuppence for me." He continued awkwardly after a moment. "However, she has made it plain over the years that she expects to marry me eventually. I know this must sound like the veriest puffery, but I think she would very much like to be a countess. Every time we meet, she seems to have more plans for the day when she becomes Lady Cordray,"

Gillian rapidly ran through her list of London acquaintances, but did not find a Corisande among them.

"When I turned eighteen or so, my parents began haranguing me to make a declaration. When they passed away, my Aunt Binsted took over the position of dragoon-in-charge."

Gillian knew she should listen to her better half and make a discreet change of subject at this point. However, her worse half was clearly in command of her emotions concerning this matter, and her curiosity—not just about Cord's evasion of his responsibilities, but about his motivation in doing so—overcame her.

"Why did you never tell them all that you simply have no wish to marry this Corisande?"

Cord sighed. "I tried. Lord knows I tried, but apparently not hard enough. It was as though my words somehow suffered a translation between my mouth and their ears, so that my continued denials struck them as mere fustian.

"When my aunt informed me a month or so ago that she had arranged for a dinner party featuring Corisande's mama and papa—and her sister and brother as well—she made it painfully clear that on this occasion I was expected to pony up. I was to by God go down on bended knee and ask for her hand in plain, unmistakable English."

"And you said—?"

"At the moment, I had rather a head and could not face another of her jobations. I said I'd think about it," Cord admitted miserably. "Well, of course, she took that as a promise and made her plans accordingly."

"And you never corrected her misapprehension?" By now, Gillian was beginning to feel like the king's prosecutor, but she plunged ahead in her unseemly interrogation.

"Again—I tried, but my aunt's ears were permanently stopped, and preparations continued apace. I even took

Corisande aside on a couple of occasions, trying to point out that I truly did not think we would suit."

"And—?" Gillian repeated.

"And, she just laughed—that tinkling, artificial titter that drives me round the bend—and said, 'Oh, Cord, you can be so silly sometimes. Now, what do you think of Italy for our wedding journey?' "

"So, on the day of the dinner party, you simply bolted?"

"Yes. I realize that at some point, I must make the betrothal official, but when I awoke on the morning of the dinner party, it was as though someone had cut off my air supply. I couldn't breathe and . . . I had to get away." The shame in Cord's voice was apparent, mixed with a certain degree of anger. At himself? wondered Gillian, or at the importunities of his family? "I could have made an appearance at the dinner party without performing the bended-knee portion of the evening, but somehow I felt Aunt Binsted would have employed anything up to and including a loaded pistol to get me into a room alone with Corisande, at which point it would have been all up with me." He sighed again. "I did leave a note, but I freely admit my behavior in the whole situation was unpardonable."

Hmm, Gillian reflected. Cord did not strike her as the kind of man who would allow himself to be bullied by his family—or the kind of man who could not face up to the critical issues of his life. She stared meditatively at him for a moment before relenting. "But, perhaps understandable," she said kindly.

Cord made no response, then said at last, "But enough about me and my travails, Miss Tate. I believe it is now your turn to unburden yourself of your maidenly secrets. Do tell me, why is it that a young woman of your undeniable beauty, charm, intelligence, et cetera, et cetera, has chosen to shun the company of men, instead creating a monument in her heart to a lost love. Surely four years is a very long time to mourn your young man, no matter how powerful your feelings for him at the time."

Gillian was at last silenced, feeling suddenly as though the ground had just given way beneath her.

Chapter Eight

Gillian opened and closed her mouth, but was unable to make a reply to Cord's unpardonable question. How dare he probe the wound that still festered in the very core of her existence? To be sure, she had gone far beyond what was seemly in her own inquiries, but this was too much.

"I'm sorry, my lord," she said frigidly. "The matter does not bear discussion. What to you is a monument to a dead love—and, by the by, I take leave to tell you your wording was boorish and insensitive in the extreme—is to me a memory too precious to be abandoned."

She cringed at her own words, experiencing again the pain and guilt that washed over her every time the subject of Kenneth's death was broached. She was now, and knew she would be forever haunted by the knowledge that she had killed him.

"I apologize." Cord's tone expressed startlement. "I did not—"

"Oh, look!" cried Gillian, her voice ragged with relief. "We are home."

She gestured toward the silhouette of Rose Cottage looming on their right.

"But—" began Cord, before subsiding into a resigned, "So we are."

"I think," said Gillian hurriedly, "that I should leave you now. I have become adept at slithering through the yard and into the stable with relatively little noise, but I think two of us trying the same thing would be stretching our luck."

Without waiting for Cord to dismount, she slid from the saddle. Looking up at him, she managed a strained smile. "I cannot say I am glad to have encountered you this night, my lord Cordray, but I do thank you for your assistance and—and your discretion. To say nothing of your promise of future cooperation, of course."

"I," murmured Cord, "on the contrary, count this as one of the most interesting and pleasurable evenings I have ever spent. I shall visit Mr. Neville at Magdalene tomorrow, and if all goes well, I'll see you later in the afternoon. Sleep well, Gillian."

He tipped his hat, then wheeled Zeus about. In a moment, he was gone, leaving Gillian to stare after him through the darkness.

Cord's thoughts, as he wended his way back to Wildehaven were a whirl of conflicting impressions. He had been right about the identity of his midnight rider! However, having solved that little mystery, several others had taken its place. What was there in the nature of Gillian Tate's seemingly prim and proper character that had prompted her to take on such a bizarre mission? To be sure, she was motivated by a desire to keep a beloved relative from plunging his family into the soup, but need she have chosen this path? There must have been some alternative—although at the moment he could not think what it might be.

And then there was the astonishing and abrupt reversal of his feelings toward her. He had begun tonight's excursion in a spirit of mischief. If, as he had hoped, she turned out to be his unauthorized visitor, he had intended to use it as leverage in his proposed game of hearts. Surely, he felt, a tincture of fear would make her more amenable to his advances. Of course, this line of thought was contemptible, but he'd planned to make it clear that no matter what her response, he would keep her secret. After all, a shared secret, as he had learned early in his career, could serve as a powerful aphrodisiac.

Something had happened, however, in the brief moment when his lips had brushed hers. Something very like a spark . . . a connection . . . a certain—tenderness? Then, he had ruined the moment with his trite, oily pronouncement. "So much more I can do for you, my dear." Lord, he had sounded like Riding Hood's big, bad wolf at his very worst.

Not that he wouldn't enjoy bedding the delectable Gillian. However, at this point friendship had reared its ugly head, tossing a large spanner into his plans. One didn't seduce a friend, after all, and he found that he wanted more from her than a tumble in the hay. He wanted her companionship. Her conversation was like fine wine, and he wanted more of it. He wanted to watch her lovely gray eyes light with that inner laughter that he found so compelling. He wanted to probe the mystery of her obsession with a dead man—to comfort her for her loss and to help her get on with her life. He had never felt an urge to protect a woman before, and he found it unsettling as well as oddly exhilarating.

His thoughts returned to that instant when his mouth had touched hers. The fabric of time itself had seemed altered, for that brief contact seemed to extend itself to an eternal moment of communion.

Tchah! He chided himself. When had he become a maudlin fool? His acquaintance with Gillian Tate was of—what?—two weeks' duration. She was undeniably one of the most alluring females he had ever encountered, but she was just that—a female, and as such very much like every other member of her sex. Pleasant enough for the occasional interlude—romantic, or in Gillian's case otherwise—but nothing more. He would enjoy her company while he was here. When he returned to his natural milieu in London, she would become a pleasant memory.

His return to London. The words settled in the pit of his stomach, chill and sodden, like the remains of a badly cooked dinner. He knew well what awaited him in London, or was perhaps even now pursuing him into the countryside. He had listened to himself in some astonishment as he spun his sad tale to Gillian, for he'd had no intention of unburdening himself so. He recalled her ill-concealed contempt for his spineless refusal to confront both Corisande and his family. The realization of the foolishness of his craven escape struck him anew, and he straightened in his saddle.

Lord, at what point in his life had he become such a spineless nonentity? He knew he had not always been so. After selling out, he had launched on a career of hedonism. He had relegated all his responsibilities to others and had refused to consider any but the lightest of decisions—except when it came to taking a wife. Because of his aunt's persistence, he had been unable to ignore this particular duty. The operative word here, he realized, was "duty," and it was one he could no longer ignore. Marriage to Corisande, he told himself, would not be so bad. She had been born into the Polite World and was fully cognizant of its rules. She knew full well that a wife must not expect fidelity in a marriage of convenience. In return for her husband's support in matters financial and social, she would be allowed her own affairs, if conducted with discretion.

In short, Cord was aware that marriage to the Viscount Rantray's daughter would not affect his pleasures. He would be free to carry on his private pursuits with no interference from his countess.

He realized that these reflections were casting him into a chill depressior. He straightened in his saddle. It was not as though he need hare off to London right away after all. He would make the most of his sojourn in the country. He was safe here in his pastoral paradise—at least temporarily. He would enjoy Gillian's company while it was available, and with any luck he could make it available for at least a few more weeks. There was his promise to her, after all, to keep her uncle out of trouble. Eventually, he would return to his responsibilities on the home front. He would take up his life as his family obligation had ordained it, but he could take comfort in the pleasures still available to a man of his wealth and status. He whistled softly as he approached the manor house and, once he was back in his bedchamber, composed himself for sleep with a clear conscience.

Cord might not have been so sanguine had he known of the events transpiring in London. In her own apartment in Binsted House, Lady Binsted lay sleeping the sleep of the just and pure of heart. Earlier that day, she had taken a step that would no doubt have profound consequences for her wretched nephew, but necessary, nonetheless.

The inquiries sent out to Cordray Park and the other

estates had proved futile. No one at any of these locales had seen or heard from Cord in at least a month.

Her lord had remonstrated with her.

"I tell you, Bessie, you had best stay out of it. Cord won't thank you for poking your nose into his affairs. The boy's done a bolt, and there's nothing you can do except wait for him to surface—which he'll do in his own good time. In my opinion, m'dear, you've done yourself no good by this incessant meddling. Cord simply don't want to get married. Maybe he will someday," he added, "but I'm beginning to agree with Wilf that he and Corisande don't suit and never will."

As usual, Lady Binsted had retorted, "Nonsense."

A chill finger of doubt had twisted inside her, but, with the complacency that was her trademark, she quickly suppressed it. The day after this conversation, she had summoned Geoffrey Tomlinson, Cord's man of affairs, to Binsted House. The instant the young man had entered her drawing room, she perceived that he knew something. The expression of guilt on his open features was almost ludicrous. However, the ensuing conversation was far from productive. Mr. Tomlinson had at first denied any knowledge of Cord's whereabouts. At last, after persistent questioning, he admitted that Cord had informed him of his precipitate departure, just before leaving Town.

"I knew it!" exclaimed Lady Binsted. "Well? Where is he, man?"

"I don't know, my lady," Mr. Tomlinson replied miserably.

"Please." Lady Binsted's voice was sharp with impatience. "Let us not go through all that again. It is imperative that I—that is, we, his family—reach him as soon as possible."

"I'm sorry, my lady." The solicitor, by now very hot and harassed, loosened a noticeably damp collar. "I truly do not know where his lordship is. I only know where he is not."

In response to Lady Binsted's lifted brows, he added hurriedly, "He said not to look for him at the Park or any of the Culver family holdings. He said merely that he was going out into the countryside."

With this, the marchioness had to be satisfied. Dismissing Mr. Tomlinson, she sat for some moments in deep thought before leaving the chamber in search of the marquess.

"Binsted," she began peremptorily, having cornered his lordship in the billiard room, "we must take further steps."

"Eh?" queried her husband in some irritation. "Look here, Bessie, you just caused me to ruin a spectacular bank shot. Been practicing it for a week."

"Never mind that now. We must do something about Cord."

To the accompaniment of the marquess's continued grumbling, she outlined her conversation with Mr. Tomlinson. "He was my last hope of discovering Cordray's whereabouts, Binsted. In my opinion, we have only one other option."

"And what is that?" asked Lord Binsted with deep foreboding.

"The Bow Street Runners."

"Oh, my God!" The expletive burst from her husband's lips like the finest bank shot he had ever attempted. "Bess, you're not serious! Cord will have my guts for garters! Bow Street Runners crawling about the countryside—asking questions of his friends—prying into his activities. Might as well spread his affairs all over the *Morning Post*."

"Don't be absurd, my dear," replied Lady Binsted placatingly. "The Runners are known for their discretion—when one impresses the necessity for it upon them. If you are not concerned about Cordray's situation, I am. I find it of prime importance to assure ourselves of his continued well-being."

Lord Binsted grunted. "You know good and well, Bess, that if something had happened to him, we would have been notified. What you find of prime importance is that he be dragged back here to make a proposal to that wretched girl."

"Wretched girl! Binsted—!"

The marquess waved a hand irritably. "All right, all right. What I meant was that who Cord marries, or if he marries at all, is simply no concern of yours."

"No concern! I am Cordray's only close relative in my sister's generation. If I do not concern myself with what is nothing less than a family crisis, who will?"

This time Lord Binsted threw up his hands in resignation. "You will do as you wish, Bessie. You always do. But, mark my words, there will be the devil to pay."

With that, his lordship turned abruptly back to the billiard table, and after a moment, his wife wheeled about and strode from the chamber.

That afternoon, a burly individual, garbed in homespuns and a voluminous greatcoat, rang the bell at Binsted House. His beard, rough-cut and sprinkled with gray, was so long it fell over a rather garish red waistcoat. Instead of being directed to the tradesman's entrance, as might have been expected, he was ushered immediately into my lady's reception salon. Here, Hamish McSorley, a member of that elite band of investigators known as the Bow Street Runners, accepted a commission from the Marchioness of Binsted, on strict orders to treat the matter with the utmost secrecy.

The next morning, Cord made it his first order of business to ride to Cambridge. Glancing with a smile at the riverbank, where he had intercepted Gillian in her nocturnal foray, he turned sedately into the gates of Magdalene College. From thence, he was led with due ceremony into the presence Mr. George Neville, its youthful master.

The first few minutes of the conversation accomplished the usual demands of courtesy with congratulations on the part of the earl to Mr. Neville on the performance of his duties, and discreet questions on the part of Mr. Neville as to the reason for the earl's unexpected visit.

"Yes, thank you, my lord. My uncle is well. He is at present resting at his seat in Norwich. He took a tumble from one of his hunters last week and sprained his ankle."

"I am sorry to hear it," murmured Cord with suitable gravity. "Lord Grenville and I have been friends for donkey's years. I understand he is closely involved with the college."

"Indeed," replied Mr. Neville with disarming candor. "It was due to my uncle's good offices that I was invited to my present position at Magdalene."

"Aided in good part by your excellent qualifications, I've heard." *Lord,* thought Cord, if either of us becomes any oilier, we'll slide right out of our chairs. "But, I do not wish to take up a great deal of your time. I know you have a busy schedule. You're wondering, no doubt, what is my purpose in calling this morning."

Mr. Neville made a deprecating gesture, and Cord continued. "Before I left London for my visit to Wildehaven, I was speaking to my good friend, Lord Maplethorpe," he said referring to another generous Magdalene alumnus. "He told me of a diary acquired by the college in the last century."

It seemed to Cord that a wary expression crept into the master's eyes, but he nodded courteously. "Yes, the Pepys Diary, a bequest of that gentleman's nephew in 1725 or thereabouts." He paused for a moment before adding. "I'm not surprised Lord Maplethorpe spoke of the diary. It has garnered some interest of late—partly due to the publication of the Evelyn Diary not long ago."

"Precisely. It is my understanding that the diary is written in some sort of code."

"Mm, yes." Mr. Neville proceeded in some haste. "However, we feel that now we have begun a methodical approach to the cryptography involved. We have an eminently suitable young man on the job, young John Smith of St. John's, and we are all sure he will decipher the thing shortly."

"Splendid!" exclaimed Cord heartily. "I look forward to reading it. In the meantime—" He paused for a sip of wine. "Well, the thing is, I've always possessed an interest in codes. I did some work for the Foreign Office during the war that proved most helpful—or so I was told."

"Indeed," responded Mr. Neville admiringly, his wary expression more pronounced.

"Yes. For that reason, I'd rather like to take a look at this mysterious diary—take it home for a day or two.

I might fail completely at its transcription—but, on the other hand, I might do you a spot of good."

"Y-yes." Mr. Neville tapped the arm of his chair in some agitation. "However, I'm not sure the diary is available at the moment for scrutiny. Even Mr. Smith does not remove it from the library. He has been hard at work here, and—"

"How very disappointing," said Cord, permitting the slightest edge to creep into his voice. "I shan't be staying long at Wildehaven, and I had hoped to peruse at least some of it before my return to London."

"Yes, of course." By now, Mr. Neville was perspiring rather freely.

"I understand the diary is comprised of several volumes. I should only remove one or two of them at a time, of course, and I would not keep them long. I do feel"—he coughed delicately—"that my request is not out of order, considering that I am a longtime friend of the college."

The words "and a juicy contributor to same" were not actually spoken, but they hung in the air like a banner. Mr. Neville capitulated abruptly, horse, foot and artillery.

"I'm sure it can be arranged, my lord." He rose from his chair. "Just let me accompany you to the New Building, and we'll have a look at the jolly old tomes, shall we?"

An hour later, Cord left the college, two volumes of Mr. Pepys's diary tucked under his arm. On his way home he stopped at Rose Cottage. Gillian flew out of the house to greet him.

"Oh, Cord," she said breathlessly as soon as he had dismounted. "Uncle is in *such* a taking. He's been ranting all day at Aunt Louisa and me. She and I had the greatest difficulty in restraining him from setting out for Cambridge to 'retrieve the material that it is his right to study.' I did not tell him of your promise to help. That is, I wasn't sure . . ." She gazed at him with a mixture of doubt and hope.

"That I would actually deliver the goods? Well, Madame Ye of Little Faith, here are Volumes One and Two of the infamous diary." With a flourish, he produced them from his saddlebag and handed them to her. "I believe these are the items purloined yesterday by Sir Henry and subsequently returned by his devoted niece."

"Yes! Oh, yes. Uncle Henry will be thrilled to have them back. Come, let us beard him in his den, where he has indeed been sulking like hedgehog with a sore paw."

Sir Henry was not precisely thrilled. His attitude instead was that of a long-suffering man of letters whose property, of which he had long been deprived, had at last been returned by a just providence. He was, however, interested in how the volumes had come into Lord Cordray's possession.

"So you see, Uncle," said Gillian slowly and with great precision, "the books are merely on loan. You may keep them for a while, but they must be returned within a few days."

"I am quite sure," added Cord hastily, "that I shall be able to borrow other volumes of your choice to replace them."

With this, Sir Henry appeared to be satisfied. Indeed, he seemed most sensible to the debt he owned Lord Cordray. In response to Gillian's tactful reminder that he had no choice but to assure the volumes' return to Lord Cordray in a timely manner, he snapped, "Well, of course, I know that. If I were to prevent the return of the volumes, it would put Cord in an untenable position. Do you think I would allow such a thing? Do you think I lack principle, Gillian?"

"When it comes to your studies, Uncle, yes," replied Gillian, not unkindly. "However," she added as her uncle opened his mouth, apparently ready to dispute this calumny, "I have every confidence in your integrity."

"In the meantime, Sir Henry," interposed Cord heartily, "I must beg your indulgence for a peek at the books myself. Would you be so kind as to let me look over your shoulder for a few moments as you peruse them? I promise, I shall do my best not to intrude, or ask inopportune questions."

Sir Henry, thoroughly diverted, picked up one of the volumes placed on the desk by Cord. "Ask away, my boy!" he cried. "Like any other academic, I relish the opportunity to answer questions, thus exposing my awesome expertise on any subject under consideration."

He drew up a chair, placing it next to his own at the desk. In a few moments, two heads, one gray and one dark, bent over one of the volumes. Gillian tiptoed from the room, making her way to the linen room, where she took up the inventory in which she had been absorbed before Cord's advent on the scene.

This is going to work! she thought exultantly. Bless Cord for his tact. Uncle Henry appeared to be fully reconciled to Cord's stipulations for Uncle's continued use of the diary. Thank God. It looked as though her moonlight excursions were a thing of the past. With any luck, Uncle Henry would potter contentedly with the volumes allotted to him. Further, perhaps he would have solved the code and begun on his translation by the time Cord left Wildehaven to take up his responsibilities in London.

A mournful thread twisted through her. It was obviously inevitable that Cord would eventually succumb to his family's prodding to propose marriage to the wretched Corisande. Gillian grimaced. She knew she was being unkind, but the young woman in question certainly seemed less than an acceptable mate for Cord. She was obviously interested only in Cord's title and the material possessions he could provide her. Gillian had nothing but contempt for a female who could so barter herself for a lifetime of ease and status. She, personally, would rather starve in a ditch than marry a man for any other reason beyond a mutual respect and affection. Nor would she expect a man to marry her for any other reason as well.

She was aware that she had not used the word *love* in her reflections. Of course, when she was young she always hoped she would marry for love. Like all girls, it had been her dream to live all one's life with a man to whom she had given her heart. It was only after her relationship with Kenneth had taken such a tragic turn that her dreams had given way to reality.

She would never marry for any reason—and certainly not for love. She had learned with painful thoroughness that love was a delusion. Certainly, some fortunate persons found happiness in that condition, but she would never be one of them. She had leaned to accept that she

was incapable of that particular emotion. The knowledge
that she was unworthy of love as well was far more difficult to absorb, but she had dealt with it.

No, not incapable of love, precisely. For she loved
Uncle Henry and Aunt Louisa. She loved her parents
and siblings, too. And they all loved her. It was simply
that special love of a woman for the only man in the
world for her that she would never attain. Surely, one
could get through life without that. She knew many people who had never shared that kind of love—who had
never married or conceived children. Here a stab of pain
shot through her. The idea of never having a child was
the one concept she could never consider without experiencing a sadness so sharp it almost took her breath away.

She turned abruptly to her task, but after a moment
her hands stilled. Her thoughts drifted back to Cord's
revelations. What, she wondered, had prompted him to
so unburden himself? She had come to think of him as
a private man, not given to exchanging the more intimate details of his life with comparative strangers.

Perhaps he had been a victim of the intimacy of their
shared adventure. Perhaps he'd merely been thinking
out loud in an effort to resolve the situation to his own
satisfaction. He no doubt thought her presence of no
account. Still, she had come away from the experience
with the odd feeling that his confidences, at least in part,
stemmed from an expectation of a reciprocating opening
of her own budget.

How ludicrous! To be sure, he seemed curious about
her, in a casual, amatory manner, but to go such lengths
to gain access to her secrets was too ridiculous to be
considered.

In short, Gillian, my girl, she cautioned herself, the
Earl of Cordray's secrets, his problems and his motives
are best left hidden. The man is a pampered product of
the upper class, with nothing better to do with his time
than seek dalliance with a female of the lower orders.
As such, he is devoutly to be avoided. She picked up
her linen list and continued her task, ignoring the treacherous surge of excitement that flickered through her at
the thought of what it might be like to respond to the
earl's advances.

Chapter Nine

Life at Rose Cottage assumed a pleasant routine following Cord's presentation of the Pepys volumes to Sir Henry. The academic's days were spent almost entirely in his study, where, surrounded by mountains of reference volumes, he perused the arcane symbols scrawled across each page. Most of the reference works contained codes and methods for deciphering them—many crafted centuries ago and employed by kings and military commanders, financial wizards, lovers, and even schoolboys.

To Gillian's discomfiture, Cord's visits became more frequent until there was hardly an evening when he was not invited to join the family for dinner. He accepted more often than not, and it had become Cook's habit to include the earl in her daily dinner preparations. The rainy spell, after its cessation in the first few days of Cord's rural sojourn, had begun again, with the result that he took to wearing oilskins on the short jaunts to and from the cottage. Still, he usually arrived damp and disheveled, giving Aunt Louisa an opportunity to fuss over him, putting him strongly in mind of his old nurse.

Gillian had noticed a marked change in Cord's demeanor toward her. Gone—or almost gone—were the polished blandishments and the suggestive glances. He treated her now with the utmost courtesy. Not that he had ever been rude, of course, but he seemed to regard her more as a friend than as a potential conquest. She was, of course pleased by this turn of events. She had no desire to be viewed by the likes of the Earl of Cordray as an object of dalliance. Still, she could not help wonder what had brought about this change. Did he no longer see her as desirable? she wondered somewhat pettishly, and completely irrationally.

She noted with interest Cord's growing interest in the Pepys Diaries. Young John Smith, the undergraduate from St. John's College, also made frequent appearances at Rose Cottage, and lively discussions among the three of them on the merits of one possible translation or another became a routine feature in Sir Henry's study.

"I must admit to some curiosity," mused Cord one evening in the cottage's parlor, "about the openhandedness Sir Henry displays toward Smith. One would think Sir Henry would look on the young fellow as a competitor. Your uncle seems determined to capture the prize of making the translation, yet he loses no opportunity to assist Smith in the same goal. He makes all his notes available to Smith and shares any new idea on the subject that occurs to him." He rose to stir the comfortable fire crackling in the hearth.

The two were alone in the chamber, John Smith having taken his leave hours ago, and Uncle Henry and Aunt Louisa having gone up to bed a few minutes earlier. Widdings had just replenished the teapot before taking himself off for a pre-bedtime nip of something with Mrs. Widdings in the kitchen.

"Yes," replied Gillian from where she sat, feet tucked under her, sipping her tea in a comfortable armchair. "It is odd, I suppose. However, Uncle Henry has always been generous with his vast fund of literary knowledge. I believe he wishes to see the diary translated, not so much for his own glory, but for the increased information it will provide concerning the Restoration. He would no doubt relish being recognized as the man who broke the code, but he would derive equal satisfaction, I think, just from being partly or wholly responsible for that achievement. As I said before, he loves a challenge."

"An extraordinary man, your uncle." Cord smiled. "He has his quirks, but he is a credit to the world of academia."

A companionable silence fell, and Cord watched Gillian covertly. She presented an enticing picture, curled in her chair, comfortable as a cat. The firelight played in the mahogany coils of her hair and cast warm highlights on the sculptured planes of her cheeks. Her slim fingers caressed the cup handle as she stared dreamily into the flames.

How, he asked himself for the hundredth time, had this diamond come to be cast among the prosaic assortment of pebbles that populated rural Cambridgeshire? He reflected again on her tale of a dead love. What was his name? Kevin? No, Kenneth something. The man must have been an absolute paragon of manly virtue and/or physical perfection. It simply was not normal for a woman to bury her heart. Was it? He could not imagine any female wearing the willow for him for any length of time should he succumb to an untimely demise, but then he was far from being a paragon of any sort.

As he continued to watch Gillian, an urge swept over him to move to her. To lift her from that cozy chair and run his fingers through those shining tresses until they tumbled about her shoulders, to press the length of his body against hers and to—

He straightened suddenly, aware that her gaze had shifted to him. Her delicate brows rose questioningly, and a cold sweat broke out on his forehead.

"Ah," he said, attempting to toss off a light laugh. "I'm afraid I was air-dreaming. Thinking of the diary, you know. I . . . well, I have been considering," he added in desperation, "there is something familiar about the 'pot-hooks' used by Mr. Pepys in his book.

"Yes," he continued, on surer ground now, for he was speaking the truth. "The first time I leafed through the pages of one of the volumes I bought to your uncle, I was struck by the notion that I had seen their like somewhere before."

"Really?" Gillian, too, came upright in her chair, her feet hitting the carpet with a soft thump. "Where? Where could you possibly have seen anything like those odd scrawls?"

"I don't know. I've been cudgeling my brain. He shook his head. "But, I don't believe I ever came up with anything like Mr. Pepys's code. Just looking at them," he continued musingly, "the symbols seem almost to form pictures."

"What do you mean?"

"I'm not sure, only to my mind they resemble slightly the picture writings of ancient languages."

Gillian frowned dubiously. "I think Uncle Henry considered that possibility some time ago, but of late, I have not heard him mention the theory."

"But what about the odd little curves, apparently affixed at random on some of the straight lines?"

Gillian simply stared blankly at Cord. He stood and stretched out his hand.

"Come, I will show you what I mean."

Gillian rose and, without taking the proffered hand, followed him to Uncle Henry's study. Here, Cord lit the little branch of candles on the desk, and the light thus produced caressed the two small, leather-bound volumes, lying where Uncle Henry had abandoned them for the day. Cord seated Gillian in the desk chair, then positioned himself above her so that he could point over her shoulder. He opened the first volume.

"See?" His finger ran over the first line on the page. The writing was neat and the lines straight as army ranks. It began close to the thin, red margin line and was clearly legible against the yellowed parchment paper.

Ů b y d ꞈ ꞓ ꞇ , ꭒ yʳ . ꞁ q r ∞ ꞁꞏᴏ

"Now, then," said Cord. "Look at the first symbol—the one that looks like a reverse J. I believe the drawing may be simply a straight line, which represents a certain letter, with the curl added to represent a specific sound—or possibly another letter, added to create a word. See? There's also a little apostrophe sort of thing at the top of the symbol, possibly indicative of yet another letter—or sound."

"Yes!" exclaimed Gillian, bending over the page. Cord's hand brushed her cheek. "Look," she continued rather shakily, "there are hundreds of symbols here, using that same vertical line. How could one possibly—? But the symbols do not group together, as letters do to form words. If, as you suggest, each symbol represents one or more sounds, then each could be a word in itself! Oh, Cord! I think you're on to something."

He chuckled. "Well, the theory is not new, of course." He stared intently at the mysterious scratchings and frowned. "The thing is, every time I look at the marks, I am more and more sure I have seen their like somewhere before."

"The only other such journal I know of, arising in the same period, is John Evelyn's Diary. It, however, was written in plain English."

"Yes. I wonder why Mr. Pepys chose to be so obscure."

Gillian laughed. "Perhaps he was revealing state secrets of the time. He reached quite a high position in the Admiralty, I believe."

"Or maybe he was merely keeping secrets from his wife."

Gillian's brows rose again, and Cord noted what he thought was a hint of disapproval in her misty eyes. She smiled, however, as she said, "Trust the confirmed rake to come up with such a theory. Of course," she continued, "I can just see the old rapscallion scribbling a calendar of assignations with his *cher amées*."

Cord rose from his chair, his features expressing bewildered innocence. "You wound me with such calumnies, madam," he protested dramatically, a hand to his breast.

At least, he can laugh at himself, thought Gillian, and does not make any serious denials. Was this really a point in his favor? she reflected the next moment. Does one applaud the predator who makes no secret of his bent? Does such an attitude not represent a challenge? *I am about to gobble you up, pretty little lamb. Stop me if you can.*

She shook herself. She was being absurd. She had pondered before on Cord's apparent abandonment of any plans for her seduction. She stepped aside as Cord came around the desk.

"It is late," he murmured, "I must go before Aunt Louisa descends on me, wondering why I have not long since taken my leave."

Gillian made no response, but followed him from the

study. In the corridor, she turned toward the front hall, but was stayed by Cord's hand on her arm.

"There is no need to summon a groom to bring Zeus around to the front of the house. I shall leave by the rear door and walk directly to the stable."

The house seemed extraordinarily dark and silent as they proceeded to the back of the house. Their only light was a single candle, brought by Cord from the study, and it sent distorted, alien shadows scampering along the walls.

The kitchen was empty, Mr. and Mrs. Widdings apparently having gone to seek their rest. Gillian became almost urgently aware of the isolation thus imposed on her and Cord. When they reached the kitchen door, Cord handed her the candle. Their fingers brushed, and Gillian drew back, startled. Cord was very close, and he moved his other hand to cover the fingers still so close to his.

Here Gillian committed a serious strategic error. She looked up, straight into Cord's face. His jeweled eyes reflected the candlelight in a primal glitter that grew and leapt forward to consume her. One part of her mind was distantly aware when he set the candle on the scrubbed oaken table that stood close by. When he grasped her shoulders gently, she knew she should move away, but she was held in that mesmerizing glint of green fire.

He bent his head to her, and even then she did not move. Her whole being seemed concentrated on the feel of his hands on her shoulders, the fire coming ever closer until his mouth covered hers with a tender urgency.

She was astonished at the response that shuddered through her. Or at least she would have been if her mind had been functioning at all. Instead, she had become a creature of sensation, reveling in the feel of his lips on hers and wholly engulfed in a desire to press herself closer. She savored the warmth of his fingers as he cupped her head, and she lifted her own hands to grasp the soft, dark curls at the nape of his neck. Now his lips left hers to press kisses down the line of her jaw and along her throat. Appalled, she listened to the whimper that came from that throat. At the sound, Cord stepped back abruptly.

"I'm sorry," he whispered huskily. "That is, I am not, but . . . but I should be."

A wave of humiliation washed over Gillian. Dear God, the man had attempted an assault on her virtue in her own home, and she had done nothing to discourage him. Indeed, she had all but thrown herself on the floor so that he might take her right there. She had comported herself like a wanton, writhing against him and moaning like a banshee in her need. What must he think of her?

What mattered more, of course, is what she thought of herself. She drew away from Cord, ineffectually patting her hair and her disarrayed gown.

"I must—" began Cord again, his voice ragged.

"No!" cried Gillian, her own throat tight with gathering tears. "Please . . . just go."

She could say no more. Instead, she whirled and ran from the kitchen, back into the house.

Cord stared after her for a moment before moving unsteadily past the door and out into the cool night air. Damn! What had possessed him to kiss her? Had he not decided that his relationship with Gillian Tate was to be platonic? He had known that maintaining such a façade would be difficult, but he had not foreseen that it would take only the slightest temptation to make his good intentions crumble like last week's stale bread.

No—the temptation had not been slight. What man, he asked himself, could resist Gillian by firelight? The flame of hearth and candles had bathed her in a seductive warmth, illuminating her smile and her cloud-colored eyes, and limning her lush curves in loving detail.

And what about Gillian's supposed primness? The picture of propriety she presented to the world? Had she made the slightest rebuff to his advances, he would have halted. But when he had drawn her to him, she'd not so much as lifted a finger to stop him. Indeed, she seemed a most willing participant in the kiss. She had responded with a passion that nearly stripped him of what little self-control he possessed. She had melted into him like quicksilver seeking a magnet, and the sweetness of her mouth pressing against his with a seeking warmth had nearly driven him wild.

So, what of her story of a heart buried at Waterloo? Was it all a lie, crafted to form a barrier between Gillian and the rest of the world? *But why?* Had she some other reason for avoiding the attentions of men? Again—why? Had she been hurt in a previous relationship, so that now she abhorred the thought of love? The concept seemed straight out of a gothic novel, but what other explanation could there be?

Don't be absurd, he told himself sharply. There could be a hundred reasons for choosing to hide away from the world. Perhaps she had committed an indiscretion in her youth, a sin so unforgivable in the eyes of society that she now felt herself an object of scorn. In which case, her guise of virtuous niece might simply be a smokescreen.

He rather liked that theory. It allowed for the hope that the beautiful Miss Tate might not be averse to a spot of dalliance, after all. The hunter in him awakened, as though from a long, dull nap. The next time he visited Rose Cottage, he must make sure the evening ended with yet another tête-à-tête before the fire. Then, he thought to himself with a chuckle, we shall see what develops.

There was only one thing wrong with this scenario. His thoughts returned to the moment when he had released her so suddenly from his embrace. Her expression had not been one of a spinster drawn abruptly from a pleasant experience. Her eyes had been wide and anguished, her gaze haunted. It was as though she felt she had somehow been betrayed. Or perhaps she felt she had betrayed herself—or the sacred memory of her grand passion.

In which case, he had no right to intrude. No matter how great the waste, one could not argue with a love so deep that neither death nor time could erase it. Even if he should entice her into a brief fling, she would be devastated afterward, and she would never forgive him. Somehow that thought left him oddly discomfited. He had known Gillian for only a short time, and his relationship with her had been, he thought, much the same as with any other woman—cordial, usually with the expectation of a satisfying liaison. Unless, of course, the liaison was over and done with, leaving both parties on amicable terms. With none of his previous connections, however, had he felt the sense of . . . rapport he experienced with Gillian. He simply enjoyed being with her. He savored her wit, her warmth, her intelligence and that indefinable grace of spirit that shone in her remarkable, translucent eyes.

He sighed. It looked as though he had talked himself back to the platonic relationship. He would enjoy her company while it lasted, and afterward . . . Cord frowned. It was becoming increasingly difficult to think of afterward— a time when Gillian would not be in his life.

Having saddled Zeus, he lifted himself onto the horse's back. This was ridiculous, he chastened himself. Gillian was merely a female. A superior specimen of her sex, to be sure, but certainly no cause for this absurd maundering.

Slapping the reins against Zeus's neck, he clattered out of the stable yard.

Chapter Ten

From the upstairs window, where she had rushed after leaving Cord, Gillian stared into the night. She observed him as he moved to the stables, and he seemed to move awkwardly, as though he were walking under water. The stable door closed behind him, the windows flickered with lantern light and then grew dark, and still she watched. At last, Cord reappeared, astride Zeus, and rode away from the precincts of Rose Cottage. It was not until he had been swallowed by blackness that she stepped away from the window and walked blindly through the corridor until she reached her own chamber.

The serving girl had left a candle burning for her on the dressing table, and Gillian sat gingerly before the mirror. She stared at the figure before her, her fingers brushing her lips. She looked the same, she thought with some surprise. No different from the hundreds of other times she had subjected herself to examination in the glass. The upheaval she had just experienced had left no outward mark.

How strange. How very peculiar that a man's touch—his kiss—could bring about such a profound change to her innermost self and not be reflected in the façade she presented to the world.

She had been kissed before. Kenneth had kissed her on many occasions, and even since his death, she had allowed one or two men that liberty—more as an experiment than a sign of her affection, to be sure. None of them, even Kenneth at his most passionate, had awaked the firestorm of emotion brought forth by that single kiss from the Earl of Cordray.

What was happening to her? She was certainly not forming one of those hopeless passions that one read about in ladies' periodicals. She knew herself to be incapable of love, after all. So, why had her pulse begun its absurd humming when his hand had brushed against hers? Why, when he drew her into his embrace, had her blood become liquid fire in her veins? And most of all, why had she responded to his kiss like a cat in heat, writhing under the attentions of her mate? Was she a wanton, then? One of those repressed spinsters who were the butt of so many cruel jokes, with fires lying banked beneath their frigid exteriors, just waiting for the touch of a man to spark a conflagration? Dear God, she thought, if Cord had attempted a full-blown seduction at that moment, she doubted very much if she would have resisted.

Her thoughts went again to Kenneth—dear, gentle Kenneth. Even in their most heated embraces, his kisses had been warm and tender, his mouth soft on hers. She had enjoyed kissing Kenneth, even if she was always left wanting . . . something. But never had she been stirred to press against him as though she might join with his very soul. Never had she welcomed his hands on her body as an ice-imprisoned flower craves the sun's heat.

She tried to gather her wildly scattered thoughts into some semblance of their usual order. It might be said, of course, that one of the features of a successful rake must be his ability to arouse wicked passions in virgin breasts. He had seemed stirred, but to him, the situation must have been merely a repetition of a hundred other such scenes in which he figured as the successful marauder—the thief of a maiden's ultimate treasure.

She stood and began to undress. She must be realistic about this. To the Earl of Cordray, a woman like her, of common birth and with no man to protect her, was simply a convenience. She'd observed ample evidence of his determination to place his pursuit of pleasure above all else. In his pursuit of herself, he no doubt sought an enjoyable interlude to while away his forced sojourn in the country. What better sport than to lay siege to the fortress that was the virtue of the neighborhood spinster? She had been warned by his demeanor on their first meeting. She had actually been amused by his presumption on that occasion.

Well, she had learned her lesson. There would be no repetition of tonight's encounter with the spellbinding earl. She knew she stood in no danger of losing her heart, for she had known for many years that she had none to lose. She refused to consider the pleasure she might derive from a purely physical relationship, for she had no wish to court ruination. It was not only she who would suffer from such a liaison, but her aunt and her uncle, and, indirectly, her parents and brothers and sisters.

No, she would steer clear of Cord's machinations. If he wished a diversion from the boredom of ruralization, he would have to seek some other female driven to mindless submission by his admittedly superior technique.

Having donned her night rail, she brushed her hair and blew out her candle. Climbing into bed, she composed herself for sleep, banishing with some effort the image of a laughing green gaze that seemed to stare down from the canopy above her.

The next day, Gillian was able to go about her usual routine with reasonable calm. She spent the morning in the kitchen garden. The chickens' recent behavior had resulted in the near-destruction of the entire patch. Luckily, it was still early enough in the year to replant the garden and, shortly before luncheon she rose to stand with arms akimbo, viewing the rows of newly sown vegetables with satisfaction.

" 'Through verdant vales, doth Ceres' golden reign . . .' "

Gillian whirled at the sound of the deep voice behind her, her hard-won serenity shattered in an instant. From somewhere she produced an insouciant laugh. "Well, as you see, the wheat, rye, barley and oats are somewhat farther afield, but behold . . ." She concluded her reference to Cord's quote with a sweeping gesture toward the corner of the garden neatly labeled PEAS.

"Ah, you are familiar with the works of Herrick."

Gillian searched Cord's face, but could find no hint of a searing kiss remembered or an instant treasured. "Robert Herrick," she responded prosaically, "born in Cheapside in 1591, died in 1674. Yet another Trinity graduate. Allow me to admit that my knowledge of his work is purely by incidental absorption, as I do not believe I've ever read the fellow's works. One does not live with Uncle Henry without becoming knowledgeable about every Restoration poet who ever set quill to paper.

She halted, but Cord showed no inclination to move past her into the house.

"You are early today," she blurted unthinkingly. "That is, I did not mean— You are welcome any time, of course, but . . ." She trailed off, inwardly cursing her absurd perturbation.

To her vast relief, Aunt Louisa appeared from the kitchen door at that moment, hailing Cord with delight.

"Of course, it is not too early to be paying a visit," she assured him, in response to the question he posed merely for Gillian's discomfiture, she was sure. "We are happy to see you any time. You will lunch with us, will you not?"

"Actually, ma'am, I came to return the diary volumes to Madgalene, as per my promise to the master. I shall, of course, procure two more, so I hope Sir Henry will be amenable."

"Of course," replied Aunt Louisa and Gillian in unison. "Indeed," continued Aunt Louisa, "Henry was saying just this morning that he thought you might be by today to collect the volumes. He is looking forward to working again on the second two. But, do come in," she concluded, gesturing the others inside.

She led them directly to the parlor, where she left them to apprise Sir Henry of Cord's arrival. Gillian had scarcely launched a rather frantic line of polite small talk when her aunt entered the room again, this time with Sir Henry in tow, a leather-bound volume in each hand.

"Good morrow, my boy!" exclaimed the academic. "Just in time for luncheon. I was thinking we might have something served in the study, for I want to talk to you about an idea that came to mind this morning as I was looking at February sixteenth," he said, referring to one of the diary entries.

"Actually," responded Cord smoothly, accepting the volumes from the older gentleman, "I must be off, for I have a few other errands to accomplish while I am in town. However," he added, turning to Gillian, "I was wondering if Miss Tate would accompany me on my journey." He gestured toward the curricle standing in the stable yard. "I could use some feminine advice on a gift I must choose for my cousin Susan's birthday. I thought perhaps we could dine in town as well. If memory serves, the Pelican provides an excellent spread."

"No!" exclaimed Gillian involuntarily. Her aunt turned to look at her in some surprise.

"But, Gillian, dearest, it sounds like a delightful outing." Aunt Louisa accompanied her words with a significant look, and Gillian realized suddenly that for some days now, in Cord's presence, her aunt had practically hurled many such glances at her. It was borne upon Gillian that Aunt Louisa saw Cord as a possible suitor for her hand. Good Heavens! How could the poor woman have conceived such a maggot in her brain? Of course, Aunt Louisa knew nothing of Cord's all but certified proposal to Miss Corisande whatever-her-name-was. Still, how could she think Cord would seriously consider an obscure spinster of low birth and no expectations as his bride? The Earl of Cordray could look as high as he might for a mate. His family, even if they had not already decided on the Viscount Rantray's daughter, would insist that he ally himself with a female of birth and breeding and substance.

Glancing at Cord, she observed that he had intercepted Aunt Louisa's look. His sea-colored eyes sparkled with mischief, and she felt a tide of heat rise to her cheeks.

"I'm sorry," she all but gasped. "That will not be possible. I have things to do this afternoon. I cannot possibly go jauntering off for—"

"Nonsense," interposed her aunt briskly. "We have nothing of any importance on our calendar for the day. Old Mrs. Frederick will undoubtedly stop by, but I can regale her with gossip as well as you, and as for the Fotheringay children, I shall just tell them to come by another day for their excursion into the woods."

"There, you see?" remarked Cord, his eyes now sparkling like sunlight on a fountain spray. "All your tasks are taken care of, and you are free to plunder the delights of metropolitan Cambridge."

"Yes, dear," said Aunt Louisa, even as Gillian opened her mouth to protest this cavalier disposition of her day. "Do run upstairs and change."

Sir Henry, who had contributed nothing to this exchange, reached for one of the volumes in Cord's hand. "That's all well and good. In the meantime, come with me, Cord, and let me show you what I have in mind."

"Yes," said Aunt Louisa, "I shall help Gillian, and she will be down again in just a few moments."

Feeling unpleasantly helpless, Gillian allowed herself to be swept along. In her bedchamber, Aunt Louisa hurried to the wardrobe and pulled out several gowns suitable for a spring outing in a gentleman's curricle.

"Which shall it be, dearest, the apricot sarcenet or the rose silk twill? I think the rose, don't you? It is such a becoming color for you, and the Pamela bonnet you always wear with it suits you admirably."

"Aunt." Gillian spoke the word austerely. "I am merely going into town for lunch. I am not planning an appointment with the Prince Regent."

"Oh, but Gillian, this is much more important!" replied her aunt in shocked tones. "It is easy to see his lordship is taken with you. Why, who knows what this might lead to?"

"Indeed," declared Gillian tartly. "It might well lead to an offer of carte blanche."

"No! How can you say such a thing, dearest? Why, the earl is a gentleman, and you are a lady."

"Only in the most general sense, Aunt. Men of Cordray's stamp seek only one thing from females of my social standing, and it is not marriage."

Aunt Louisa's chins quivered in distress. "Oh, you are mistaken, my love. You are not some common woman of the streets, after all. You are gently bred. You are so lovely and so dear, and you have received so many offers. There is no reason his lordship should not be as smitten as was Mr. Willoughby last spring—or Squire Pendenning all last year. They would still be paying calls if you had not turned them off so coldly. And there's Mr. Cadwallader. He hasn't given up yet, even if—"

"Even if I haven't made it as clear as I'm able that I have no interest in marrying. Aunt, there are a great many foolish men in this world, but I do not believe Lord Cordray is among them. If he finds me attractive—well, that's very flattering, but I hope I am more than seven and can take his Spanish coin for what it is worth."

Gillian was aware she was counseling herself as severely as she was her aunt, and she went on. "I find the earl an amusing companion, and that is the only reason I let you persuade me to pelter off with him to Cambridge today. Now, please do not read any more into the expedition than that."

Aunt Louisa sighed. "Very well, dearest. I think you are very wrong, but I shall say no more."

The old woman, however, had much more to say. As she assisted Gillian in donning the rose ensemble, she unburdened herself of several pithy comments on the foolishness of females of a marriageable age who discarded earls as though they were a piece of bad fruit in the apple basket.

At last, Gillian pronounced herself ready. Adjusting her skirt and settling the Pamela bonnet on a casual arrangement of her sable curls, she planted a loving kiss on Aunt Louisa's cheek.

"Please do not worry about me, best of all my aunts. I wish you would believe that I am happy with my single state. I'll be pleased to continue my, ah, association with the earl—so long as he does not become importunate. I know you value his friendship—as does Uncle Henry, even more so. And I do, too," she added in some surprise. She had not considered the earl in those terms, though now that she thought about it, she had come to enjoy the banter that sparkled between them like froth on tossing waves.

"But it's such a waste!" her aunt wailed. "You should be married to a fine young man by now, with babes in your nursery."

"You know how I feel about all that, Aunt, and now," said Gillian, surveying herself in the mirror one last time, "his lordship awaits." Picking up her reticule, she dropped another light kiss on her aunt's cheek and ushered her from the chamber, treading lightly right behind her.

She felt awkward in the extreme as Cord handed her into the curricle. The presence of a diminutive tiger perched on the back of the dashing vehicle precluded private conversation, for which Gillian was heartily grateful. She maintained a light flow of chatter until shortly after they emerged from the gates of Wildehaven, at which point Cord drew the curricle into a roadside spinney and pulled the horses to a halt.

Turning to Gillian, he said in a low voice. "I must speak to you."

She lifted a hand in protest, but Cord had already descended from the carriage and given the tiger instructions to walk the horses.

"I don't think—" began Gillian as he came round to assist her to the ground. Cord, however, smiled rather tightly, and tucking her hand in the crook of his elbow, led her a little way into the trees.

"I do not plan to bend your ear for any length of time, but it is apparent that I owe you an apology."

Gillian merely stared at him.

"My behavior last night was inexcusable," he began

with what Gillian could only describe as a marked dis-
comfort—astonishing in one of the earl's usual urbanity.
"I . . . I don't know what happened—I can only blame
it on the lateness of the hour—and being alone with you,
and—confound it, Gillian, you're not going to make this
easy for me, are you?"

Gillian started. "My lo— Cord, it is not my intention
to make you feel guilty. As you say, you were merely
taking advantage of a convenient situation. One would
expect nothing else from your sort. No, no," she added
hastily as Cord flushed a deep red. "I did not mean that.
That is, I no longer believe you to be the degenerate
sort of rake who takes advantage of every unprotected
female in his path. I simply think you a normal member
of that class who seeks his dalliance where he may find
it, and I do not blame you for it— at least, not wholly."
She smiled stiffly. "And, in all fairness, I must say that
I did not find the encounter entirely unpleasant." She
felt the smile broaden and relax. "I beg to assure you
that I have not formed a *tendre* for you, but you are
very good at your art, my lord. While I do not believe
I was ready to succumb altogether, I do not wish a repetition of the occurrence."

Cord breathed a long sigh and took Gillian's hands
in his.

"Now, there we are in agreement, Miss Tate. I thank
you for taking a tolerant view of my behavior and I
promise you most sincerely it will not happen again. On
the other hand"— he tightened his grasp on her fingers
as she began to withdraw them in startlement—"I have
grown to value your friendship, and for that reason, I
hope you will allow me to continue my visits to Rose
Cottage without any awkwardness between us."

Gillian could not have been more surprised had he
suggested they dance a quadrille in the middle of the
Trumpington Road. Of all the conversations she had envisioned following last night's heated encounter, this was
the last thing in the world she'd expected of him. Friendship! She had concluded that this was all she wished
from the earl, as well, but to hear him voice the same
desire—a man like the Earl of Cordray—was quite
unbelievable.

She eyed him narrowly. Was this merely a ploy to induce her to lower her defenses? He stood before her, his mien open and his gaze sincere. His customary poise seemed to have deserted him completely, for he shuffled uneasily, and the flush that had risen to his cheeks at his declaration showed no sign of diminution. In short, he looked like a schoolboy who had just said something he feared was going to get him in a good deal of trouble, but was hopeful of a satisfactory outcome.

Gillian found within her an appallingly strong desire to continue seeing him. She already had friends, she told herself. She had been supremely content before he galloped onto the scene, she told herself. In addition, she admonished herself further, the man might well be up to no good. On the other hand, he would not be in the area for very long, and one could not have too many friends—particularly friends who seemed to understand one so well, friends with whom one could laugh at an unspoken joke or who seemed to sense one's mood without being told.

Gillian capitulated. "Very well," she said shyly. "We shall forget the incident ever happened—and I look forward to your brangles with Uncle Henry and John Smith."

"To say nothing of our lively conversations over dinner," Cord added modestly.

"That, too," agreed Gillian gravely. She was aware that he had not yet released her fingers, but now he slid his away to raise his hand in a gesture to his tiger. A few moments later, they had remounted the curricle and were on their way to Cambridge.

Afterward, Gillian could not remember an afternoon so enjoyable. After a visit to Magdalene College and a pleasant chat with young Master Neville, she and Cord strolled through the winding medieval streets of the town to lunch at the ancient Pelican Inn, located on another patch of riverbank.

They spoke on many subjects, discussing poets—Restoration and otherwise. They discovered that each thought the Corn Laws an abomination, found their Prince Regent less than admirable, and deplored the antics several years ago of Lord Byron and his paramour, the less-than-ladylike Lady Caro Lamb.

Cord divulged something of his childhood, and Gillian learned that his relations with his parents had been amicable, but nothing more. He told her of exploits at Eton and Cambridge with friends either long forgotten or still part of his life. She regaled him with tales of life in the small village of Netheringham, where she had grown up.

Of Saint Kenneth, Cord noted, she said little. His careful prodding resulted only in more revelations of his purity of character.

"You must have loved him a great deal," he said at last, reaching to touch her hand.

She stared enigmatically at him for a moment before replying. "Yes, I did," she said simply. "And he loved me—with an unselfish devotion I've never encountered since," she finished almost fiercely. She blinked as though startled at her own vehemence, then drew a deep breath and said in calmer tone, "You have told me a great deal about your early life, Cord, but on the day we met you said something about an army career. I don't think I have heard you speak of it since. How long did you serve?"

Cord stiffened, experiencing the tightening in the pit of his stomach that always occurred when his stint in the army was mentioned. "I would hardly call it a career," he said lightly. "I bought a pair of colors when I was just down from Oxford, in '05. I thought it would be a glorious adventure to give old Boney a drubbing." He laughed shortly. "I found it very much to the contrary. In fact, I must tell you, my dear," he drawled, "I found the whole thing tedious in the extreme."

"But, you must have taken part in some of the battles. Surely, they were hardly, er, tedious."

"No." Cord found that he was having difficulty with his breathing. "They were, in fact, unspeakable." With a monumental effort, he dredged up his former lightness of tone. "Literally—for I most assuredly do not wish to speak of the matter anymore. It was a part of my life I would just as soon forget."

He picked up one of the volumes that lay between them on the sturdy wooden planking of their table. "I wonder if these will provide Uncle Henry with any new insights into the mystery of the coded diary." He laughed somewhat unsteadily. "Goodness, that sounds like the title of a very bad play."

Idly, he opened the book.

"I see no great difference in the character of the symbols from those of the first two volumes," he said. Suddenly, he frowned. Something—a wisp of memory flashed into his brain.

"What is it?" asked Gillian. "Have you—?"

"I . . . I don't know." Cord continued to stare at the strange scrawl. "I . . . I don't . . . That is . . . there's something." He sighed. "No, it's gone." He looked up to laugh into her eyes, an action that, to her vast annoyance, caused her knees to turn to soup. "It's just that the more I study these marks, the more I am sure I've seen something like them before, but I cannot for the life of me think where."

Their conversation on the drive home was light, interspersed with fits of abstraction on Cord's part. The sun was warm and the breeze scented with the first blossoms of a burgeoning spring. Gillian knew she would remember this magical afternoon as long as she lived.

Chapter Eleven

The enchanted days of long drives and idle conversation continued. On the occasions, frequent in number, when it rained, Cord usually braved the elements to spend hours before a cozy fire in the cottage parlor. Though Gillian absorbed the pleasure of Cord's company like a watered flower, as time passed she noticed within herself some feelings of . . . irritation? As much as she enjoyed being with Cord—as much as she felt herself thriving under his interest in her—a friendly interest, of course—she wondered why he had made no move to return to London. He had responsibilities there, after all. His Corisande might not be the bride of his choice, but surely he owed the woman an explanation of his desertion of her on the eve of their betrothal. Not that she believed the earl to consider the sensibilities of anyone other than himself.

He had behaved admirably in the matter of the diary, of course. His actions had not involved much effort on his part, to be sure, but his decision not to turn her over to the authorities on the night of her last unauthorized entry on the sacred precincts of Magdalene College, and his subsequent efforts to secure access to the diary for her uncle bespoke a man willing to help his friends when he could.

Still, it seemed to Gillian that, although a marriage between Cord and Corisande would be a disaster, the young woman in question had been left in a most unpleasant lurch, and it was up to Cord to set matters right. Which he showed no sign of doing.

Gillian acknowledged to herself that she had not the slightest right to regulate the earl's affairs. Indeed, even if she were in such a position, her own life choices left her little room to point fingers or call kettles black. Was she not herself a drifter? All her life she had been a dutiful daughter to her parents. When Kenneth had moved into the neighborhood in her eighteenth year, a union between the two was soon looked on as inevitable.

But Kenneth went off to war and never returned. And it was all her fault. Gillian shook herself. No, she would not think of all that now. She had not made a conscious decision to turn away from life, but that was what she had done. Other men had stepped up to take Kenneth's place, but, having been brought to the realization of her elemental flaw, she merely smiled politely and allowed them to fall back again, either through a lack of persistence or interest in thawing out Miss Tate's reputedly cold heart.

Not that she was unhappy. When it became apparent that her favorite relatives, Uncle Henry and Aunt Louisa, were in need of assistance, slight though it was, she'd been eager to escape the turmoil she had created to come live with them. She had never regretted that decision and had made a new life for herself in the quiet backwater that was Great Shelford. This life suited her, she declared stoutly to herself, and though the advent of the Earl of Cordray had caused a definite upheaval, this was where she belonged. This was where she would stay—or someplace like it when Uncle and Aunt reached the end of their days.

She could not, however, allow the same latitude for the earl. He was an important man. He had duties and responsibilities, and it seemed wrong that he should forget them, all for an idyllic sojourn—a lengthy sojourn—in the country. She was uncomfortably aware that a part of her would like to assume it was her own beguiling self that kept Cord here. But she was no Circe, compelling Odysseus to forget his obligations. No, she feared Cord was simply one of life's lillies of the field. He toiled not, neither did he spin, instead leaving it to others to clean up the chaos he created.

This rather dismaying concept of Cord's character was further strengthened one evening at dinner. Cord had joined them, as usual, and the conversation was convivial—as usual.

"Do tell us, Cord," said Aunt Louisa, accepting a second helping of trifle from Widdings, "how long do you plan to stay at Wildehaven?"

Cord cast a rather shamefaced glance at Gillian before answering. "I really don't know, Mrs. Ferris. I planned to stay for only a few days, but I am enjoying my stay vastly. I don't know when I shall return to London."

"But, surely your family and friends must be missing you," persisted Aunt Louisa. "And what about your responsibilities? Surely a man in your position—"

Cord lifted an impatient hand. "But that is one of the perquisites of being a man in my position, Mrs. Ferris. One can pay a great many people to take those responsibilities from one's shoulders. As for my family and friends, I am sure they are doing quite well without me for the moment."

Cord realized that his tone had been sharper than he'd intended, and he felt a twinge of compunction on observing Mrs. Ferris's chastened expression. "But, you are right, dear lady," he continued. "It is time for me to think about returning to my duties."

"Nonsense," interposed Sir Henry gruffly, "you've only just got here. I've enjoyed your company, young man, and you've given me a fresh insight into translating the diary. Surely, your family won't miss you for another few days. If they do—why let 'em come here."

At this, Cord nearly dropped his fork. He had felt secure in his little bolt-hole, but what if Aunt Binsted happened to think of the obscure bequest made to him two years ago. The next moment, he relaxed. There was no reason why she should make any such leap of intellect. At any rate, he had already decided that it was high time he confronted his aunt with his newly formed determination not to marry. On the other hand, he would much rather beard the marchioness in her own den. The thought of her striding up to the front door of Wildehaven, with his uncle at her back—to say nothing of Corisande and her family—sent a shiver down his spine.

At that moment, Mrs. Ferris lifted her hand for silence.

"Listen!" she exclaimed. "It has come on to rain again, and it sounds a perfect torrent."

Indeed, the rain could be heard pelting against roof and windows. The wind had risen as well, and the sound moaned in the chimneys. Lightning could be seen flashing intermittently against the drawn curtains, accompanied by booms of thunder. As they finished dinner and repaired later to the parlor, the storm grew in strength. As the usual time for Cord's departure approached, it showed no sign of abating.

"Well, you'll just have to spend the night here," said Mrs. Ferris at last.

"No!" cried Cord and Gillian together.

Good heavens, thought Gillian, Cord and she sleeping under the same roof? The idea made her extremely uneasy.

As though echoing her thoughts, Cord declared, "Nonsense, Mrs. Ferris, I think I won't melt under a little rain."

However, when, a while later, the little family stood en masse at the door to bid Cord good night, as Sir

Henry opened the door, a gust of wind took it from his hands and blew it against the wall with a window-rattling crash. A shower of rain entered with the wind, drenching the assembled group. Sir Henry retrieved the door and slammed it shut.

"Phew!" he exclaimed. Hurrying to a window, he pointed dramatically. "M'sister is right, Cord. You won't be going anywhere tonight."

Cord followed the direction of his pointing finger. Little could be seen in the inky blackness outside, but occasional lightning flashes illuminated the outline of trees, tossing wildly in the wind. Enough light flowed from the room to the driveway to reveal, not a neatly graveled carriageway, but a swirling river, rushing past the house.

"We'll hear no more about it, Cord," stated Aunt Louisa firmly. "You're staying here. I doubt if your people at Wildehaven will be expecting you home, but will realize you could not leave here."

Cord was forced to agree that only a madman or a fool would venture into the storm and so capitulated with suitable expressions of gratitude. Glancing at Gillian's stiff countenance, he tried to reassure her with a small but meaningful smile that he would not use the situation to avail himself of a repetition of that heated encounter in the kitchen.

As it turned out, neither Cord nor Gillian need have concerned themselves with visions of another tête-à-tête in the parlor before an intimate hearth fire. A small flurry ensued, with Aunt Louisa summoning the serving maid with instructions as to the bedchamber his lordship would be gracing with his presence that evening. Uncle Henry took Cord upstairs to provide him with a nightshirt. A fresh toothbrush and other essentials were also forthcoming, and Cord barely had a chance to bid Gillian a hasty good night before he found himself ushered into a pleasant bedchamber, evidently kept in readiness for unexpected visitors.

Later, lying between fresh-smelling sheets, he lay staring up at the canopy over his head. He had no idea in which direction Gillian's bedchamber lay. In other circumstances, with any other woman, he would most probably have made this determination one of his priorities before retiring for the night. He wondered how she might greet a midnight visitor in search of a little conversation—and a little something else as well. He almost laughed aloud. He could just imagine his reception. She'd comb his hair with a joint stool and send him on his way. Not, of course, that he had any intention of going back on his vow of a purely platonic relationship with Gillian, but, Lord, he thought, nobility of soul could be a severe trial to a man. He thought of Gillian, undressing and donning a night rail—possibly one of those filmy things that revealed every delicious curve—with rosebuds embroidered along an enticingly low neckline. She would brush that glorious mane before climbing into bed, and once under the covers she'd compose herself for sleep. He pictured her moving sensuously beneath her quilt, turning her face into a scented pillow, and, finally, he imagined her lashes fanning over her cheeks of purest alabaster as her breathing grew deeper.

His own breathing was about to choke him, he discovered, and he made a valiant, if not wholly successful attempt to expunge the image of Gillian at bedtime from his thoughts. He wondered muzzily, just before he drifted off, if Gillian might be thinking of him as well.

It might have surprised Cord to learn that, indeed, thoughts of the unwanted guest were spinning through Gillian's mind like miniature whirlwinds stirring leaves in the park. After donning her night rail, a prosaic garment of sturdy cotton, and dragging a brush several times through her hair, she climbed into bed. She attempted to read the book currently occupying her bedside table, but on this night Mrs. Edgeworth failed to grip her attention. Tossing it aside, she blew out the candle, scrunched down beneath the covers and attempted to sleep.

She punched her unscented pillow and turned her thoughts to the upcoming church fête, in which she had promised to participate, and of how Cord's hair had looked in the candlelight that evening. She thought of the laundry inventory she must take tomorrow, and of her conversation with Cord that afternoon in Cambridge. The words had seemingly spun about them in a glistening strand. It was not until a determination to subject

Uncle Henry's library to a thorough dusting somehow phased into a contemplation of Cord's remarkable emerald eyes that she realized the futility of trying to sleep.

She gave herself up to a thorough, albeit singularly profitless examination of her feelings for Cord. She liked him—she had already admitted that much. She had enjoyed his kiss—although perhaps "enjoyed" was not the *mot juste*. She had dissolved into a molten puddle of desire at his touch, and would probably do so again should he make another attempt on her virtue. Could she trust his promise to maintain his posture of friendship? Perhaps it was not a mere posture, she mused. She knew little of the workings of a man's mind, particularly that of a gentleman of the beau monde. However, experience had taught her that once a male on the hunt had chosen his prey, he was not likely to be too nice in his methods. Cord had seemed sincere, but she could not be easy. In fact, even now she found herself listening for the sound of a door latch being softly raised. What would she do if he came to her? Could she dredge up a show of maidenly outrage and send him to the roundabout with a hearty slap across his honeyed mouth?

She rather thought so, because if Cord *were* to prove himself so importunate and so disregarding of his host's trust in him, she would be truly angry. She hoped her wrath would enable her to drive him from her chamber with a fiery sword before he had a chance to practice his alarmingly effective blandishments on her.

No such invasion of her virginal chamber occurred, however, and after some time, when the door handle remained unturned, she finally drifted into an uneasy sleep.

The next day dawned brilliant with sunshine and birdsong, as though Nature were apologizing for her behavior of the evening before. Cord had been informed that it was the family custom to dine together at what he could only consider the impossibly early hour of seven of the clock. Emerging from his chamber a little before that hour, he unexpectedly encountered Gillian, just leaving the room next to his. He almost cried aloud, clapping his hand to his head in a "Had I but known!" gesture, but contented himself with a courteous nod and a solicitous hope that she had enjoyed a good night's sleep.

Nodding sedately, Gillian informed him that this was the case, and the two made their way to the dining parlor. Making his way through a repast of eggs, kippers and ale, Cord assured Aunt Louisa, in response to her anxious questions about his night's rest, that he had slept like a log. To Gillian, he spoke little, merely commenting on the beauty of the day and requesting the pleasure of her company on an early morning ride.

Thus, shortly after eight o'clock, the two, appropriately garbed and mounted, cantered from the stable yard.

"Ugh!" exclaimed Gillian, examining her boots. "What a morass! The rains last night apparently turned everything to soup."

Cord nodded in agreement. "We'd best stick to the high ground on our ride."

"Yes. Perhaps we could travel northward. Your estate is mostly forested in that area. We might see—or at least hear—a few grouse. I love to listen to them, thumping messages to their ladyloves."

"Is that what it takes to get your attention? Pounding on a log with one's feet? If that is the case . . . All right." He flung up a hand in response to Gillian's austere glance. "Consider that last unsaid. Although"—he continued with some might have called a foolhardy insouciance—"had I known that your chamber lay next to mine, I might have attempted a spot of wall thumping last night. Just to assure myself that you were resting comfortably," he added hastily. His smile was of the blandest purity, but Gillian had no difficulty in detecting the mischief sparkling in the jade depths of his eyes.

"For heaven's sake, Cord," replied Gillian in irritation. "Is the hope of seduction never five minutes from your thoughts?" She pulled on the reins, preparatory to turning about. "If you don't mind, I believe I should like to return home. You will want to be on your way, of course, so—"

In response, Cord placed a hand on her reins. He laughed contritely. "Please, Gillian. Do not desert me. I spoke out of force of habit, I fear." The laughter in his eyes was a gentle onslaught, and Gillian felt herself

weakening. "It is difficult for me to be in the company
of a woman who is both beautiful and charming, without
spouting gallantries—all right—meaningless gallantries. I
shall desist. I promise."

"The awareness is creeping over me, my lord Cordray,
that your promises are as these mud puddles—creations
of the moment that will dry up and vanish under the
glaring scrutiny of the sun."

Her tone was amused rather than angry, but Cord felt
unaccountably stung. No one had ever questioned his
commitment to a promise. He was a gentleman, after
all, and was scrupulous where his honor was concerned.
Surely Gillian must know that he had been merely amusing himself—that he was not considering a serious attempt on her virtue.

"Really, my dear—" he began, but was silenced as
Gillian help up her hand.

"Listen!" she exclaimed. "What on earth is that
sound?"

Cord did as she bade, and immediately became conscious of a strange, roaring noise, coming from directly
ahead of them. As they quickened their pace, the roar
intensified. Rounding the curve that led to a small bridge
across the river, they halted abruptly, mouths open in
astonishment.

Before them lay the river—not the placid stream that
one could cross easily on the little bridge, but a roaring
torrent that tumbled and foamed in its fury. The water
had risen mightily, raging over its banks like a ravening
monster, seeking to engulf the countryside. The little
bridge was gone.

Chapter Twelve

"My God!" breathed Cord. "I had no idea . . ." He was forced to shout above the roar of the water. "That was a terrible storm, but how could this have happened overnight?"

"I . . . don't know," Gillian shouted back, pale and shaken. "I suppose it's a culmination of all the recent rains. It's been the wettest season in years, but, I've never seen anything like this. The bridge—it's simply been washed away as though it had never existed."

"I must tell Jilbert to get something temporary constructed until we can build a new one. Or, no—I suppose that will have to wait until the spate slows and the water level falls. In the meantime, we must erect some sort of warning. Anyone driving at a fast pace here—coming around that curve without notice—might well tumble into the torrent."

He turned to ride back along the curve in the road. Dismounting, he began to gather rocks, piling them in a small cairn at the side of the road. He patted his clothing, searching, then lifted his eyes to Gillian, who still sat astride Falstaff, watching him wonderingly. She had never seen Cord move so briskly and with such purpose.

I wonder, my dear, would you be willing to contribute that extremely fetching scarf to a good cause?"

Glancing down, Gillian lifted her hand to her throat. In place of the stock she usually wore with her cinnamon-colored riding habit, she had chosen a scarf of a brilliant orange-red. She removed it and handed it to him. Working quickly, Cord secured the strip of brightly colored cloth to the top of the pile with one more large rock. He stepped back.

"There. We cannot do anything for riders coming

from the other side of the river, but I hope we have warned those approaching from this side."

Once astride his horse again, he made as though to wheel about, but stopped suddenly, frowning.

"Jilbert mentioned the tenants' cottages—and the danger of flooding."

Gillian gasped, raising a hand to her mouth. "Dear Heaven, do you think—?"

"What I think is that I'd better get over there." His gaze met hers. "Do you mind riding back to Rose Cottage alone?"

"Of course not, but I'm not going to do any such thing!" In response to the question in his eyes, she flushed. "I am coming with you, of course. I may not be of much help piling sandbags, but perhaps there is something else I can do."

Cord said nothing. He merely stared at her for a moment, then nodded.

The two found it difficult going as they retraced their steps to the washed-out bridge. They turned to ride along the path that led along the river, but soon had to make their own way farther from the rushing waters. As they progressed, on a slight decline, the area of flooding grew broader. By the time the first cottage was sighted, the horses were slogging in water up to their hocks. Gillian and Cord drew up abruptly as they absorbed the scene of chaos before them.

The sandbags could still be seen, piled in rows between the river and the cottages, but they had proved completely inadequate. Indeed, it was difficult to ascertain the river's channel, so wide had it spread beyond its banks. Water swirled in sluggish wavelets in a newly formed lake that encompassed nearly every one of the twenty or so dwellings that formed a line along the now-invisible lane. The inhabitants of the cottages could be seen splashing through the water, crying out to one another as they loaded possessions into several wagons that had been brought about. Cord, with Gillian close behind, galloped up to the nearest of these.

At his approach, a burly man turned to greet him, thus losing purchase on the wooden table he was attempting to pile into an already laden wagon. His wife, carrying a chair, screamed. Cord leaped from his horse to assist the man.

"Good God, man—Findley, isn't it? When did all this start?"

The man lifted his head, startled. His arms full of table, he was unable to remove his cap, and instead performed a hobbled bow.

"G'morning, me lord! Wull, it was only muddy when we arose earlier. Then, the rush came. We could hear the awful noise of the river as it swoll and swoll. We could tell it wouldn' be long before it bust its banks and we begun getting our things together, and sure enough, by seven of the clock it started flooding in earnest."

Findley cast a worried glance toward the other houses. "Trouble is, we an't got enough wagons fer everybody, and I'm afeared we won't be able t'pull 'em out when we do get them loaded."

"Has anyone sent for Jilbert?" asked Cord, also gazing about assessingly.

"No—but we thought 'e'd be here by now, anyways. He knows how it gets here when it rains. Howsomever, 'e lives on t'other side of the river, and we figger 'e must be stranded. Ee—what're ye doin', me lord?" Findley asked in consternation as Cord began to dismount. "Ye can't go walkin' about in this."

"I've walked about in far worse than this," retorted Cord. He called to a young boy, manfully attempting to haul a cupboard from a nearby home. "What's your name, lad?"

The boy splashed over to where Cord stood with Findley.

"Jim, sir—my lord, that is. Jim Deggs."

Cord handed him Zeus's reins. "Jim, I want you to ride to Wildehaven. Go immediately to the stables and tell them to bring over every available conveyance—carriages, carts, wagons—and men to drive them. Get the servants from the house over here, as well. Tell them to don boots and serviceable garments. Gillian, can you—?"

But Gillian had dismounted as well. Holding up the skirts of her habit as well as she could, she approached Findley's wife, a young, plump-cheeked matron, who was now struggling with a rocking chair. After assisting her to get the chair atop the other furnishings in the wagon, Gillian followed her back into the house. Here two young girls bundled pots and pans and other kitchenware to safety in the upstairs loft. From this direction could be heard the sound of a baby wailing.

"Oh, Betty," cried Gillian, "what a dreadful mess! But you seem to be managing."

"Yes, Miss Gillian." Betty paused to tighten the rope she had tied about her waist to hitch up her skirts. "I can't think why they built these places so close to the river in the first place. Almost every spring, our yards become mud holes, but this is the first time it's flooded." She gestured to her daughters. "We're carrying the small things upstairs, for I don't think the water will rise that far. The larger pieces—tables and settles and such are what's going in the wagon—though I don't think it will hold everything. Oh, dear, miss, just look at yer gown!"

Gillian was already aware of the state of her clothing, since her habit was already so sodden that she could scarcely move. However, she said merely, "Have you another piece of rope?"

Having wrung out her skirts to the best of her ability and secured them to a more workable level, she moved to a small cupboard. "I think we can manage this, don't you?"

"Oh, but miss—you can't—that is, you're Quality!"

"I think I'd be of pretty poor quality if I couldn't help my neighbors when they need it," retorted Gillian, smiling. The two women pushed and hoisted until they had the cupboard safely aboard the wagon. She paused a moment to glance at Cord, again surprised at the swiftness with which he had taken charge of the situation. As she watched, he strode from the Findley environs to the next house in the row. There, he spoke to the family briefly, issuing instructions, before moving to the house beyond. Since most of the wagons were by now almost fully loaded, he brought together the strongest men in the little community to haul them to higher ground. There they were unloaded and brought back to be laden again.

Gillian returned to the task at hand. She, too, moved from house to house, helping where she could. She gathered the babies and smaller children into the upper story of the largest of the dwellings, instructing two of the older children to mind them so that their parents could devote their energies to salvaging the family belongings. Then she helped where she was most needed in dragging precious possessions aboard the wagons.

She saw Cord only intermittently during the coming hours, which passed quickly. More wagons, horses, men and women arrived within an hour from the Wildehaven manor house and from Rose Cottage. Mr. Jilbert arrived at last from his home in Great Shelford.

"I'm that sorry, my lord," declared the agent. "Every bridge between here and Trumpington is either under water or washed away altogether. I had to travel several miles upstream before I could find a place to ford the river." He looked around in some astonishment. "I see there was little I could have done that you have not already accomplished."

Cord flashed a grin. "One does one's humble best," he said, pausing only momentarily in hitching a farm horse to one of the wagons already on the site.

Lunch was provided by Mrs. Moresby from the manor house and Aunt Louisa, and eaten standing, sitting in wagons and even perched on low-hanging tree branches by the workers. Cord gobbled a hasty sandwich on the move, as did Gillian some distance away.

By the end of the day, matters were under control. The lower floor of each cottage had been emptied and families temporarily relocated to the estate barns. Ned Gudge's ninety-year-old grandmother screeched a running stream of direction to the men who carried her from her tiny bedchamber to a comfortable accommodation at Rose Cottage.

It was just an hour or so short of sunset when Cord and Gillian and Silas Jilbert collapsed in the drawing room at Wildehaven. Aunt Louisa and Uncle Henry, who had both served as far as their abilities would allow had taken themselves off to Rose Cottage for a well-earned rest. Gillian would have accompanied them, but stayed behind at an unwontedly earnest request from Cord.

"I have some ideas I wish to discuss with Jilbert, and I'd like your opinion as well. Please stay."

His words were accompanied by the very lightest clasp of her hand. His green eyes were unreadable, but she thought she detected a barely suppressed excitement there.

"Of course," she said simply.

Now the three sat before the fire. Gillian had sent for a change of clothes from the cottage, and felt herself in reasonably prime twig. The cinnamon habit in which she had started out the day now reposed in the Wildehaven trash bin, and she wore a becoming walking dress of dark blue kerseymere. Her feet were dry for the first time in hours and were unexceptionably shod in a pair of jean half boots.

Cord, too, had changed into dry clothing; thus Mr. Jilbert was the only one among them who remained damp and bedraggled. His coat hung over a chair by the fire, gently steaming.

"I shan't keep you long, old man," promised Cord. "I just want to set one or two things in motion before you head off for home and hearth. Do sit down and share a bite to eat with us."

Mrs. Moresby had bowed to Cord's orders that she put her feet up for the rest of the day, but insisted on first preparing a light supper, which she brought in at that moment on a tray.

"Now then, Jilbert," began Cord, "how soon do you think it will be before we can get the new bridges up over the river? What was it you said—three of them will need replacing?"

"Yes, my lord." Mr. Jilbert then added somewhat anxiously, "I wish to take this opportunity to assure you, my lord, that the bridge near Rose Cottage is the only one to have collapsed under the rush of water. All three were well maintained, and I feel it is only that the torrent was so—"

"Devil take it, man," interposed Cord impatiently. "I certainly do not fault you for this turn of events. You have done an excellent job here—all the more remarkable for having performed your duties despite a lack of direction from the top—so to speak."

Gillian gazed at him, her brows lifted. Was this Cord, actually admitting that he might have been lax in his duty?

"No," continued Cord, "I'm merely asking what needs to be done now."

Mr. Jilbert ran a hand over his thinning hair. "I shall check on the condition of the remaining bridges, of course, before proceeding with any necessary repair. As for the cottage bridge, the river has crested and has already started to recede. We should be able to contrive a temporary span tomorrow or the next day. A more permanent structure will take more time, of course, but I shall set men to work as soon as possible."

Cord nodded. "Good. Now, about the cottages."

Mr. Jilbert drew a deep breath. "I should think the water will have drained away by next week, but the houses themselves—well, we shall have to look at the foundations, and at the condition of the wattle with which they are sided. In addition . . ." He paused. "I believe they will require extensive work to be rendered habitable again."

"Actually," said Cord slowly, "I was thinking of rebuilding the whole lot in another location."

Gillian uttered a small gasp, and Mr. Jilbert's eyes grew round.

"Apparently everyone save myself has known for years that the homes should never have been built there in the first place. Even if this flood was an unusual event, the tenants tell me that the whole area becomes a morass every year."

"My, yes," sighed Mr. Jilbert, his prim mouth pursed in dissatisfaction. "I don't know how many times Mrs. Clearey has complained about her ruined laundry, or Mrs. Matcham about the mud her husband and their sons track inside. And, of course, the tenants can never plant a garden until June or thereabouts because the soil remains too damp. But," he continued, his eyes widening again, "to rebuild them? *All* of them? Why, that would take a fortune, my lord."

"Yes," replied Cord gently. "But, as it happens, I have a fortune. Several, in fact. So, I think the estate could run to—how many is it?—twenty-two cottages without plunging me into ruin."

Mr. Jilbert exhaled gustily. "My lord, I don't know what to say!"

"And while we're at it, perhaps we could incorporate some improvements. Cook stoves? Gardening sheds out back? Ask the tenants what they require."

At this, Mr. Jilbert's features took on the expression of one experiencing a beatific vision. "I shall consult with them, my lord. They will be ecstatic!"

Cord rose. "I'm pleased to hear it. Now, Mr. Jilbert, it's time I let you go. Get yourself home and into some dry things. Your good wife will no doubt have your pipe and slippers at the ready."

The agent jumped to his feet. Donning his still-damp coat, he departed with multitudinous expressions of gratitude and good will.

Cord sank back into his chair. "I've never been so 'my lord'ed in one afternoon before, I don't think."

"I'm not sure," responded Gillian, her eyes twinkling, "that they were not capital L's. At any rate, your tenants will have elevated you to sainthood by tomorrow evening."

"Good God!" exclaimed Cord, startled. "May I hide out at Rose Cottage for the duration?"

"Of course. For as long as you like." Gillian sighed contentedly, finishing the last of her chicken sandwich. "Goodness," she declared. "I was famished at lunch and I quite stuffed myself on Mrs. Widding's cold roast beef. I didn't think I would be ready to eat again until tomorrow, but I seem to have managed quite nicely."

Cord cast her an affectionate glance. "From the way you worked today, I should think you might have downed twice as much."

"I worked no harder than everyone else." She smiled. "You, for example, literally saved the day."

Cord stared at her for a moment, his sandwich suspended in midair. He grinned then. "I guess I did phase into my military character, rather. It's been a long time since I did that," he murmured.

Gillian had pondered all day on Cord's seeming reversal of personality. The man she had seen today—decisive, efficient and energetic—was not the Earl of Cordray with whom she had been acquainted for the past two weeks. Which, she wondered was the real Cord? What had happened to his almost trademark indolence?

"You did appear in a different light today," she began carefully, placing her empty plate on the table before the fire. She poured a cup of tea for herself and one for Cord. "Indeed, at times it appeared you were almost enjoying yourself."

Cord looked at her, startled. "Yes," he replied musingly. "In a way I was."

He stared off into space for several moments, and Gillian became aware of the intimacy of the scene. She knew that Moresby and his wife were busy about their duties in another part of the house, and that various other servants toiled nearby as well. However, she heard only the silence that surrounded them, broken by the muted crackle of the hearth. She watched a progression of emotions play across on Cord's features, and it seemed as though they were, at that moment, alone in their own universe.

She searched Cord's face. What was it she saw there? A certain intensity, she thought, and an awareness. But—awareness of what?

"You know, Cord," she said, again choosing her words with care. "I cannot help wondering if today I saw the real Earl of Cordray, and that the careless, pleasure-seeking rake I've known up till now—charming though he may be—is a lie—a role you're playing."

Cord glanced up. "Pleasure-seeking rake!" He laughed. "Somehow, I don't believe you mean that as a compliment." He sobered almost immediately. "No, of course you don't, and why should you? I have hardly presented and admirable character, have I?"

He rose and paced the carpet in front of the fire. "However, you are right. Actually, I did not realize until today how changed I have become from the man I was when—" He halted abruptly.

Gillian said nothing, but gazed at him with a calm expectancy. Cord stood for some moments, staring into the fire. Then he flung himself into a chair near Gillian. His emerald gaze seemed to bore into her.

"Yes, I used to be different. Not that I was a model gentleman, by any means. I was a hey-go-mad youth when I badgered my father into purchasing a pair of colors for me. I thought it a glorious adventure to participate in the crusade against the Corsican monster. My father thought I needed steadying, and a stint in the army would be just the thing to accomplish that goal.

"But it wasn't a glorious adventure," he whispered. "It was a sojourn in hell, and when I returned to England, I was another young man altogether."

Chapter Thirteen

"You know," said Cord haltingly. "I never thought of myself as one of your exquisitely sensitive fellows—the ones who cry over a violet drooping in the woods or blanch at a cut finger, but in my first battle at Ciudad Rodrigo—" He gazed directly at Gillian. "I was frightened—almost out of my mind."

"But surely that is normal, particularly for a very young man."

"Yes, I suppose, but, of course, I was ashamed of my terror and strove to overcome it. And I did—or at least managed to stuff it far enough back in my soul so that I could function. No," he continued in a low voice. "It was not so much my fear of dying a horrible death that made the war a living hell. For me it was watching others die. To see men killed—many of them my friends—with unspeakable brutality . . . Arms, legs, even heads were shattered in nightmare explosions of blood and tissue. It seemed sometimes as though I swam through the battle in a sea of blood. Men did not always die instantly, of course, and the air was always filled with sounds of screams and moans—death rattles and pleas for help.

Sometimes they cried out to be put out of their agony with a ball."

He stopped suddenly, his face pale. "Forgive me, Gillian, I don't know what caused me to talk of such things to a female."

Gillian could hardly speak for the tears that had gathered in her throat, but she reached for Cord's hand. "Please, Cord. This is not a time for social niceties. I think you need to talk about this, and . . . I am here. Please . . . please go on."

Cord caught her fingers in a painful grip. He did not look at her, but stared once again into the flames. He continued as though he had not broken his chain of thought. "Once—at Orthez—a man ran next to me. He caught a ball in the stomach and fell. He lurched against me, and I grasped him as he crumpled to the ground. I cradled him in my arms for what was probably only a few moments, but seemed like an eternity. Gillian, his guts spilled out into my hands, but he could not die. He screamed and screamed. There was nothing I could do." Cord's breath came in harsh spurts. "I could not even stay with him until he expired. The battle was in full spate, and I was forced to rejoin the fray."

"Dear God," whispered Gillian, tears hot on her cheeks.

"Of course, being proper English gentlemen, none of us could ever display our grief or our horror. When someone was killed, it was, 'I say, where's Simpson? Haven't seen him about this evening.' 'You didn't hear? Old Simpers snuffed it today. Some frog got him with a bayonet.' 'Ah. Pity. He'll be missed the next time we're out to hounds. He was one of our best front men.' After that, his name would rarely be mentioned."

"In how many battles were you involved?" asked Gillian brokenly.

"I never counted, but I suppose seven or eight—not counting the skirmishes and ambuscades." He paused, still staring sightlessly before him. He kept Gillian's hand imprisoned in both his own, clutching her fingers as though he gripped a lifeline. He continued at last. "The worst was Badajoz. God, if ever the devil spent a night above ground with all his fiendish minions, it was there.

And he brought all the pain and anguish of hell with
him. It was blood and fire and bedlam from beginning
to end. From the time the French began firing on the
Forlorn Hope creeping up the glacis, all through the
siege of the escarpment through a booby-trapped, water-
filled moat, to the pounding the men took as they scaled
the walls, there was never a moment of respite. Every
kind of punishment known to man and a malevolent
God was flung at us from the ramparts. For hour after
hour, we fought our way up those damned walls, through
musket ball, exploding grapeshot and a hundred other
missiles of sure death. Our eyes stung with smoke from
the artillery and from the oil spilled into the moat by
the frogs and set ablaze. Men—both French and English—fell from the ramparts, some lodging on top of us,
some clinging to us as though we might prevent them
from plunging to the death that awaited them at the
bottom. I heard of one fellow who spent the night in the
foul, flaming cesspool that was the moat, trapped by one
of the siege ladders that fell on him with three dead men
still attached to it. He lay there with fire and the stink
of death all around him, forced to watch his best friend
drown two feet away because he couldn't move to
reach him.

"Even the next day, when we finally emerged victorious, the nightmare did not stop. Our men—our fine,
brave English troops—stormed into Badojoz and began
a campaign of the most brutal, unbridled pillage and
rape I've ever seen and never hope to see again. It
ended only when Wellington arrived on the scene and
put a stop to it."

A sob escaped Gillian, and Cord at last turned to look
at her. "I am so sorry, my dear. I had no right to inflict
my own private hell on you."

"No . . . oh, no—"

"And I suppose you must be wondering," he continued as though she had not spoken, "if there is a point
to this long, distressing tale." He drew a shuddering
breath. "As I told you, I sold out after Toulouse, and
came home to join a good many of my comrades-in-arms
who had also just returned to the pleasures of the London scene. None of us would have admitted under tor-

ture that we were having difficulty readjusting to life as
gentlemen of leisure. Instead, we buried our memories
in drink—or gambling—or outrageous escapades—or in
the arms of women of a certain sort—or in some cases,
all of the above. Most of my fellow roisterers eventually
regained their balance and returned to whatever had occupied them in their prewar existence.

"I was unable to follow their example. A night spent
alone in my chambers in quiet pursuits inevitably resulted in unpleasant recollections and culminated in
nightmares. I returned to Cordray Park and spent a few
weeks attempting to familiarize myself with the running
of the estate, to no avail. I thought that burying myself
in work would be my salvation, but it brought me no
solace. I was miserable in my enforced solitude, and
even when I was busiest, images of death and destruc-
tion rose before me, almost overwhelming me. I bore
the company of my worthy neighbors—none of whom
had participated in the war and who had not the slightest
inkling of what it had been like—with gritted teeth and
false bonhomie until I thought I would go mad. It was
borne on me at last—though not consciously, I realize
now—that it was only in the most frenetic pursuit of
pleasure that I could find a certain surcease from the
pain of memory. I craved the glitter of the city and my
life of frivolity there as a starving man might seek sustenance." He smiled thinly. "A few weeks later, I gave in
to my baser needs, and returned to London. I've been
driving myself to hell in a handbasket ever since, as my
relatives put it so succinctly."

With these words, Cord's face settled back into its
habitual expression of bored amusement. Appalled, Gillian released her hand from fingers that still clasped
them tightly. She leaned forward to grasp his arms.

"No!" she cried. "Not sustenance, but escape! Escape
from memories that were too awful to bear."

"A convenient theory, that, my dear," he drawled.
"But, I rather think—" He halted, arrested by the consternation in her eyes. He began again, this time in a
serious tone. "I thank you for your concern, Gillian. If
you will forgive what I know must sound like blatant
self-exculpation, I will tell you that I wasn't always so

self-absorbed. My family—even when I was quite young—used to think of me as one of those chaps who strides into a problem, searches for a solution and then proceeds to try to fix things." He smiled. "My efforts were not invariably successful, but it seemed I was always up to my eyebrows in some sort of commitment. If your sister was a wallflower, it was good old Chris—as I was called in my salad days—who would seek her hand for the next country dance. Your sow was stuck in her byre? Good old Chris to the rescue with pulley and hoist! Your punt was sinking? Why, young Chris would see to it in a moment—well, no, perhaps that's not a good example, for as I recall, all concerned emerged from the River Cam soaking wet on that occasion."

Gillian was forced to laugh through her tears. "Yes, I see what you mean."

"But after the war," Cord continued musingly, "I could not bear to turn my thoughts to serious purpose. It was as though only in the most frivolous pursuits could I avoid the depression that haunted me. I must say that for a long time I had a very good time. London provides fertile ground for the pleasure seeker. Friends from my army days eventually drifted away to get on with their lives, but they were replaced by a jolly set of fellows always ripe for a spree, always willing to accompany me on any lark."

"Always at your expense, I would imagine," Gillian murmured.

"Well, yes, there was that. I've endured my share of leeches and hangers-on, but I wouldn't let that matter. Lately, however—well, I've become dissatisfied with my habits. Even pleasure begins to pall eventually, I suppose. I began to think seriously of marriage—though not to Corisande, for God's sake. Still, I suppose that is why I wasn't more forceful with Aunt Binsted. In addition, I felt guilty for being such a constant disappointment to her and the rest of my family."

He rose again and began to pace once more, this time seemingly in a burst of nervous energy.

"But today I felt really alive for the first time in years. The flood created a horrendous mess for all concerned, but, you're right—I enjoyed it. I relished the need for action—the sensation that I was needed and that I was accomplishing something worthwhile." He flung himself into his chair again and looked at Gillian. It seemed to her that his jade-colored eyes had taken on the fire of flawless gems.

He laughed.

"You see what you have done to me, Miss Gillian Tate? I fear that my life as a professional hedonist is ruined."

"I?" Gillian hiccuped in surprise. "What on earth had I to do with your volte-face?"

"My dear, who do you think it was who caused me to embark on my tedious self-examination? I have enjoyed your company since we met. I have come to look on you as a friend; a real friend, not my usual sort of fair weather companions. You, in turn, have been more than kind—but do you think I have not sensed the mild contempt you feel for—'my sort' as I think you phrased it? You may have chosen to hide yourself in a backwater, which I think the height of folly—" He flung up a hand to halt the protest forming on Gillian's lips. "But you have made something of that choice. You have made yourself indispensable to two people whom you love, and who love you in turn. You are busy almost every minute of every day in some useful enterprise, whether it's organizing a church fête or gathering materials for the village school. You made me ashamed of my lack of purpose and my mindless adherence to a life of frivolity. I was forced to take stock of myself—or at least to begin to do so. Today was just the kick in the behind I've been needing—almost searching for, I think."

Gillian was almost afraid to breath. Was he being truthful—with her and with himself? Was he saying that he planned to change his life from this moment forward? Could a man make such a profound decision in the course of one short day? The questions whirled in her brain, with more joining them every moment. Cord had said that the need for change had been growing in him for some time, but had she truly been an influence in this final revelation? Even if he was serious in his purpose, could he remain steady on his path to reform?

"B-but the memories . . ." she began.

"Mmm, I see what you mean—but it's the oddest thing. If I'd been paying attention, I might have noticed that time has at last begun to do its work. Oh, I still think of the bad old times now and then, but they have receded. I find that now I can bear to contemplate the ghastliness without becoming physically ill. My emotion is sadness, chiefly, for all the young lives wasted."

"Cord, I . . . am so very happy for you," choked Gillian.

Cord placed his hand under Gillian's chin. His laughter was soft, when it came, but held a genuine joy, which Gillian had always felt absent before.

"Now, my dear, no more tears. They are surely wasted on 'my sort.' I am not about to become a monk, after all. I imagine I might indulge in the odd orgy now and then. I can only promise that I look forward to a more productive future—and I have you to thank for it."

Before Gillian could utter a blushing rejoinder, Cord rose to his feet. "It's getting late," he said abruptly. "Your aunt and uncle will think I've kidnapped you."

"Why, so it is!" exclaimed Gillian in surprise, glancing at the darkened windowpanes. She stood as well, brushing sandwich crumbs from her skirt. She felt suddenly awkward, and when, a few moments later, they stood in front of the house, bathed in moonlight, waiting for their horses to be brought around, she sought refuge in bright, empty chatter.

"Yes," agreed Cord somewhat bemusedly, "I do think the weather will hold fair for the fête next week. They rode in silence during the short journey to Rose Cottage, and when they arrived and had dismounted, Gillian would have turned quickly into the house. Cord placed a gentle hand on her arm, and Gillian experienced a shock of awareness.

Oh, my, she thought, her heart beginning to pound. Here you are, alone with him again. In the dark, in the moonlight, and you, you wretched idiot, stand here waiting—hoping he will take you in his arms again and . . .

And he did. With what sounded like a moan, he gathered her to him. For several moments, he simply held her close. She fancied she could feel the beat of his heart through the layers of cloth that separated them, and she imagined that the heat from his body might consume her. He brushed his lips against her temple in a soft whisper of a kiss. But then, when his mouth came down on hers, she opened to meet him.

He kissed her, not with the urgency of their last encounter, but with a yearning tenderness that, oddly, made her want to cry. His mouth moved over hers as though tasting her, absorbing her very essence. She felt herself opening to him, inviting him to explore the very depths of her being. His hands moved slowly along her back as though he were memorizing the contours of her body. She pressed into him, her body limning his as well.

His mouth moved away then, to press warm, slow kisses along her jaw and throat, leaving little rivers of fire in their wake.

"Dear God, Gillian," he whispered, "I don't know what is happening to me. I've never felt this way about anyone."

He drew back to look at her, and in the moonlight his eyes were green flame. He laughed softly. "Lord, that was original, wasn't it? But I mean it. I've spoken many pretty words to many pretty women, but you are unique—and so are my feelings for you."

All the while he spoke, his hands caressed her hair, her cheeks, the tender nape of her neck until she thought she would simply dissolve in a puddle of mindless desire. At his next words, however, she came to herself with jarring abruptness.

"Gillian, I have never said this before—and I really don't know how to say it so that you will believe me, but I think I'm fall—"

Panic surged through Gillian in an icy wave, and she thrust herself from Cord's embrace. "Falling under my spell?" she asked brightly. "Goodness, Cord, you're right. For a man of your charm and experience, you are being dismally trite."

Cord stepped back as though she had struck him.

"Do not discompose yourself, however. I am, of course, flattered by the attention of a man of the world such as yourself, but I fear that if I do not take care, I shall become another in one I am sure is a long line of your conquests. I shall therefore bid you good night, sir."

With those words, still spoken in that light, brittle voice, she whirled from him and darted into the house. Cord was left staring at the closed door, his eyes dark pools against the whiteness of his face.

Chapter Fourteen

Cord's first reaction to Gillian's incomprehensible behavior was anger. He stood before the house with clenched fists for a long moment, until the groom came around to claim Falstaff. He mounted Zeus then, and cantered away from Rose Cottage in a fog of wrathful bewilderment. Good God, he had told her things he had never revealed to another living soul. He had poured out the anguish that had festered within him for years. His pain had moved her, he was sure. Later, the mood of that soul-sharing still upon him, he had kissed her with an ardor more sincere than any he had ever experienced before. He had spilled his heart into that embrace. And she had responded with a sweetness and an innocent passion such as he had never known. Then, when he'd tried to tell her of his feelings for her, she had turned him off like a spigot. No. She had drained cold water from that spigot and dashed it in his face.

To be sure, he had spoken awkwardly. He had never before, after all, tried to reveal his deepest emotions to a female—emotions he had not even been fully aware of before he began to speak.

He could not say when he had come to want more from Gillian than either a temporary liaison or, later, a simple friendship. He had been attracted to her physically from the first moment of their acquaintance, of course, but it was only later that he had come to realize that she had taken up permanent residence in his heart.

The full force of this reality had not become apparent to him until he began to speak, but he knew as soon as the words formed on his tongue that they were true. He was falling in love with Gillian Tate!

How many women had he known? he wondered sardonically. He had enjoyed them all—some for their beauty, some for their charm, others simply because they wanted him. But none of them had inspired in him a desire to protect—to make them a part of his life. Gillian had become part of the fabric of his being. He felt somehow empty when he was not with her, and complete when he was.

He had begun to think she felt the same way. Surely, her lovely eyes took on a special sparkle when they laughed together. Her smile seemed to hold a warmth that was just for him. And she had welcomed his embraces. She had responded to his kisses with what he was sure was a genuine passion.

What, then, had caused her to speak to him just now as a hardened flirt might address an importunate swain?

By the time he rode into the Wildehaven stable yard, Cord's anger had subsided into a cold melancholy. He could only conclude that he had been mistaken in Gillian's feelings for him—her seemingly ardent response to his embrace. Apparently, she wanted no more from him but a mild friendship, and when he left Cambridgeshire, her memory of him would be no more than that of a pleasant interlude.

So be it. If she wished no more than shallow platitudes from him, that's what she would receive. No more shared confidences, no more laughter together in cozy intimacy. From now on, he would mouth pleasantries that reached no further than trivialities exchanged between acquaintances—people who barely knew one another.

Entering the empty house, he climbed the stairs and prepared for bed.

At Rose Cottage, Gillian lay in her bed, staring yet again into the canopy above her. Her heart was still pounding, her pulse leaping with fear as she contemplated the scene so recently played out before her front door.

Lord, she had behaved like a simpering widgeon. Cord must think her completely heartless at best—or, at the very least, a fluttering spinster, unable to so much as admit to carnal needs. Why had she reacted in such a ludicrous fashion?

Because Cord had been about to speak of love. And she could not allow that. She had pegged him as a de-spoiler of women on their first meeting. This may or may not have been true—she had come to believe that she might have been harsh in her judgment—but tonight he had spoken with an undeniable sincerity. She had not expected this turn of events. To be sure, her own feelings had undergone a change, but she never thought that Cord . . .

She stilled suddenly. Her own feelings? She had not given much thought to that matter, except to ponder occasionally on the enjoyment she was taking in Cord's company—to say nothing of his kisses. She drew in a sharp breath. How could she have been so stupid as to allow the earl such liberties? She might have known no good would come from those stolen moments of magic.

She'd had no fear that she would succumb to his charms. She was aware, of course, of the danger in such dalliance to a susceptible spinster. It would never do for the likes of a nonentity like Gillian Tate to fall in love with a handsome, worldly peer. That way lay ruination, but she knew there was no danger of such an occurrence. Her heart was inviolate.

But what of Cord? It seemed unthinkable that he had actually formed a *tendre* for her. Yet, he had been about to confess such a sentiment. She was sure of it. She could not, of course, warn him away from her in so many words, but she must take steps to protect him from the tragedy that would surely ensue were he to come to love her truly.

For I am cursed.

She almost breathed the words aloud, words she had not spoken since shortly after receiving the news of Kenneth's death. She drew in another deep breath that was almost a sob. She had vowed at that time that she would

never allow a man to love her again. She had experienced little difficulty in keeping that promise, for, although she was apparently attractive to men, she had
found that without her active encouragement, the at-
traction usually withered at the outset.

That was the problem, though, wasn't it? She had not
discouraged Cord—though she had not flirted with him,
certainly, or given him cause to think his advances might
be welcome. Had she? No, of course she hadn't. It was
simply that his overtures of friendship had overcome
her. Good Heavens, she *liked* the man. She liked being
with him and conversing with him and sharing moments
of laughter and . . . Yes, above all, she liked being in
his arms, her body pressed against his and his mouth
on hers.

This *must* not happen again! She had said that before,
only to be utterly undone when it had happened a second time. She resolved anew to avoid the incidents of
temptation—intimate, candlelit conversations and horseback rides after dark.

She would not have to keep her guard up for long, she
considered, with what should have been a sense of relief.
Now that Cord had decided to assume his responsibilities,
he would be leaving Wildehaven soon. He would return
to London to search for a bride—Corisande or otherwise.
In which case, the sneaking thought crept into her consciousness, *what was he doing mouthing words of love
to you?*

She gasped, startled. Had she been mistaken? Had
Cord been pursuing his own agenda? Was he in reality,
as she had first thought, simply after a little light dalliance and was about to use a spurious declaration of love
as a path to her virtue? Attractive to men, indeed. Was
she so set up in her own estimation that she could per-
ceive a love light in a man's eyes, where only a prurient
gleam existed? She remembered Cord's halting words
and their almost painful intensity. She was so sure he
had spoken honestly.

Suddenly weary, she abandoned this line of thought.
She returned to her reflections on Cord's imminent departure from Great Shelford. Though he might consider
the upkeep of Wildehaven part of his new program of

responsibilities fulfilled, his main efforts would surely focus on his seat at Cordray Park, with forays into London to see to business matters. She would likely see little of him in the future.

She turned her face into her pillow and at last drifted into an uneasy sleep punctuated by dreams from which she awoke with tears on her cheeks.

The next morning Gillian went about her routine in a mood of abstraction. After her treatment of Cord last night, she was not sure he would ever visit Rose Cottage again. On further reflection, however, she decided that she owed the man an apology. He had tried to make what she was sure was a sincere declaration, and she had stepped on it like an unwanted bug in the kitchen larder.

She was in the still room, making an inventory of the herbs and medicinal plants needed in a household that contained two old people, when Peggy, the serving maid, entered to tell her the Earl of Cordray had come to visit. Gillian responded swiftly. She hurried to the little parlor, where she found Cord with Uncle Henry and Aunt Louisa, discussing the events of the day before.

"My, yes," Aunt Louisa was saying. "I'm sure everyone is situated nicely. Of course, no one wants to live permanently in one of your barns, Cord, or in the village church, but for the time being—"

"Yes, yes," rejoined Uncle Henry impatiently, "but I've spent too much time away from my work already. Is it necessary for us to stand here nattering about what went on yesterday? Come, my boy, let us repair to my study."

Cord looked up swiftly at Gillian's entrance, and he bade her a pleasant good morning. Searching his face, Gillian was unable to read anything but the most fleeting courtesy.

"I'm afraid I cannot do that, Sir Henry," replied Cord. "I merely came by today to see how you were faring after yesterday's, er, upheaval. I have promised myself to Mr. Jilbert for the rest of the day. There is still much to do to repair the damage incurred by the flood. Not just in the rebuilding, but in some of the fields, as well."

He picked up his hat in preparation for a swift departure, but Gillian, gathering her courage, spoke up. "We can certainly understand your need to be off and doing, Cord, but I wonder if I might have a word with you on your way out."

Ignoring Cord's expression of surprise, she laid a hand on his arm and led him from the room. Walking swiftly through the corridor, they proceeded outside, where Zeus awaited his rider. Gillian turned to face Cord.

"About last night—" she began, and when Cord raised a hand in protest, she continued hurriedly. "I behaved abominably. I must say that I have no wish to discuss what prompted that behavior." She cursed herself momentarily for the blush she felt rising to her cheeks. "However, I had no right to respond so to what you said afterward. I believe you were in earnest in . . . in what you said, and I . . . well, I behaved abominably."

Aware that her little speech lacked anything resembling a coherent expression of her feelings, she looked in vain for a reaction to her words. Cord's expression remained blank and courteous, but he said, "Are you now telling me that you did not mean what you said, Gillian?"

Gillian's heart flew into her throat, where it lodged in an uncomfortable lump. "About falling under my spell?" she said chokingly. "Yes. I mean no. No, I did not mean that, for such an idea is patently absurd."

"How about the part about being dismally trite?" he asked colorlessly.

Gillian's gaze dropped to her shoe tips. "No, of course not," she said at last. "You were—apparently—paying me a compliment. How could that be considered trite? Cord," she said miserably, "I don't know how I came to speak so, but I am truly sorry."

Cord surveyed her gravely. He had done some reflecting as well that morning and had come to some rather different conclusions from his heated judgments of the night before. He had thought long and hard about his short acquaintance with Gillian Tate. He recalled all the qualities that had drawn him to her—to the person that lay beneath the beautiful woman. They included her warmth, her intelligence, her charm, her wit—and not least of all her rock-deep kindness. The Gillian he had come to know would never have cut off a declaration of honest sentiment so brutally.

So what was going on? he wondered. Now that he had thought about it, he was sure he'd detected a certain note in her voice—one that in any other circumstances he would have called fear. But how could that be? He had merely been trying to tell her he was falling in love with her, not threatening her with a beating. His most honeyed phrases had never brought that reaction from a female before. What was there in what he said that could have frightened her?

If she had told him she felt nothing for him because she was still mourning her lost love, he might not have believed her, for the memory of her response to his kiss still thundered in his blood. However, he would have accepted her statement—for the present.

Somehow, he did not feel that flicker of alarm was directed at him—that is, she'd not been fearful he was about to harm her. He was sure it was something else. But what? Something within herself? Or how about Saint Kenneth? Gillian had spoken at length of his gentleness and his kindness and his mawkish devotion. Had she merely been trying to obliterate her memory of a streak of brutishness in his nature? Cord's hands clenched. Had the swine in reality harmed Gillian physically, so that she now feared all men who came to her with words of love?

His thoughts by now had been running in circles, and he realized the futility in trying to crawl inside Gillian's mind. He'd finally ceased his ruminations with a decision to revert to his original plan of maintaining friendly relations with Gillian and nothing more. Well, perhaps a little something more, for he planned to probe—ever so delicately. Whatever it was that had caused Gillian to withdraw from him so precipitously, he was, by God, going to get to the bottom of it.

Thus, as Gillian concluded her unhappy apology, he smiled. "Please, Gillian, there is no need for this. While I might wish you had chosen less abrupt phraseology to deter me from my pretty little speech, your message came through with extreme clarity. I am sorry to have so discomposed you." He paused awkwardly. "I know that after that, er, encounter in your kitchen, I vowed not to attempt such intimacies with you again. I broke that vow last night. I must say in my own defense that the temptation was irresistible. You are a beautiful woman, Gillian, whom I have come to, ah, admire greatly. After our shared ordeal yesterday, I fear I let my, um, emotions overwhelm me. So you see," he concluded, perspiring heavily, "it is I who owe you an apology. I hope you will say we can remain friends, however, for I would miss your company."

Gillian stood rooted for a moment. This was not at all what she had expected. He still wanted to be friends? In her head she repeated what had almost become a mantra. *He will be leaving soon.* She took a deep breath and smiled brightly. "I would like that very much, Cord, for I have come to value your friendship as well."

She held out her hand, and as Cord took it in his own, he faltered suddenly. He gazed into Gillian's eyes and felt that he had become unaccountably lost in their misty depths. A strange, prickling sensation enveloped him, as though he had been struck by lightning, and for a moment it seemed as though time had stopped, leaving him suspended in an alien universe where nothing was as it had been before.

He mumbled something—he did not know what—and turned from Gillian to mount Zeus. He clattered off down the driveway, with barely a wave, rocking in his saddle as though he had never ridden a horse before.

Good God! He was not just falling in love with Gillian—that pleasant state between dalliance and a more involved arrangement—the state in which a man moved from kisses to an acknowledged liaison. He loved the woman! As in a church and flowers—and a lifetime spent with each other—and children! The thoughts spun about in his mind in a hundred variations as Zeus, through lack of direction, meandered home. At length, Cord took himself in hand. Why the devil was he so surprised? He had spoken of falling in love with Gillian just the night before. Somehow, however, falling in love signified a pleasantly vague state of mind. The words did not have the same ring as "I love Gillian Tate." No, the prospect of falling in love did not involve a blinding flash

of revelation that even now threatened his equilibrium,
to say nothing of his sanity. All he knew was that he did
not want to think about spending the rest of his life
without Gillian. He wanted her—no, needed her—by his
side in this new phase of his life. She had become as
important as air to breathe and water to drink. When
he was not with her, he felt as though some critical part
of him was missing, and he was complete only when they
were together.

How this state of affairs could have come about after
only a few weeks' acquaintance, he could not fathom.
He had remained happily heart-whole for well over a
quarter of a century, but after little more than a fort-
night in Gillian's company he had toppled like an oak
to the woodman's axe.

So—what was he to do now? Under ordinary circumstances, when a man found the only woman in the world
for him, the next step was to ask for her hand in marriage, was it not? A cloud of depression settled on Cord.
He had no idea of Gillian's feelings toward him. She
had just told him that she valued his friendship, but that
was a cold substitute for what he really wanted from
her. She apparently feared the idea of his loving her,
and he had no idea how to overcome this problem. To
be sure, many women formed friendships with men for
whom they would never have deeper feelings.

But there had been that response to his kisses. His
blood stirred at the memory of her pliant, willing body
in his arms. Cord straightened in his saddle. He must
ascertain where that spark of fear had come from. Then,
perhaps he could deal with it—erase it.

Somewhere in his consciousness the thought stirred
that his family—or rather, Aunt Binsted—would not en-
dorse this program. Even if he was able to persuade
Corisande that they would not suit, Cord was well aware
that the daughter of an obscure country squire would
not be seen by his aunt as a valid candidate for the
position of Countess of Cordray.

That was unfortunate, but would not hinder him in
his goal. He thanked God that he had not actually proposed to Corisande. She would be disappointed, of
course, and he was sorry for that, but he was more than

sure that her heart had not been touched. Corisande would just have to look elsewhere for her suitable parti.

Cord sighed. He could not think of returning to London at this point, but. . . . He wondered grimly what steps had been taken so far by his redoubtable aunt to discover his whereabouts.

Chapter Fifteen

"It's as if the ground opened and swallered 'im whole, my lady," pronounced Hamish McSorley in a dismal tone. The Bow Street Runner perched uneasily on one of the small, elegant occasional chairs in the morning room in Binsted House. Opposite him, the Marchioness of Binsted tapped an impatient foot.

"Surely, he must have left some trace on the way to wherever he went," Lady Binsted protested. "One cannot leave London for a journey of any length without passing through toll gates and stopping at inns."

"That's true, my lady, but apparently that's just wot your nevvy did. I've checked with every toll gate and innkeeper on every main road leading from London, and none of 'em have seen anybody who looks like the description I gave of the Earl of Cordray."

The marchioness clicked her tongue irritably. "So, what you are saying is that so far you have not earned a farthing of the sum I paid you last week."

Mr. McSorley turned his misshapen hat in broad, stumpy fingers. "Well, I wouldn't say that, ma'—my lady. "I traveled up to the estates you mentioned and made discreet inquiries. Ain't anyone at Cordray Park, or either of the other two places seen hide ner hair of the earl. He ain't been in contact with anyone there, neither. If 'e's out and about in the country, 'e's somewheres else altogether. Tell me, my lady"—he hunched forward a little in his chair, producing an ominous creaking as he did so—"does 'e 'have any p'ticular friends who live outside the city—but not too far?" He coughed delicately. "A lady friend, p'raps?"

The possible answer to the question of her nephew's whereabouts had already occurred to Lady Binsted, but she stiffened in outrage. "Good God, are you suggesting, my good man, that my nephew—?" She sat back, abruptly abandoning her stance. "Of course, Cordray has many acquaintances in all parts of the country. And, yes," she admitted grudgingly, "he does have his little connections—as do most gentlemen. However, nearly everyone with whom he might be, er, visiting is here in Town. We are approaching the height of the Season, you know," she added for the benefit of one who she assumed would know no such thing.

Mr. McSorley merely grunted. "Wull, I'll keep on with my inquiries. Are you sure it was 'is lordship's curricle that he took with 'im?"

"Why, yes, or so said his head groom. Of course, his favorite hack is missing, too. One would expect him to take—Zeus, I think his name is—if he planned to stay at his destination for any length of time. He would not use the curricle for short jaunts about the countryside."

The Runner rubbed his chin. "It occurs t'me, my lady, that mebbe 'is lordship *rode* out o'town, instead o' drivin'. That way, he could avoid the toll gates—and he may not have traveled far enough t'avail 'isself of an inn."

"But, the curricle—"

"Mebbe 'e rode 'is 'orse and sent the curricle along with somebody else. His valet, I'd think, since that feller seems to 'ave gone missing as well."

Pulling out a grimy bundle of papers from a capacious pocket, Mr. McSorley commenced making notes in what he called his Occurrence Book. Lady Binsted, in response to his questions, furnished him with descriptions of Hopkins and Cord's little tiger, of whose name she was unaware.

Thanking her ladyship, McSorley rose and made a courteous farewell, leaving the marchioness to stare unseeing before her. Had Cordray ridden out of London on horseback, like an escaped felon? Had he been so determined to avoid the efforts of his family in buckling him to Corisande Brant? Surely, he must see that his relatives—well, all right, it was she, herself, who was the most vocal in this project—sought only his best interests.

She thought of Cord as a child, an open, warmhearted boy. He had loved his parents, if rather distantly—much as any other youngster raised in an upper-class family. Again, like many such children, the greater part of his affection had been given to and returned by his nurse. He still visited old Mrs. Bender frequently and never forgot her at Christmastime or her birthday. As an adult, Cord was generally deferential to his older relatives—except in the case of his proposed marriage to Corisande.

The countess frowned. When had Cord, always so active and energetic as a child, changed into the bored, indolent specimen who fairly sulked at her when she so much as mentioned his responsibilities to his family.

Lady Binsted sighed. Why could her nephew not see that Corisande was the perfect mate for him? In recent years, she had convinced herself that Cord had come to the same conclusion and that his resistance was only the token objection expected from any bachelor of lively habits. Though he had disputed her intentions at every turn, Cord had always capitulated in the end to her various plans to throw them together.

Now, she was forced to ponder the question—had she wholly misread Cord? Had her refusal to listen to his objections forced him into headlong flight?

She shook herself. What nonsense! If she was the only member of this family willing to put forth the effort to bring Cord to his responsibility, so be it. It was up to her to find Cord and bring him to the point, and she would not shirk her duty.

Thank the Lord, Wilfred had taken up the slack occasioned by Cord's absence. He had squired Corisande to Lady Forstead's ball and to Mrs. Beaumont's Venetian Breakfast. He planned to escort her to the Wilton's rout this evening. For Cord's all-but-betrothed to appear in his brother's company was perfectly unexceptionable, and the girl was saved considerable embarrassment at

Cord's disappearance. How fortunate it was that the two seemed to enjoy each other's company.

Lady Binsted rose and moved to the bellpull. A strong cup of tea, she felt, would assist her in marshaling the next move in her offensive.

At Rose Cottage, Gillian went about her routine in an oddly unsettled mood. She had presented her usual serene, loving visage to her aunt and uncle, assuring their comfort as she always did, and driving out with Aunt Louisa in the afternoon to pay the calls in which the old lady so delighted. Now she sat in the little room behind the stairs that she used as an office, going over the accounts for her little family. She had not seen Cord since his departure from Rose Cottage three days earlier. She knew he had been busy with Mr. Jilbert, and would most probably return to the bosom of the Folsome family when his duties permitted.

At least, that is what she told herself. His behavior when he had left her standing before the cottage had been most peculiar. After his apology for yet another stolen intimacy, he had then apologized for his subsequent loverlike speech. This was followed by a declaration of only the most platonic of future behavior. What was really odd, however, was the way his jaw had then fallen open as though someone had struck him a blow to the back of the head. He had all but careened off down the drive with barely a word of farewell. Had he regretted his words?

Her concerns were laid to rest late that afternoon when she was interrupted in her little office by the sounds of an arrival. Hurrying to the hall, she intercepted Widding's welcome of the Earl of Cordray. Cord, handing him hat and gloves, raised his head at Gillian's entrance. For a moment, his eyes lit like emeralds in sunlight. He lowered them almost immediately, and when he looked at her again, they were merely their usual deep green.

She was absurdly glad to see him. The reason being, she told herself, was that she had become used to seeing him almost every day, and thus missed his appearance at the cottage.

"I'm so glad to see you!" she exclaimed before she could stop herself. He turned abruptly from Widdings, lifting his head to gaze directly at her. That unsettling light sprang again into his green eyes and he started toward her.

"Gillian!" He grasped her hands in his, and for a moment she thought he meant to gather her into an embrace.

Whether or not this had been his intent, he glanced back at Widdings and, after dropping a brief kiss on her fingers, released them and stepped back. Widdings, bearing the hat and gloves with appropriate reverence, silently exited the hall.

"I . . . I suppose," said Gillian rather breathlessly, "you have come to see Uncle Henry. John Smith arrived about an hour ago, and they are closeted in the study." She turned to accompany him from the hall, but he placed a hand on her arm.

"I cannot stay," he said. "I am on my way to Great Shelford to consult with the man who is going to start construction on new bridges next week. I merely came to—ah, good day, Mrs. Ferris."

Aunt Louisa, who had hurried to greet the earl on hearing of his arrival, accepted his casual embrace. "How very nice to see you dear boy!" she exclaimed. "How early you are up and about, but we have missed you. Sir Henry and Mr. Smith have been at their work for some time. They—"

"Actually, Mrs. Ferris, as I was just explaining to Gill—Miss Tate, I must be on my way. I have merely stopped to invite you all to a small dinner party I am planning for a few days hence. In fact, I was hoping you would act as my hostess, dear lady."

Aunt Louisa grew quite pink with gratification. "Why, of course, Cord. I would be delighted. Is there anything I can do to help with the planning of your party?"

Cord smiled ruefully. "I'm glad you offered, for I'd greatly appreciate your conferring with Mrs. Moresby on the guest list—and the menu. I was thinking of a week from Thursday. Is that enough notice, do you think? I don't want to leave it much later, for I must return to London."

Aunt Louisa's face fell. "So soon?" She sighed. "I suppose it's to be expected, for I'm sure you've left many duties unfulfilled in your absence. But, we will miss you, Cord."

"And I you," Cord replied gently. "All of you," he added, though his gaze did not leave Aunt Louisa's face.

"Ten days should be quite enough notice," said Aunt Louisa after a thoughtful pause. "In any event, I should imagine that if any of your proposed guests have a previous engagement, they will cancel it. To a man—and woman—they'd rather die than miss the opportunity to further their acquaintance with the Earl of Cordray."

Gillian watched with amusement as Cord absorbed this apparently unpalatable information. He merely bowed, however, and promised to pay a visit of longer duration within a day or two.

And he did. The very next day, the earl presented himself at the cottage, and spent the afternoon in lively debate with Sir Henry, following which he was persuaded to stay for dinner.

Conversation was general around the table, and Gillian did not allow her gaze to stray to Cord any more than was seemly. Nor did Cord direct more than a modicum of conversation her way. After dinner, he stayed for only a few minutes, taking himself off after a promise to make himself available for the next day for a visit from Aunt Louisa for the purpose of drawing up a guest list for the proposed dinner party.

Later that evening, as he prepared for bed, Cord congratulated himself on a few hours well spent. Though he would have preferred to stay longer at the cottage, envisioning another conversation with Gillian before the fire, he realized the folly—to say nothing of the danger—of such a course, and had contented himself with the pleasure of simply watching Gillian by candlelight. She had worn her chestnut hair in a loose knot atop her head tonight, from which a few glossy tendrils escaped to frame the delicate features of her face in a charming filigree.

As always, she had made her aunt and uncle the primary focus of her attention, chuckling at Sir Henry's ancient witticisms and bending her head to catch each of Mrs. Ferris's tidbits of local gossip.

With some effort Cord wrenched his thoughts from Gillian and the charming pictures she formed in his mind. Most important, he mused with some satisfaction, he had arranged for Mrs. Ferris to visit Wildehaven on the following day, *sans* Gillian, for a conference on the guest list for the proposed dinner party. His interest in the function was minimal, but he realized that it was incumbent upon him to make himself known to his neighbors. That it presented the opportunity for which he had been searching was sheer serendipity—all going to show, he reflected virtuously, that doing one's duty provided its own rewards.

Mrs. Ferris appeared on schedule the next morning, a sheaf of papers in her hand.

"Just a few notes," she explained, "on some of the families hereabouts."

Cord led her to his study, where he deposited the little bundle on his desk and drew up a chair for Mrs. Ferris. The next hour was taken up with an exhaustive study of the notes and other information culled from that good lady's brain.

"I know you will want to meet Sir Arthur and Lady Beecham. It is fortunate for us that they are in the area right now, for they usually repair to their estate in Scotland at this time of year. Oh, and, of course, the Wentleys. Such a nice family. They will be leaving soon for London, for their daughter, Emily, is to make her come-out this year. Lovely girl, but somewhat spoiled to my way of thinking. Now," she added somewhat doubtfully after a moment, "there are also Mr. and Mrs. Drublingham. She comes from a good family, but I cannot like him. And their son, Reginald—he is four-and-twenty now, and a perfectly dreadful young man. A loose fish I think you would call him."

Cord listened patiently to all Mrs. Ferris's suggestions, and at last a list of thirty unexceptionable persons was drawn up. Cord rang for a fresh pot of tea and urged Mrs. Ferris to a more comfortable chair near the fire.

"I do appreciate your taking time from your day to assist me in a task that I would certainly have made mincemeat of," he began, offering her a plate of cucumber sandwiches.

"It is my pleasure, dear boy," replied Mrs. Ferris, making a modest selection. "I know how confusing it can be, coming into a strange neighborhood. It's too bad Gillian could not be with us, but she had promised Mr. Ellison to help him choose the music for the children's choral recital. That's coming up in two weeks. Do you think you will be here then?"

"I rather doubt it." Cord arranged his features into an expression of regret. While he was sincere in his determination to assume his responsibility as one of the areas more prominent landlords, he drew the line at a local children's choral recital. "I have noticed," he continued smoothly, "that Miss Tate seems to take an active role in village activities."

"Oh, yes! She is always the first one called on whenever a volunteer is needed. Why, I don't know how Mr. Ellison—he's the schoolmaster, you know—or Reverend Bollings and his wife would manage. Gillian makes herself available for everything from visiting the sick to arranging mothers' meetings to distributing baskets to the poor. She especially enjoys her work with children, however." Mrs. Ferris sighed. "It is such a pity that she does not have little ones of her own. She would make an admirable mother."

Ignoring the speculative glance she shot at him, Cord grasped at this, the opportunity he had been waiting for.

"To tell you the truth, Mrs. Ferris, I am rather surprised that Miss Tate has chosen such a . . . a contained existence. Not that I believe she is unhappy," he continued hastily, noting signs of distress on the old woman's features. "She obviously loves both you and Sir Henry very much and relishes her life with you. It's just that— frankly, one would have expected a young woman of her beauty and . . . and character to have been married by now."

Cord glanced assessingly at Mrs. Ferris. Had he gone too far? He did not wish to be seen as prying into Gillian's private concerns. A second look told him he need not have worried, for apparently Sir Henry's sister was concerned as well.

"Oh, you are right, Cord! She should have wed some nice young man years ago. She claims to be perfectly happy in her present state, but how can any woman actually choose to remain a . . . a spinster?"

"Well," said Cord, progressing with care, "she told me of her betrothal some years ago to a young man who was killed at Waterloo."

"Oh, yes, Kenneth Winthrop. Such a nice boy. He was utterly devoted to Gillian. We were surprised, and so disappointed when she broke off the engagement. He died a hero, you know."

"Broke off the engagement?" Cord echoed in astonishment. Why had Gillian given him the impression that she mourned Saint Kenneth as a woman would for the man she intended to marry? "Do you know why she severed the connection? Was it something in their relationship then that could have turned her away from men in general? No unpleasantness or character flaws on Mr. Winthrop's part?"

"Oh, no!" replied Mrs. Ferris in a shocked voice. "Young Mr. Winthrop was a perfect paragon of virtue. He would never have so much as contemplated any action that was not above reproach. That is—I did not know the gentleman very well personally, but I received glowing reports from Gillian's parents. They were so happy at the betrothal!" Mrs. Ferris paused to dab at her eyes with a lace-trimmed handkerchief. "No," she continued uncertainly, "if anything—that is—it must have been that Gillian, having known one perfect love, cannot bring herself to search for another. It is so very sad," she sniffed.

"But understandable," Cord concluded comfortingly.

It was apparent that no more information on the possibly perfidy of Saint Kenneth would be forthcoming from Mrs. Ferris, so Cord sought a subject with which to turn the conversation. The old woman was before him, however. She set her cup down on its saucer with a little clatter and turned to face him, her plump features serious.

"Cord, I hope you don't mind, but I have been wishing to thank you."

Cord stared blankly. "Thank me?"

"Yes, for the kindness you have shown to Henry.
know you discovered Gillian's part in his ridiculous esca
pades with that diary. You could have made life very
difficult for us, but you did not."

"Oh, but I—"

Mrs. Ferris lifted a hand. "Instead, you arranged fo
the loan of a few of the volumes at a time. I really do
believe, my dear boy"—she groped in her skirt pocke
and once more brought out her handkerchief—"tha
Henry would have gone mad if permanently deprived o
the diary."

"Now, now, Mrs. Ferris." Cord patted the old lady'
hand. "It was my pleasure to help. In any event, I cer
tainly would not have wished to make life difficult for a
family who have become my very dear friends."

At this, Mrs. Ferris was almost overcome. Sniffing
noisily, she blew her nose and wiped her eyes with grea
thoroughness. "Oh, dear," she gasped, "I can only hope
that Henry will finish his dratted translation before you
leave. Although, neither Gillian nor I have much hope
in that. If he hasn't made sense of all those little line
and crooks and squiggles in the years he's already spent
I shouldn't imagine another two weeks will help. Why
what is it, Cord?" she asked in some confusion, for the
earl had stiffened, his brows snapping together in a puz
zled frown.

For a long moment he did not respond, remaining in
an unseeing trance. "What?" asked Cord in response to
another question, as though returning from a great dis
tance. "Oh. Forgive me, Mrs. Ferris, I—something jus
occurred to me." He rose from his chair. "I hope you
will excuse my rudeness, but I'm afraid I must leave
you."

"Oh, dear—is something wrong?"

"No. Oh, no. I just remembered something of . . . o
great importance—something that requires my immedi
ate presence elsewhere."

Mrs. Ferris had by now risen as well, and with more
profuse apologies, he bundled her from the room and
out the front door. "I must leave Wildehaven for a few
days," he explained as he handed her into the gig that
provided transportation for the Folsome family.

"But . . . but the dinner party!" Mrs. Ferris spluttered.

"Oh, I shall be back in plenty of time for that. In fact, I shall no doubt return by the first of next week."

Though obviously not contented with this explanation, Mrs. Ferris allowed herself to be driven off, looking backward in startlement at Cord, who remained standing in the middle of the driveway, staring before him in abstraction.

Chapter Sixteen

Gillian took the news of Cord's departure from Wildehaven with a reasonable degree of equanimity. She felt unaccountably distressed that he would leave so precipitously, without bidding her farewell, but she told herself this was nonsense. The earl was certainly under no obligation to discuss his comings and goings with her. At any rate, he had said he'd only be gone for a short time. He would soon be out of her life forever, so why should she mope at the prospect of spending a mere few days without him?

She found the time dragging, however. Every time a clatter on the drive announced a visitor, she looked up expectantly.

"Did he say where he was going?" she asked her aunt at last.

"No, dearest, but, as I told you, something occurred to him suddenly. He could hardly wait to get me out of the house. Though, of course, he was the soul of courtesy," she added hastily.

"And he did not say where he was going?"

"No, only that he had just thought of something that required his immediate attention. But, never mind, dear, he promised to be back in time for the dinner party."

With that, Gillian tried to force herself to her usual

routine. She was also forced to admit that dinnertime at the cottage had become a dull affair, and she found that her uncle's interminable discourses on the diary and other matters of the Restoration period had become irritating in the extreme. She even found it difficult to attend her aunt's blameless gossip about the doings of their neighbors.

In fact, it seemed as though she were living in some sort of gray limbo. No matter how she chastised herself for this witless behavior, she waited in almost breathless anticipation of Cord's return.

Thus, when she was sat in her office one sunny afternoon four days after Cord's departure, a mound of ledgers surrounding her, she lifted her head at the sound of the front doorbell. It seemed she scarcely breathed as Widdings shuffled to answer it, and when a clear, deep, very masculine voice drifted back from the entry hall, she thrust papers, notes and ledgers away from her. Stopping only to remove her apron and tidy her hair, she picked up her skirts and ran to the front of the house.

Gillian caught herself up in the corridor outside the hall and skidded to a stop. She took one last look at herself in a nearby mirror, then moved sedately into the hall. Cord had just greeted Widdings, and at her entrance, he looked up swiftly. An unsettling glow leaped to his eyes, and she walked toward him without knowing that she did so.

"You're back," she breathed, immediately biting her tongue on her blatant inanity.

However, he answered in kind. "Yes."

Under Mr. Widdings's interested stare, they stood for a moment, locked in each other's gaze.

"I—we missed you," Gillian said at last, coming to herself with a little jerk. She turned to lead him farther into the house. "Uncle Henry is in his study. I expect—"

"No. I came to see you," interposed Cord quickly. "That is—I have brought something." He withdrew from his coat a slender volume and handed it to her with an air of suppressed excitement. "Gillian, I believe this little book may provide the answer to our mystery!"

She stared up at him, startled. "Cord! What is it—and where did you find it? Uncle will be beside himself."

Again, she turned to lead the way to the study, but once more, Cord detained her.

"No. I . . ." He stopped uncertainly. "I'd like to discuss this with you privately first. Is there somewhere we could speak for a moment uninterrupted?"

Gillian hesitated. Her first instinct was to avoid so much as five minute's worth of uninterrupted privacy with the Earl of Cordray. Despite his declarations of the purity of his intentions, she did not trust him. She did not trust herself. The next moment she chided herself. She was not a siren at whom men threw themselves in wild abandon at the slightest opportunity. She smiled and led the way to the little office.

Cord glanced around him. "So this is the working heart of Rose Cottage," he murmured. Briefly, he touched the ledgers scattered on the desk.

"Yes, indeed," replied Gillian with a smile. "I have been hard at work all day, and have only now persuaded these wretched figures to stay in their proper columns and add up to their proper amounts." She moved the account books into an untidy pile on one corner of the desk. "But what is this miracle you have brought us?"

"No—to y—" began Cord, before halting himself. He turned away in some confusion to bring up Gillian's chair at the desk. He pulled one up for himself as well. He placed the little volume on the desk and, with Gillian, spelled out the faded letters on its cover.

"*A Tutor to Tachygraphy,*" murmured Gillian, "by T. Shelton."

"Yes!" exclaimed Cord. "It finally dawned on me where I had seen the little symbols used by Pepys. I remembered a book I had once seen in the library at Cordray Park—my home. It must have been years ago—when I was just a boy, I suppose. I don't know how I happened to come across it, or why I so much as picked it up. I suppose it was the word *Tachygraphy.* I hadn't the slightest idea what it meant, and I probably hoped it was something wicked and forbidden. At any rate, that's where I went—back to Cordray Park to look at it again."

Cord opened the book. "As you can see, it's an instruction book on a form of shorthand."

"Shorthand!" echoed Gillian. "You don't mean—?"

"Yes. You see? It was published in 1635—by the Cambridge University Press, no less—and must have been on the bookseller's shelves when Sam Pepys strolled the streets of London. And look—" Slowly, Cord leafed through the pages of the booklet.

"Oh, my," breathed Gillian. "The marks are just like those in Pepys's journal."

"Yes," replied Cord excitedly. He fished in one of his pockets for a moment, bringing out a sheet of paper. "And see? On my last visit to your uncle, I copied several lines from the first page of the diary. "Gillian," he breathed. "The shorthand worked! I was able to translate the first sentence."

Reverently, he passed the paper to Gillian, and she read aloud. " 'Blessed be God, at the end of the last year I was in very good health, without any sense of my old pain but upon taking of cold.' "

She turned a wide gaze on Cord. "You've done it, Cord! You've solved the mystery! If this is truly the source of Pepys's code, the translation of the diary should be the work of—well, several months, I should think." She halted suddenly. "But why did no one ever think of this before? I mean, if this book has been around for almost two hundred years, why did no one think to—?"

"That's precisely the point. The Shelton system was undoubtedly known in Pepys's time. Perhaps it even became a popular method of transcription, but then it went out of fashion, eventually to be forgotten. Who today has even heard of this book? Even in academic circles I should imagine no one knows of it anymore."

"Cord, I don't know what to say. To think that the secret of decoding the diary has been buried all these years in such an unremarkable fashion. Uncle will be so pleased!" She started to rise. "We must give it to him at once!"

"Um," began Cord, who had remained seated. "Perhaps we want to think about that for a bit."

Gillian sank back into her chair, sending him a puzzled look.

"If we just hand Sir Henry the book," continued Cord,

"we will have taken the challenge from him. He will think of it as . . . well, as my accomplishment. I know you said he's interested in simply seeing the journal translated, but it seems to me he very much wants to be the source of the solution."

"Yes," said Gillian slowly. "I see what you mean."

She lifted her gaze to his, astonished. This aspect should have occurred to her immediately, for she had known Henry all her life. Surely, she should have realized at once how he would feel. Instead, it was Cord, a relative stranger, who had put himself so neatly in Uncle Henry's shoes. She had not suspected the earl of such depth of understanding, and she felt slightly shamed.

Watching her, Cord knew a pang. She was surprised at his consideration of an old man's feelings. She must think him a self-absorbed idiot.

"So, what shall we do?"

Cord came to himself with a start. "I've been thinking about that, and it seems to me that we must arrange for your uncle to stumble across the tachygraphy book on his own—or, rather to *think* it is on his own."

Gillian frowned dubiously. "But how are we to do that? Uncle knows every book in the house. If a strange title appears on his shelves, he will grasp at once that he did not put it there."

"That's true. Well, then, we must get him out of the cottage. He will be coming to Wildehaven tomorrow for that confounded dinner party. Yes," Cord continued, warming to this theme, "I shall invite him into the library and tell him to treat it as his own. Knowing Sir Henry, he will take me at my word."

"Actually," interposed Gillian, "Uncle Henry visited the library at Wildehaven on many occassions—when your uncle was in residence."

"I had not thought of that."

"However, this is a small volume, and it might very well have been overlooked by even the most dedicated of book browsers. We need only to place it in a conspicuous location—"

"And your uncle's insatiable literary curiosity will do the rest! Yes, I think that's the solution."

Cord rubbed his hands briskly. "Well, that's that

then." He rose. "Now, I'd best go inform Sir Henry of my return."

"John Smith is with him," said Gillian, also getting to her feet. "I think they came up with a new avenue of investigation last night, so they will have much to tell you."

"I've missed our little gatherings these last few days. I . . . I've missed you." They were very close together as they stood at the desk, and Cord's breath caught in his throat. Would he ever *not* feel an urge to kiss Gillian Tate every time he came within two feet of her? He had vowed—to Gillian and himself—that his behavior toward her would be that of one friend to another. Bah! He could think of none of his other friends whose very scent he found intoxicating. Would the day ever come, he wondered again, when Gillian would accept a declaration of love from him? Would she ever confide in him the story of her short-lived betrothal? More to the point, would she explain her strange reluctance to tell him that she had broken it off before Kenneth's death?

Ah, well. He'd given his word—and he was stuck with it—for the time being, at least. He drew away from her and turned to leave the room.

Gillian followed, feeling oddly deflated. She had been almost certain Cord was going to kiss her in that moment when they had stood within inches of each other. No—try to kiss her, for she certainly would have thwarted any such attempt. Wouldn't she?

Declining to delve further into this murky area, she hurried after him.

Sir Henry and young John Smith were indeed pleased to welcome Cord back from his travels. In a few moments, the three were back at the old stand, deep in discussion of the diary and its secrets. Gillian watched for a few moments, smiling, before tiptoeing from the room.

Cord stayed for dinner, and the conversation around the little dining table in Rose Cottage was lively.

"But do tell us, Cord," said Mrs. Ferris at length, "where did you hare off to so suddenly? Were you called to London?"

Gillian sent her aunt an admonishing glance, but Cord laughed.

"It was necessary to make a flying visit to my home in Bedfordshire—to Cordray Park. Some trifling business there required my attention."

"Ah." Aunt Louisa nodded wisely. She laughed. "I was afraid you might just go directly to London, and not return to us at all." She blushed a little as though aware of what she no doubt thought of as presumption. "At any rate, we are so pleased you are returned to us."

"But, my dear lady," he declared in wounded innocence, "I told you I would return in plenty of time for our famous dinner party."

Aunt Louisa brightened, and the rest of the dinner conversation was taken up in relating the returns brought in by the invitations Aunt Louisa had written so painstakingly.

"It's as I told you, Cord," she said, beaming, "all the world and his donkey will be there."

As it turned out, this statement proved a slight exaggeration, but two nights later, as Cord gazed out over his drawing room, he realized that every neighbor of any consequence within twenty miles of Wildehaven had put in an appearance. Many of the faces were new to him, but he had already met enough of them so that he felt comfortable. There, by the hearth, stood Sir Septimus Babbacombe, his wife and two daughters at his side. Chatting amiably with them were Mrs. Mitford and her daughter, roughly the same age as the Babbacombe chits. Hmm he mused. Glancing about, he spied at least three other young women of marriageable age. He smiled to himself. He'd better be careful or he'd find himself committed to one of these misses before the night was out.

Indeed, Cord found himself surrounded by ladies of varying ages, as well as their hopeful mamas for the rest of the evening. He began to feel rather like the maypole at a spring festival, enmeshed in soft words and giggles, smothered in a swirl of muslins and flowery perfume.

When Sir Henry and his family arrived, Cord moved to greet them with some relief. His gaze first went to Gillian, who was garbed tonight in a cerulean blue silk

that deepened her gray eyes to the color of smoke
against a night sky. His breath caught in his throat, but
he managed to greet her with only a casual courtesy
before turning to Sir Henry.

"I am pleased to welcome you to my home, Sir Henry.
It seems as though I have spent a great deal of time at
Rose Cottage, but this is the first time you have visited
me. I certainly hope it will not be the last."

"Yes, well, I do not get out a great deal these days.
When Frederick lived here, I used to pop over every
now and then. Your uncle had an excellent library."

Grateful for the opportunity presented to him, Cord
spoke quickly. "The library is still extant, Sir Henry. In
fact, I was hoping that while you are here tonight you
would peruse the volumes there once more. Please," he
added with the most charming smile at his disposal, "I
hope you will treat my collection as your own."

He exchanged a significant glance with Gillian, giving
her to understand that he had already put their plan in
motion. Earlier this afternoon, Cord had placed the
Shelton tachygraphy book in a prominent position in
the library.

"Umph," responded Sir Henry. "I've been over every
volume in that library—more than once. However, I must
say that I wouldn't mind renewing my acquaintance with
some of them. As I recall, Frederick possessed several fine
volumes of commentary on verse by The Court Wits, as
they were called. Rochester, Sir Charles Sedley, the Earl
of Dorset and all that lot. After dinner, perhaps."

Cord all but rubbed his hands in satisfaction. He had
selected these volumes as the ones most likely to be
searched out by Sir Henry, and he had placed the Shelton book in their midst. He breathed an inward sigh of
relief. It looked as though all would transpire as he and
Gillian had planned. He caught her eye and winked. He
was rewarded with an answering smile of such engaging
mischief that he ached with the need to sweep her into
his arms.

The conversation turned to more general matters then,
and Cord congratulated Mrs. Ferris on the arrangements
she had made for tonight's festivities. All the while, his
glance strayed to Gillian. She seemed aware of his re-

gard, for a delicate flush rose to her cheeks, and after a few minutes she turned away to converse with one of the young females who, with their mamas, continued to circle the earl like vixens closing in on a spring lamb.

It was not until dinner time that he was offered some surcease, for Sir Septimus was seated at his right hand, with his lady on Cord's left. Their two offspring, however, a little farther down the table, spent the greater part of the meal leaning over their plates to converse with him, fanning their food with great sweeps of artfully curled eyelashes.

Mrs. Ferris sat at the foot of the table, and from her place nearby, Gillian observed the activity at the table's head.

Cord, lifting his head as though she had reached out to touch him, intercepted her glance and returned it with one of amusement—tinged with some anguish. Gillian almost laughed aloud. She had earlier experienced an entirely unreasonable qualm at the sight of the earl almost submerged in a sea of feminine fluffery. She had soon realized that he was not enjoying the siege. Now, however, as she watched Cord turn his gaze to the Misses Babbacombe, her smile faded. The older sister, Horatia, was plump and more than somewhat plain. Eighteen-year-old Eleanor, on the other hand, was undeniably attractive. Small and vivacious with a cap of crisp auburn curls and sparkling blue eyes, she flirted outrageously, using her lush fringe of lashes, and giggled appreciatively at Cord's every pleasantry.

Surely a man of Cord's years and experience would not be caught in the toils of a girl barely out of the schoolroom. In any case, he was scheduled to marry the awful Corisande. But then, he did not really wish to wed his childhood playmate. He was, he said, reconciled to the idea that he must marry someday, and given his shiny new resolutions to uphold his family responsibilities, perhaps he was even now seeking another candidate. While Eleanor was notably lacking in the birth and breeding usually considered essential in a prospective countess, she was young and biddable and—pretty.

Gillian shook herself. For heaven's sake, what difference did Eleanor's impact on the earl make to her?

After all, she had no interest in Cord's matrimonial plans. A cold thread of honesty coiled unpleasantly within her. She was forced to admit that Cord's plans mattered very much to her. Good Lord, not only did she cringe at the idea of Cord's leaving, but the idea of his marrying some biddable little chit was enough to make her want to spit like a cat.

Instead, she turned determinedly to make conversation with Mr. Delacroix, seated next to her.

To Cord, dinner seemed to lurch in eternal increments. Why had Mrs. Ferris seated Gillian at the foot of the table? If ever he needed her at his right hand, that moment was now. If the little Babbacombe giggled one more time at the inanities he seemed to be spouting like some damned deity in a fountain, he would be sore put not to fling his wine in her face. The only person in the room with whom he wanted to talk was Gillian, and she may as well have been dining on the moon.

After another year or two, the last bite of Mrs. Moresby's excellent trifle was spooned up, and at Mrs. Ferris's signal, the ladies rose to depart for the drawing room. Cord found some relief in the masculine conversation that ensued, but rose with alacrity when the decanter had made the prescribed number of rounds about the table.

As they moved to join the ladies, Cord maneuvered to a position next to Sir Henry.

"If you would like to visit the library, sir," he said smoothly, "this would be as good a time as any." He accompanied his words with a slight pressure on Sir Henry's elbow.

"Eh? What?" The old gentleman spoke somewhat groggily, having indulged rather heavily, not only in the buttered lobster and the pigeon pie featured at dinner, along with the trifle, but in the postprandial brandy as well. "Excellent suggestion, my boy. Can't say as I look forward to an entire evening of mindless nattering with a parcel of clotheads who probably don't know Charles II from a China orange."

Cord, in some satisfaction, led Sir Henry to the library.

Chapter Seventeen

"Ah." Sir Henry rubbed his hands in satisfaction. As Cord held his breath, the old man moved to an eye-level shelf near the center of the room. Cord breathed a relieved sigh. This was where the commentaries would be found, and the Shelton book of instruction on tachygraphy lay in plain view right next to them.

Lovingly, Sir Henry picked up the commentaries, inadvertently knocking the Shelton to the floor in the process. Cord retrieved it hastily and replaced it on the shelf, almost pressing it into Sir Henry's hands. Absently, Sir Henry brushed the book aside and turned toward the light. Cord watched in frustrated silence as the elderly academic, apparently lost to his surroundings, turned the pages of the first volume of commentary slowly and intently. Of the little volume on tachygraphy, he took no notice. At last, he regretfully replaced the commentary on the shelf and moved toward the door, still ignoring the little volume lying so close to his hand.

"The ladies will be wondering what became of us, and Louisa will no doubt poke her head in the door any minute to bring me to a sense of duty she knows very well I do not possess."

"But—" expostulated Cord. "The commentaries!"

Sir Henry sighed. "Some other time perhaps. Unless—" He stared hopefully up at Cord. "Do you suppose I could borrow them for a few days? It's been donkey's years since I've been through them."

Cord fairly leaped on this suggestion. "Of course, you may. With my blessing. I'll tell you what. I'll put all four of these volumes on the table—right here. We can collect them later when you go home. Nothing simpler."

Sir Henry expressed his gratification at this program,

and the two made their way to the drawing room, where he was immediately surrounded by what he was beginning to think of as his personal harem. From across the room, he caught Gillian's questioning gaze and sent her a rueful grimace.

Oh, dear, thought Gillian. Was his expression indicative of a failure in the tachygraphy scheme or his dismay at finding himself once more the target of a feminine assault? Her answer came a few moments later when, with some difficulty, he made his way to her. He explained Sir Henry's failure to take their bait, and Gillian's heart fell momentarily, until Cord went on to detail his plan to lend Uncle Henry a stack of volumes, on top of which, Cord assured her, would rest Shelton's small book on tachygraphy.

Cord had been informed earlier by Mrs. Ferris that some of the guests would be asked to perform in an impromptu concert following dinner. Thus, as signs of preparation became evident, he deftly guided Gillian to one of the chairs being pulled into a comfortable arrangement near the pianoforte. Settling himself into one next to her, he launched into a commentary on the procession of singers and players of various instruments.

"But, are you not going to favor us with a song?" he asked at last, as Miss Hester Selwyn drew her vocal selection to a close—a lively, if somewhat shrill rendition of "Keys of Canterbury."

"Oh, no," replied Gillian quickly. "I am quite tone deaf, you see. I do play the piano, but indifferently at best. I am, however," she concluded with a laugh, "known far and wide for my talent as a listener, and with that, I am content."

Gazing at the play of candlelight in her glossy, nut-brown curls, Cord marveled at how little he really knew of this woman. She had captured his heart, but she had yet to reveal hers, or the many other fascinating details that made her the exciting, wholly desirable female he was determined to make his own.

Unthinking, he reached to brush back a tendril of hair that had escaped the Clytie knot in which it was contained. Abruptly, the smile dropped from her lips, and she stiffened as though he had struck her. Startled, he dropped his hand and murmured something inconsequential about the duet now under way between Sir Walter Finnaby's son, Rutherford, and a very nervous Miss Charlotte Anstey.

He sighed inwardly. How was he ever to penetrate the fortress Gillian had built around her emotions? For, he told himself once more, he was willing to swear she was not totally indifferent to him. The memory of her lithe body pressed against his in the kiss they had shared not two weeks ago shot through him again like a Roman candle. He did not think she was the sort of woman who could respond so givingly if her heart was not involved. Why, then, did she treat his slightest gesture of genuine warmth as though he were suggesting some sort of sordid liaison? Was that what she thought? That he wanted her merely for a bit of dalliance while he sojourned in the country? She had categorized him on their first meeting as "that sort of man," meaning the type of high-born despoiler of women who took his pleasures where he found them with no thought of the consequences.

His heart lightened. Surely, he could convince her—if she would give him the opportunity—that, while the idea of dalliance with Gillian sent him into a spiral of wanting, his intentions were almost painfully honest. He must make her understand that he wanted to marry her at the earliest opportunity in a church full of blazing candles and fond well-wishers. He wanted to make a family with her, to fill a nursery with their offspring, and . . .

He discovered that his collar had tightened, and he turned his attention with some effort to the duet.

At his side, Gillian upbraided herself. She *must* learn to suppress her absurd response to Cord's very touch. Just now, when his fingers had touched her cheek, it was as though lightning had brushed her skin. Not that he should have been taking such an intimate liberty, of course, but it was evident she must increase her guard against such invasions of her equanimity.

She turned to address a remark to old Mr. Burgess, seated on her right before speaking to Cord again.

"Uncle Henry really took no notice of the Shelton book?" she asked, grasping for a safe topic of conversation.

Cord sighed. "No. He was so absorbed in Lawford's poetic commentaries that he had no eyes for anything else. Of course, I couldn't press the Shelton on him, for then he would have realized that I had found something of value."

"No," agreed Gillian. "That would not do at all. He must feel he's made the discovery on his own."

"Precisely. However, I nipped into the library a few moments ago and placed the Shelton atop the pile of commentaries he will be taking home with him. Even if he doesn't notice it then, surely when he begins examining the commentaries, he will observe the Shelton. I cannot imagine Sir Henry opening an unfamiliar book without perusing it."

"You're right, of course," breathed Gillian. "At least, we can only hope."

At that point, Lady Babbacombe, who was seated on his left, claimed Cord's attention.

"Our little Eleanor is going to sing now," she whispered stridently, her hand in a death grip on his sleeve. "I know you will enjoy her lovely soprano."

Eleanor did indeed sing with a pretty sweetness, and Cord clapped appreciatively at the conclusion of her song. Lady Babbacombe simpered fatuously. "Isn't she just the most darling girl? There are no end to her talents, you know, and she's a fine little householder, as well. Lucky indeed the man who weds my Eleanor."

Cord pasted a sickly smile on his face, and with some effort disentangled himself from Lady Babbacombe's hold. He turned again, almost gasping in relief, only to discover that Gillian was once again in conversation with Mr. Burgess.

The procession of amateur musicians—the operative word, thought Cord dismally, being "amateur"—trouped on. Conversation with Gillian proved elusive, for she apparently preferred to chat with Mr. Burgess. Thus, Cord was left to Lady Babbacombe's blatant machinations.

At long—very long—last, the final singer tweetled a rendition of "The Lass with the Delicate Air," and Mrs. Ferris rose to indicate that the assemblage was now on its own for entertainment for the rest of the evening. Cord turned immediately to Gillian, but she had swept away to join a group of ladies near the window.

Feeling forlorn and abandoned, Cord attempted to move to Sir Henry, but was intercepted by yet another phalanx of mamas and their daughters. He perceived there was no escape, and, with one longing glance toward Gillian's straight back, he gave himself up to the wearisome chore of being pleasant.

At last, by mutual consent, Cord's guests began to take their leave. Drifting to the door at a glacial pace, with declarations that this had been one of the most pleasant evenings they'd ever spent, all the ladies and gentlemen and assorted marriageable daughters eventually departed.

The Folsomes were the last to leave.

"I thank you, Mrs. Ferris, from the bottom of my helpless soul," said Cord, "for putting the party together. That it was a huge success is wholly your doing."

Mrs. Ferris blushed. "Why, it was my pleasure, Cord. It has been many years since I was called on to perform hostess duties, and I enjoyed it vastly. You will be receiving return invitations, of course, so I trust you are not planning to leave us very soon." She laughed slyly. "Lady Babbacombe, for example, will take it very much amiss if she does not snare you for a dinner party of her own—or at the very least, a picnic."

Cord bent a twinkling glance on her. "I would, of course, be loathe to miss such a festive occasion."

At this point, Sir Henry apparently bethought himself of the promised largesse of Cord's commentaries. Cord himself went to retrieve the volumes stacked on the table in the library. When he returned, he handed the volumes ceremoniously to Sir Henry, with a significant glance at Gillian. On top of the pile, conspicuous by its very inconspicuousness against the fine leather of the commentaries, lay the pasteboard-covered Shelton book.

Gillian returned Cord's glance with a barely concealed anticipation. Surely, Uncle Henry could not overlook the slim volume that differed so strongly from the rest in the little armful. Her pulse quickened at Uncle Henry's next words.

"Thank you, my boy. I shall derive great pleasure

from a reacquaintance with these old friends. Here, what's this?" Juggling the commentaries in one arm, he removed the Shelton. "Where did this come from?"

"Ah," declared Cord smoothly, "I must have placed it with the others by mistake. But do take it along as well. Perhaps it's something you haven't read."

"No thank you, but I shall have enough to occupy myself with these. I don't want to keep them from you longer than necessary." Without looking at the Shelton, he set it on a nearby table, only to have it slip to the floor.

Gillian scooped it up and opened it before handing it back to her uncle.

He merely glanced at the pages disinterestedly before passing it along to Cord. He turned to his sister. "Well, come along then, Louisa, Gillian. Mustn't keep Cord from his bed any longer."

It was obvious that his haste to leave was prompted more by an eagerness to peruse his borrowed treasure than from a desire to relieve his host of the last guest.

More significant stares were exchanged between Cord and Gillian. With raised eyebrows, glances sent to the ceiling and shrugged shoulders on Cord's part, Gillian was given to understand that he considered further prodding on the part of either of them unwise. Nodding to indicate her understanding, she accepted the wraps handed to her by a servant and assisted her aunt and uncle in donning their outerwear.

Outside, as Sir Henry and his sister mounted their gig, Cord drew Gillian aside.

"Well, so much for our grand plan," he muttered in exasperation.

"Indeed," she replied in a similar tone. "What are we to do now?"

"I shall make another effort tomorrow to press the book into his possession in an unobtrusive manner." Cord sighed. "If that doesn't work, I suppose we shall be obliged to simply thrust the book at him—to tell him that it is the means to the translation of Pepys's diary."

Gillian sighed as well. "I suppose. It seems such a shame, though, to take his triumph from him. He has worked so hard."

Cord touched her hand briefly. He knew that his response to the sadness in her eyes was almost wholly on her behalf rather than Sir Henry's, but he was swept by a desire to lighten her concern, to solve this and any other problems that might cross her path for the rest of her life.

"I will find a way, Gillian," he whispered. "I don't know how yet, but I'll manage something."

To his surprise, Gillian covered his hand with hers. In the dim light of the flambeaux, her eyes were misty pools, but he thought he caught the glitter of tears and a trace of unguarded warmth. "I know you will, Cord," she murmured huskily. "You are very good."

At Sir Henry's peremptory command for Gillian to "for Lord's sake, stir your stumps, girl," Cord handed Gillian into the gig and waved the little party off down the drive. Bemused, he entered the house.

What had caused Gillian's about-face? he wondered. She had stiffened like a church steeple when he had merely brushed her cheek earlier. Just now, however, she had actually returned his gesture of affection. Several explanations whirled through his mind as he made his way upstairs, his favorite being that on this occasion, Gillian had acted with her heart instead of with whatever skewed logic she had crafted in her mind.

As he readied himself for bed, Cord's thoughts drifted to Sir Henry and to the abortive attempt to thrust the Shelton book on him. He scratched his head. How the devil was he to get the old fellow to notice the little volume with all those Restoration poets thundering in his brain?

It occurred to him that prior to his recent contretemps with his Aunt Binsted, he had scarcely given Wildehaven a thought since it had come into his possession. Now, a scant three weeks after his precipitous flight from London, he was thoroughly embroiled in the doings of his neighbors. He had fallen in love with the nearest of these, and had made himself responsible for the well-being of her aunt and uncle. He had immersed himself in his duties as a landlord, and had become the target of what appeared to be a concerted effort on the part of a number of others to get him married at the first possible opportunity.

Oddly enough, he mused as his valet slid a nightshirt

over his shoulders, he was enjoying himself. He relished
having his tenants rely on him and having his neighbors
welcome his new efforts to improve his estate. In fact,
all he needed now to make his life perfect was to convince Miss Gillian Tate that what she needed in her life
was his own humble self.

He crawled sleepily into bed and soon fell into a deep
slumber, troubled only slightly by dreams of maypoles
and dancing maidens and a pair of clear gray eyes that
surveyed him critically from afar.

He did not know how long he had been asleep when
the dancing maidens began to race toward him. Grown
larger and somehow menacing, they tucked up their
skirts and ran with pounding feet over an earthen path.
As in so many nightmares of this sort, he found himself
unable to move, and it was not until the pack was almost
on him that he woke, wide-eyed and sweating. His confusion was not lessened, however, for the pounding continued. It was several moments before he realized the
sound came from someone pummeling the front door of
the manor house. Hastily donning a dressing gown, he
hurried downstairs to find Moresby hobbling across the
floor from the servants' wing, wearing a nightcap and a
voluminous shawl over his nightshirt. The old man carried a candle before him like a sword, and with some
indignation threw open the door.

To Cord's astonishment, the visitor was none other
than Sir Henry Folsome. He was garbed in night attire
and still wore his nightcap, but had stuffed his nightshirt
into a pair of breeches. He was in a high state of
excitement.

"Cord!" he gasped, lurching into the house. He ignored Moresby's presence and almost hurled himself
into Cord's arms.

"Good God, Sir Henry! What's toward? Is something
amiss at the cottage?" Cord led the old gentleman
toward the drawing room.

"No, no!" cried Sir Henry impatiently. "It's that book!
The one I almost took home by mistake. Where is it? I
must see it at once!"

Chapter Eighteen

"The book?" asked Cord stupidly.

"Yes!" cried Sir Henry, almost dancing with impatience. "Surely you must remember. It was atop the commentaries. I almost took it home with me."

"Of course." Cord nearly stumbled in his eagerness to steer the old man into the library. "I returned it to its shelf. But, my dear sir, you needn't have come out in the middle of the night. I would have sent someone over with it in the morning, had you asked."

"Eh?" Sir Henry glanced about as though surprised to find the household plunged into darkness. "What time is it?" He glanced at a wall clock, barely visible by the light of Cord's single taper. "Good Lord, it's three o'clock!" He whirled to face Cord. "I say, my dear fellow, I am sorry. But, you know, it was the most peculiar thing. I awoke from a sound sleep with a picture in my mind of the open volume, and there I saw—well, I can hardly believe it—but I'm sure I saw marks very similar to the ones Pepys used in his diary!"

"No!" exclaimed Cord.

"Yes! I rose immediately, of course, and made my way here as quickly as possible. Oh, by the by," he added distractedly, "would you have someone see to my horse? I rode old Sukey. She's the oldest animal in our stable, but she was closest to the door. I did not saddle her, but merely threw a blanket over her back. I'm afraid she may wander off if . . ."

Cord gestured to Moresby, who still stood near the entrance door, gaping in affront. At Cord's signal, he opened the door with weary resignation. Peering into the gloom outside, he turned with a nod before moving outside, slamming the door behind him.

Cord turned back to Sir Henry, but the elderly academic had appropriated the candle and had hurried to the library, where he was already hunting among the shelves.

Cord went immediately to the spot occupied by the Shelton. "Here you are, sir," he said, drawing the book from its place.

"Ah," replied Sir Henry, beaming in gratification. He read the title aloud in slow wonderment. Taking the book to a nearby table, he flung himself into a chair and opened the volume. He became at once lost to his surroundings, and for some minutes, the only sounds to be heard were the shuffling of pages and the excited murmurings of the old scholar.

Cord watched with bated breath, until at last Sir Henry rose. He blew out a sigh of vast satisfaction and peered at Cord.

"Yes, my boy. I can hardly believe my eyes, but I think this is our answer!" He examined the book's title sheet again. " 'Shelton's Tachygraphy.' Good God, boy, this was published in 1635! Pepys was no doubt familiar with it. Perhaps it even attained some popularity in his time. Has it lain in old Frederick's library all these years since? Like a buried treasure! How could I have missed it?"

Cord cleared his throat. "Well, it is a very small book. Easily missed."

Sir Henry slapped the table delightedly. "Well, I have it now! Unless I am much mistaken, the diary may very well be translated by this time next year. Of course, I must take it home immediately—with your permission, of course. The first thing to do is to make absolutely sure that this is the true key."

With the book clutched to his bosom, Sir Henry prepared to make his way back to the hall.

"Wait, Sir Henry!" Cord laid a hand on the old gentleman's arm. "You may have the book with my good wishes, of course, but I cannot allow you to return to the cottage at this hour."

"Nonsense," returned Sir Henry briskly. "I want to get started immediately." He turned from Cord's grasp, but was immediately reined in again.

"Sir, your sister would comb my hair with a joint stool, as would you niece, if I were to let you set out on that spavined old mare at this hour. You will spend the remainder of the night here. I'll send a message to the cottage apprising the ladies of your whereabouts. You can return home to start on the translation first thing in the morning. After breakfast," he amended. "Please, sir," he said, cajoling, as Sir Henry opened his mouth in expostulation. "The diary has been waiting for two hundred years. One more night cannot make any difference. It will be there for you in the morning—when you are fresh."

It took some moments to convince Sir Henry of the wisdom of this program, but at last the old man, apparently realizing that he was, indeed, very tired, capitulated. Cord instructed Moresby, now reinforced by the presence of his wife; also in night garb, to lead Sir Henry to a guest chamber.

A few minutes later, Cord climbed the stairs and settled once more into bed. Sleep eluded him, however, for he realized that with Sir Henry's discovery of the method for translating the diary, he himself had come to a watershed point in his rural sojourn. He could no longer delay his return to London. To be sure, Geoffrey Tomlinson, his man of affairs, was no doubt handling matters of importance to his well-being, but there was the matter of Corisande. How was he to expunge his obligation to her? He knew now that he would never make that long-awaited proposal, but how was he to disentangle himself from Corisande's expectations and those of their families?

He was determined to win the heart and hand of Gillian Tate. When, he wondered, had the idea of marriage been transformed from a life sentence to a goal to be ardently pursued? When had he first pictured Gillian ensconced at Cordray Park as the Countess of Cordray? Or envisioned walks with her through the estate park— long, intimate evenings spent before the fire—nights with her in a scented boudoir, her mahogany hair spread over the pillow next to his?

He turned abruptly to pull the covers about his shoulders. Oh, indeed, these maunderings were all well and good, he reflected savagely, but at this point he had as much chance of making them a reality as he had of flying to the top of King's College Chapel in Cambridge. Not only was he still committed to Corisande, but Gillian seemed in no way inclined to listen to his words of love.

A thought occurred to him, so startling that he sat bolt upright in bed. How could he have been so stupid? He had surmised earlier that Gillian considered him simply another rake in search of a conquest. He had not so far made the slightest effort to disabuse her of this misconception! He would go to her tomorrow! He would lay his heart at her feet, and his title and all that went with it. He was sure she would be unimpressed by the title and the wealth and the status, but he hoped—oh, God, how he hoped she would accept his heart.

Cord slept at last, but his dreams were so tumultuous that he woke early. Not, however, so early as Sir Henry, who had risen before the servants. Cord found him waiting in the drawing room, pacing the floor impatiently. He held the Shelton book in one hand, and every few seconds stopped to examine one of the pages though which he shuffled rapidly.

"Ah!" he exclaimed as Cord entered the room. "You are up at last. I trust you have breakfasted? If so, let us be on our way."

He made as though to brush past Cord on his way to the door, but Cord stayed him with a hand on the old man's arm.

"No, indeed, I have not breakfasted, sir. Nor, I'll warrant have you, since none of the servants is yet stirring."

"Yes, but that is no matter. I have slept and I am rested and it is imperative that I get to work! You can breakfast at the cottage if you're concerned about the state of your stomach." The old man was hopping up and down like a child in his eagerness to be off.

Cord smiled. "Very well. Just let me have a note for Moresby, so he won't think we've been kidnapped by brigands."

"Tchah!" snorted Sir Henry, but he contained himself with reasonable calm as Cord took pen and paper from a small desk nearby and scratched a swift message.

They moved to the rear of the house and out to the

stables, where they found Sukey, apparently the better for a few hours' repose. Cord saddled Zeus, and in a few moments they were on their way.

At the cottage, all was silent. It was barely seven of the clock, and the sun had peeped above the horizon not an hour before. Sir Henry, however, took no notice and burst past the front door, bellowing at the top of his lungs. "Louisa! Gillian! Where are you? Widdings! Breakfast for his lordship!"

On receiving no immediate response to his commands, he repeated them, again at full volume. It was not until he had begun on a third verse of the litany that Gillian appeared at the top of the stairs. To Cord's delight, she, too, was still in her night rail, over which she wore a pretty sprigged dressing gown. Her hair tumbled about her shoulders in enticing disarray, and from beneath the dressing gown, her bare toes peeped entrancingly.

"Uncle! What is it?" She gasped on catching sight of Cord and tried to withdraw both feet at once under the dressing gown, almost catapulting herself down the stairs.

"Where the devil is everyone?" roared Sir Henry. "We need breakfast. Tell Widdings to serve it in the study."

He wheeled about and strode from the entryway toward the study, leaving Cord to explain things as best he might to Gillian.

"Oh, good Heavens!" she squeaked when he had concluded his tale of the night's stirring occurrence. She plumped down on the top step, drawing her dressing gown more securely about her. "Our plan worked, Cord! Not quite as we envisioned it, perhaps, but nonetheless, he has the book and he's hot on the trail of the diary translation."

"Indeed," began Cord, mounting the stairs toward her, but he was interrupted by the arrival of Mrs. Ferris, who pattered into view at that moment from her own bedchamber. She was encased in a sturdy cotton dressing gown, and wore a lace-trimmed nightcap, from which a few strands of gray hair escaped like wispy exclamation points.

"Goodness, what is the commotion? Cord, my dear

boy, what has happened? Has there been an accident at the manor? Did I hear Henry's voice? What—?''

"Yes, indeed, Aunt," interposed Gillian. She related to her aunt the tale of Sir Henry's discovery of a book on shorthand, omitting, of course, any mention of the source of the book.

"Well, my stars!" gasped the old lady. "Do you mean Henry now has the means to translate his precious diary?"

"Yes," replied Gillian and Cord in unison.

"Sir Henry estimates that the actual work will take a year or so," added Cord.

"Oh, my," breathed Aunt Louisa, "Oh, my," she said again, apparently unable to formulate an appropriate response to this momentous news.

"In the meantime," said Gillian briskly, rising to her feet, "Uncle Henry wants breakfast sent into the study."

"Oh, that wretched man!" exclaimed Aunt Louisa. "If that isn't just like him, so taken with his all-important diary that he can just put the whole household at sixes and sevens—and he doesn't even care! Well, I imagine Mrs. Widdings is already in the kitchen. I'll tell her what Sir High-and-Mighty desires this morning. After," she concluded in some dudgeon, "I am properly dressed."

She glanced severely at her niece. "And what in the world do you think you're doing here, Miss Gillian, appearing in your nightclothes in the presence of a gentleman. Off with you now!"

Gillian laughed over her shoulder at Cord as Aunt Louisa herded her along the corridor with word and gesture. Warmed by the scene, Cord watched her go, and when the two ladies disappeared from view, he betook himself to the kitchen. Here he found Mrs. Widdings directing a young maid in the making of coffee and frying of ham. She displayed some surprise at seeing the earl in her domain—"and at such an ungodly hour!" she later related to her husband. "And dressed all anyhow!" However, she received Sir Henry's wishes with equanimity and promised sustenance in short order.

Cord then made his way to Sir Henry's study, where he found the elderly academic poring over the book on tachygraphy. He had covered a piece of paper with words and symbols, and beside him lay one of the volumes of Pepys's Diary, currently in his possession. Sir Henry looked up at Cord's entrance. His plump face was wreathed in smiles, and his eyes glowed behind his spectacles.

"See here, my boy. It works! I have here before me proof that Pepys used Shelton's system of tachygraphy to write his diary! Look! I have already transcribed three words using the method. See?"

He turned the paper so that Cord could read the words, " 'And so . . . to . . . bid.' No, no. That must be 'bed.' "

Sir Henry's voice sank to a broken whisper. "I cannot believe it. After all these years . . . And to think the solution lay not two miles from here in Frederick Deddington's library. Who would have thought?"

The old man appeared not to hear Cord's assenting rejoinder, but returned to his task, becoming oblivious to Cord's presence. In a few moments, Mrs. Ferris and Gillian joined him, both now dressed with impeccable propriety.

"But, of course, you will not eat in here, Henry," were Mrs. Ferris's first words. "Henry! Lift up your head and attend to me. Breakfast will be served momentarily—in the dining parlor, and that is where you will eat—with the rest of us."

Sir Henry protested mightily, but in the end, accompanied by a steady stream of invective, rose to join the rest of his little family as they trooped out of the study. At table, over a hearty meal of ham, eggs, kippers and toast—and, of course, ale for the gentlemen, conversation centered on Sir Henry's grand accomplishment.

"For now, dearest, the people at the college will realize that you were right all along. The book was indeed translatable—just awaiting a man with intelligence and experience to find the key."

"Tchah!" responded Sir Henry gruffly. "As though I care for what that pack of dunces thinks."

Nevertheless, the old man could not conceal his gratification. He rubbed his hands briskly, thereby leaving his knuckles smeared liberally with butter.

Unheeding, Aunt Louisa burbled on. "What do you

suppose John Smith will say when you tell him you have
found the secret? He will no doubt visit this afternoon,
as it's been a few days since his last call."

At this, a sudden stillness fell upon the table. Cord
and Sir Henry, forks suspended in midair, glanced at
each other. The next moment Cord swiveled to face Gillian, who in turn stared at him, startled.

"Yes, indeed, John Smith," murmured Sir Henry, as
though to himself. He was silent for a long moment before coming to himself. At last, he lay down his napkin
and rose from the table.

"I . . . I may not be home if John calls this afternoon."

"But, dearest . . . ! exclaimed Aunt Louisa.

"I must go into Cambridge in a little while," Sir Henry
responded brusquely. He pushed his chair back. "But,
for now, I must get back to my desk. Join me when
you've finished," he added to Cord before stumping
from the room.

The three remaining at table gazed at each other in
mystification. They consumed the remainder of their
meal in relative silence, until Aunt Louisa stood, saying,
"I'm sure this is a red-letter day for Henry, but life must
go on. I have a hundred things to do this morning. No,
no—" She gestured to Gillian, who had also risen to her
feet. "You stay with Cord. I'm sure Henry doesn't really
want his company—for he will be oblivious to the world
for the rest of the morning. Perhaps, since the day is so
fair, you two might enjoy an early ride."

So obvious was the old lady's desire to see the pair
off on their own that Gillian blushed.

"Oh, I don't think . . ." she began, her heart fluttering
like a wind tossed leaf. "I'm not dressed for riding,
and—"

Cord, observing her, felt his own heart twist. Now!
he thought exultantly. But he spoke calmly. "An early
morning ride sounds delightful, Mrs. Ferris." To Gillian,
he said, "I hope you will agree, for there is a matter I
would discuss with you."

Her expression remained discouraging, but she made
no demur. Breathing an inward sigh of relief, Cord continued. "While you are changing, I shall stop for a few
moments with Sir Henry."

He left the room swiftly, before Gillian could protest. Gillian turned to Aunt Louisa. "Aunt, how could you?"

Aunt Louisa was all bewildered innocence. "Could I what, dearest?" Deftly, she steered Gillian out of the room and up the stairs.

"You know very well, 'Could I what?' How could you throw me into Cord's company—alone in his company, that is?"

"But surely you have been alone in his company before. Never tell me that he has comported himself in an ungentlemanly manner, for that I will not believe."

They had by now reached Gillian's bedchamber, and Aunt Louisa rummaged in her niece's wardrobe, producing in short order a riding habit of Cheshire brown.

"N-no," mumbled Gillian hesitantly. "No, of course not. However, his manner to me of late has been . . . That is, he has said some things . . . that I would rather he not repeat," she finished, feeling hot and harassed.

"What sort of things?" asked Aunt Louisa eagerly.

"Oh, dear . . . I should not have . . . that is, I would rather not discuss them."

"Now, Gillian, you know I have never pried into your affairs—at least, not excessively so—but I wish you would tell me what is troubling you."

Gillian searched her mind for a noncommittal but courteous response. She was not the sort of person to reveal her private thoughts to another—no matter how dear to her that other was. To her surprise, however, what came out was a brittle laugh.

"Would you believe, Aunt? The earl would have me understand that he's enamored of me!"

Aunt Louisa's eyes grew round, and the lace on her cap fairly quivered with excitement. "Oh, my dearest girl, what a wonderful thing! Has he propo—?"

"Oh, of course not, Aunt. Nor do I expect him to. He's just like any other man. Setting his sights on a pretty face, he feels he must make it his own."

"Oh, I don't think so, Gillian. I have seen how he looks at you. You cannot tell me his feelings are not genuine."

Deep within, Gillian felt a flutter of panic. They were,

she knew, approaching the crux of the matter. "Even if that were true, Aunt, he has a commitment elsewhere. In any case, he would certainly not consider a connection with someone of my background."

"Why, that's just nonsense. You are of gentle birth, for heaven's sake. Your father may not have been a lord with status and wealth, but one hears more and more of titled gentlemen marrying to please their hearts rather than their purses."

"All right, Aunt. Let us say for the sake of argument that the Earl of Cordray has tumbled head over heels for an obscure little nobody in the wilds of Cambridgeshire. I'm extremely flattered, to be sure, but—oh, Aunt, have you forgotten Kenneth?"

Her question hung almost visibly in the air while Aunt Louisa stared blankly at her. "Gillian," she said at last, her voice low and wondering. "I know you loved Kenneth. Anyone who looked at the two of you together could not help but be aware of the devotion you shared. "But, my dear, Kenneth is gone. No, hear me out," she added hastily as Gillian lifted a hand in protest. "I have watched you over the years since Kenneth's death, rejecting love and, it sometimes seemed to me, life itself. You know—and please do not mistake my meaning— your uncle and I are supremely grateful that you came to us. But, oh, Gillian, my dear girl, I could not help wondering if in doing so you were using Rose Cottage as an escape—a sort of cave in which you could hide out from the world—or perhaps from your own demons."

Gillian could only stare at her aunt. She had always known that the older woman, though somewhat flighty, possessed a certain shrewd ability to assess human nature. However, she had not realized until this moment how thoroughly her aunt had read her niece's reasons for coming to Rose Cottage.

"Of late," continued Aunt Louisa hesitantly, "I thought—hoped that you were emerging from your slough of despond. It has, after all, been four years since Kenneth died so valiantly in battle. It is time, my dear, to lay the past aside—to get on with your life . . . to—"

Gillian felt she might explode in her despair. The very air seemed to press down on her, combining with her burden of guilt to smother her. She leaped to her feet, preventing Aunt Louisa from finishing a sentiment she did not at all wish to hear.

"How can you say that, Aunt? My only thought in coming to the cottage was to be with you and Uncle. You are the dearest people in the world to me aside from my parents and brothers and sisters. Yes, you are right in that I welcomed the opportunity to be away from my family—for a while. For they, too, despite their disappointment in me, urged me to 'get on with my life,' dropping one eminently suitable male after another in my path. Why can no one understand that I do not want a male—suitable or otherwise? Kenneth was the one and only love of my life, even though . . ." Gillian halted, unable to complete her sentence. She continued in a rush. "And I cannot so much as contemplate loving another."

Aunt Louisa sagged. "Then I suppose there is no more to be said, dearest—except that I hope you will listen with an open mind and an open heart to what the earl has to say. Sometimes," she concluded, "love creeps up on one despite all one's barricades against it. Here, let me help you with that." She reached for the Cheshire brown habit and assisted Gillian in scrambling into it.

Within a few minutes, Cord and Gillian galloped down the drive, the cool morning air bringing a flush to Gillian's cheeks.

"Would you mind?" asked Cord as they rounded the pillar posts that marked the end of the drive. "I have been doing some exploring of my estate on my own, and I'd like to show you my favorite spot so far."

With some misgivings, Gillian nodded and followed Cord as he led her in an opposite direction from the manor house. Their path took them cross-country toward a hilly wooded area just past the home farm. Cord drew to a stop on the crest of one of the highest hills.

"Look!" he exclaimed with a sweeping gesture. "You can see the spires of Cambridge from here. With the woods at one's back and the whole county spread out before one, I think this must be one of the most beautiful spots in all of England. And," he continued, assisting

Gillian to dismount, "the place even boasts an ottoman-sized boulder for our comfort."

To Cord's dismay, Gillian seemed to shrink from his touch, and her back was stiff and resistant as he settled her on the boulder. What did she think he was up to? Did she think he had a spot of rapine planned for this lovely morning? He seated himself beside her, careful not to so much as brush her arm. He was silent for a moment as he gathered together the speech he had crafted in the small hours of the night before.

Chapter Nineteen

"Gillian," Cord began hesitantly, "I must speak with you."

Gillian felt a tide of panic rise within her. "But, we have been speaking," she responded brightly. She turned away from him to face the view from the hilltop. "You are right, Cord. This view is absolutely spectacular. I wonder that I have never—"

"Gillian, please," said Cord in a firmer tone. "Please don't try to put me off again. I merely wish to tell you that I will be leaving Wildehaven in a day or two."

She knew she should be pleased at this news. She needed very badly for the Earl of Cordray to remove himself from her life—and she was pleased, of course, that he had come to a sense of his responsibilities. Why, then, did she feel as though something large and unpleasant had just exploded in the pit of her stomach?

"A day or two?" she asked falteringly.

"Yes. To be sure, there is much I still wish to do here, and I will return at some time in the future to attend to the repairs and improvements that Jilbert has set in motion. However, I feel the need to see about my other estates. They have not been neglected, precisely, for I have an excellent staff, but it has finally been borne on me that there are many matters I should be seeing to myself."

Matters such as his proposal to Corisande, Gillian muttered inwardly, suppressing the tears that rose in her throat. She berated herself. She had kept her emotions firmly in control for the last four years. Why, at this point, was she thrown into a vaporish maelstrom of longing for she knew not what, all over a man for whom she didn't care a button? Not really, at any rate.

She started, as she became aware that Cord was speaking again.

"But I cannot go without telling you how I feel about you, Gillian. Why—what is it?" he blurted as Gillian leapt to her feet.

"Cord, please," she said breathlessly. "Please don't spoil everything."

Cord, too, rose, and she was startled at the expression of pain that flashed in his green eyes. She had convinced herself that, despite his aborted declaration of the other night, Cord had no real feeling for her beyond that of an amatory gentleman and his designated prey of the moment. Could she have been wrong? Oh, please God, surely she could not have been wrong. She *must* not allow him to entertain any stronger emotion for her.

"Spoil everything?" he asked softly. "Is that how you see my feeling for you? An inconvenience that must not be allowed to ruin a sunny morning?"

"No! Of course, I did not mean that, but—" Gillian laughed unsteadily. "I'm sure we both agree that we have enjoyed each other's . . . company. This has been a lovely idyll—for us both, I think, but we have always known that your sojourn here would be brief. In truth," she continued, feeling a little desperate, "I am pleased that you are returning to take up your duties. For, I have seen *such* a difference in you of late—a vitality and sense of purpose—and, yes, a new happiness."

"Yes," he replied seriously. "I am happier than I have been in years in my decision to start living rather than rattling about in a meaningless existence. But—" A tentative smile curved Cord's lips. "It is you who has brought about this metamorphosis—and an undeserved joy to my life."

He took her hand in his. Gillian knew she should have withdrawn it—immediately. When he moved closer, she knew she should have sidled away—immediately. And when he bent his head over hers, she should have avoided the kiss she knew he was about to press on her lips. Instead, she remained motionless. She felt that time had slowed, encasing the two of them in a lovely golden bubble of sunshine and the warm breeze that lifted a midnight feather of hair from Cord's forehead. The humming of the bees and the exultant song of the birds and the scent of leather and soap and Cord filled her senses. She lifted her face to him.

His lips were warm and urgent, moving over hers to create a firestorm of wanting within her. A voice far in the back of her mind cried out that what she was doing was insane. She had meant to discourage Cord, and here she was participating with the utmost enthusiasm in her own ruination!

Unheeding, she pressed closer to him, reveling in the feel of his hands. Dear God, it was as though she wanted to crawl inside his very soul, to absorb him into hers. The voice faded and was silenced, and when Cord's fingers, warm and strong, moved to her breast, she cried her pleasure aloud. It was this sound that made her draw back with a frantic suddenness that almost toppled her to the ground. She found that her knees refused to support her, and she sank back upon the boulder. She put her hands to her hair in a mindless gesture, appalled that she had so lost herself.

Cord felt as though a critical part of his being had just been peeled away. He sank to a seat beside her. Once again, he took Gillian's hand, but this time she snatched it away to knot it almost fiercely in her lap.

"Gillian," he said softly, "after that—I can only call it a communion of spirit—can you honestly say you are indifferent to me?"

"Indifferent?"

Cord quailed before the anguish in her eyes.

"Of course, I am not indifferent! It is just that . . . well, I am not a wanton, after all, and despite the feel-

ings you have no difficulty in calling from me, I do not
wish to . . . join you in this dance to my own downfall."

"Downfall!" Cord could hardly believe his ears. "Is
that what you think? That I seek to ruin you? Do you
think that is what I have been about since we met? I
thank you for your pretty reading of my character,
Miss Tate!"

He could have bitten his tongue. What a cloth-headed
thing to say! Had it not already occurred to him that
Gillian might have come to this conclusion? At their first
meeting, she had seen unerringly through his efforts to
charm her. Why should she see him now as anything but
an unregenerate rake?

He grasped her shoulders, turning her toward him.
"Gillian, listen to me. I will admit that when we met,
my first instinct was to make a conquest. That is the way
I've been living for some time, I regret to say. But as I
came to know you . . ." He drew a deep, shuddering
breath. "Gillian, I love you. I love you with everything
that's in me. I want you to marry me—and come back
to London with me—and then to the Park—and have
my babies—and spend the rest of your life with me. Oh,
God, you have to believe me. I love you!"

Gillian stared at him for a long moment, her eyes wide
and—yes, terrified. He held her gaze, trying to pour his
heart into the clear gray eyes that looked back at him.
The next moment, to his utter dismay, tears welled, first
to sparkle in the thick forest of her lashes, then to spill
down her cheeks.

"Gillian! What is it? What have I said to so distress
you?"

"Oh, Cord, you cannot mean it! You do not love me.
You *cannot* love me!"

"But, what is this?" Cord's forehead creased in bewilderment. "Gillian, I'm offering you my heart—and my
soul and my body and everything else that goes with it.
Is the thought of marriage to me so repugnant?"

He tried for a light tone, but knew he was unsuccessful
in concealing the unhappiness that seemed to fill him
with the bleakness of death itself.

"You're serious!" she choked. "Oh, dear Heaven,
this . . . this *cannot* be!"

He suppressed the urge to pull her to him. Instead, he released her. Reaching into his pocket, he produced a handkerchief and began mopping her cheeks. He forced a smile.

"I'm afraid, my dear, you're going to have to explain that remark. It is becoming painfully clear that you do not reciprocate my artless sentiments, but a simple, 'Thank you, sir, but no thank you,' would suffice."

Gillian gasped. "Oh, Cord, I would not have you hurt for anything in the world—but, no," she sobbed, "I do not love you." She twisted to face him. "Don't you see? You are worthy of any woman's love. It's—" She broke off for a moment, unable to speak, but concluded at last in a low, harsh voice. "It is I who am at fault."

Cord could only gape at her. What the devil . . . ? What was she saying? Had she lain with her beloved Kenneth and now felt herself soiled? Or worse, had she consoled herself in the arms of another man—more than one, perhaps?

Apparently the tenor of his thoughts conveyed itself to Gillian, for she drew away from him a little. She bent a twisted smile on him.

"It is not what you think, my lord earl. I am pleased to tell you—since it seems to matter so greatly—that I am still pure. No, my sin—to my mind at least—was much worse. You see—" She drew in a deep, shuddering breath. "I killed Kenneth."

Again, Cord experienced the feeling that the universe had suddenly tilted on its side. "What!"

Gillian lifted a hand. "Forgive me. I am being unduly melodramatic, I suppose. I did not physically take his life, but I might as well have, for I was wholly responsible for his death."

The world was still tilted sickeningly around him, but Cord took Gillian's hands in his. "Can you tell me about it?" he whispered, barely able to force the words through the lump that had formed in his throat.

Gillian's gaze fell to her lap, where she carefully pleated a fold of skirt in trembling fingers. She said nothing for a long moment, but at last lifted her eyes.

"I have never spoken of this to a living soul," she whispered. "You see, as I think I told you, Kenneth and

I met when his parents moved into the neighborhood. His father, like mine, was a country squire. Our parents became friends almost immediately, and Kenneth and I were thrown together. To tell the truth, I was highly pleased at this turn of events, because Kenneth was such a handsome young man, and universally liked from the start—not just because of his looks, but because he was all that was good in temperament, character and mind. He was gentle and kind, always doing for others. I'm sure you know the sort. People were attracted to him as to a beautiful garden.

"He told me later that he loved me from the first moment we met. He was so openhearted and direct that I became aware of this almost immediately. I could not help but respond. He was so eminently loveable, you see. And, I must admit that there was the extra fillip of being the woman selected by the most sought-after man in the county. I basked in his affection, and when my parents noticed and began to talk of marriage, I fell in with their plans."

"How long did it take this paragon to propose?" asked Cord, unable to contain the acid that seemed to be eating a hole in his heart.

Gillian glanced up at him swiftly. "Not long. Six months after we first became acquainted, he asked me to be his wife. It was a lovely summer afternoon, and we had come out to stroll in the orchard. I said yes, of course, and we sealed our betrothal with a long, loving kiss. Our families were ecstatic when we brought them our news. We made plans for a wedding the following summer."

"A year?"

Gillian faltered. "Y-yes. Kenneth wished to be married right away, but something in me—that is, I told him we should take the time to get to know each other better."

"What nonsense," interposed Cord roughly. "One may recognize one's love in a much shorter time than six months." He forced a painful smile to his lips. "Three weeks, for example, may sometimes suffice."

Gillian hurriedly returned to pleating her skirt. "In any event, Kenneth, with the thoughtfulness that was his

hallmark, bowed to my wishes. I was sure that in time
my love for Kenneth would grow and . . . and mature.
However, as the months passed, I found myself . . . dissatisfied. All at once, the fun seemed to have drained
from Kenneth's soul, to be replaced with a sort of respectful worship. His kisses were warm and tender
and . . . and loving, but they stirred no passion in me.
Dear Heaven, despite his every evidence of devotion, I
wanted more.''

"Not surprisingly," grunted Cord.

Ignoring him, Gillian hurried on. "When he visited me
at home, he behaved with the utmost propriety, laying
kisses on my lips, humbly, like a supplicant seeking favors from his goddess. When he spoke of our married
life, he made it sound somehow dull beyond belief,
dwelling on hours spent by the fire reading to each other
and the years he would spend making my every dream
come true.

"I should have been ecstatic at this evidence of his
devotion, but I was very young—and I wanted sparks to
fly when he kissed me. I wanted him to steal my very
breath. I wanted . . .''

"To know the fire and the fine madness of first love."

Gillian sighed. "I tried flirting with other young men
in hopes of provoking his jealousy, but all he ever did
was smile a sad, sweet smile and tell me he did not
begrudge my liveliness of spirit. It was what he loved
most about me, he said.

"I'm afraid I became petulant. Nothing he did suited
me. His flowers did not go with my dress. The poetry
he wrote to praise my fine eyes was insipid. His plans
for my enjoyment at the fair or a day at the seaside were
too tame by half.

"Arrangements for the wedding proceeded, and as the
time approached I began to experience a kind of panic.
In Kenneth's presence, I exhibited all the maidenly anticipation of a caged she-wolf.''

Cord placed his hand on hers. Her description of her
behavior, so different from the Gillian he knew, was obviously the product of her own self-loathing. Lord he
wished he could assuage her anguish.

"It was inevitable," Gillian continued, "that Kenneth

would notice my obvious change of heart. He even asked one day if I were sure I wished to marry him. If I'd had an ounce of resolution, I would have ended the betrothal right there—with all the tact at my disposal, of course, but still put an end to it. But he stared at me with his great blue eyes, as though preparing himself for a death-blow, and—"

"And you couldn't do it—at least, not then. You succumbed to one of the strongest tyrannies in existence, that of the weak over the strong."

Gillian gasped indignantly. "Kenneth wasn't—" She sagged abruptly. "Well, yes, I suppose he was when it came to me. At any rate, I assured him I was in alt over our coming marriage. But then, I added in what I'm sure was an unpleasant whine, 'Could we not make our wedding journey in Spain or Italy? Papa has said he would gift us, and I'd like to do *something* exciting before we settle down to our lifetime of rural placidity.'

"Kenneth's lips tightened, but he said only that he would look into it."

Gillian paused, and her eyes took on a faraway look.

"At last, however"—she drew in a ragged breath—"though I couldn't end the betrothal at that time, as the wedding date approached, I became panicky. Finally, only a week or so before the ceremony was to take place I took him aside one evening and blurted out in the most tactless manner possible, that I had decided not to marry him after all." Gillian's voice broke. "As I expected, he was devastated, but he made no attempt to change my mind. Instead, he said nothing for a very long time, merely sitting there with his head bowed. At last he rose and thanked me gravely for my honesty—and turned on his heel and walked out the door."

Gillian slumped in her seat, her misery almost palpable.

"There was a tremendous uproar. My parents were appalled, and my friends mystified and angry. Indeed, it seemed the only friend I had left in the whole village was Kenneth. He defended my decision at every turn, and still visited me at my home with steadfast regularity, behaving as a good friend. It was almost as though we had never been betrothed, except that I was aware every moment of his heartbreak."

"I expect he made sure of that," murmured Cord dryly.

"No," Gillian replied, her voice quiet. "Kenneth was not like that."

She drew a long breath. "This was in '13, just when Napoleon was making a strong push in Spain. The war seemed a thousand miles away from our little green paradise in Lincolnshire, but, still, we read the news in the papers.

"A week later, on the day we were to have been wed, word spread around the village that Kenneth planned to join the army. I ran to find him, and he told me that it was true. His father had bought him a pair of colors, and he would be joining the British forces in the Peninsula within the week.

"The village buzzed with shocked disapproval—all aimed at me. My parents were at first dumbstruck, but soon rallied to bewail his decision. They railed at me for driving Kenneth to this disastrous decision. They flew to consult with Kenneth's parents, who were equally appalled. They were furious with Kenneth, but, of course, they were even more furious with me, fully comprehending what had prompted him to take such an action.

"I knew, of course, why he had made this decision. He realized that I thought him dull and wished to prove to me that he could be as dashing and heroic as the next fellow. I tried to dissuade him, but to no avail. Within another week he was gone," Gillian concluded with a whisper.

"It wasn't that I didn't love Kenneth," she wailed. "I did! I loved him—for who could not? I just could not love him in the way a woman should love the man with whom she is prepared to spend the rest of her life. For me there was no fire! I felt no connection with him! And I needed that."

"Of course you did," said Cord. "And I think I am beginning to see where this is leading."

"Yes," replied Gillian dully. "I suppose you are. For, indeed, Kenneth earned his colors. Word filtered back to us of his deeds of courage in battle. Not from him, of course, for though he wrote to me nearly every day, not a word of his heroism filtered through his pen. No, two of the lads from the village were stationed in the same unit as Kenneth, and they faithfully reported his glorious deeds to their families. From whence, of course, they spread round the village like a catchy tune."

"And were you gratified," asked Cord dryly, "that Kenneth was at last living his life with all the passion and verve he had kept hidden from you?"

"Yes—in some dark, despicable corner of my heart." Gillian's voice was harsh and grating. "But I was afraid for him, too. I lived every day in terror that one day he would go too far. That one day he would sally forth with trumpets blazing and never return."

"And that's just what happened." The words came raw from Cord's throat.

"Yes," Gillian replied tonelessly. "He was sent to America after Toulouse, but he said he would be coming home soon. However, Napoleon escaped from Elba, and Kenneth was called back to fight in Belgium. The news came to us that he had died—gloriously—saving the lives of several of his comrades-in-arms at Waterloo."

"And it was all your fault."

At the bitterness in Cord's voice, Gillian lifted a startled gaze. "Yes, of course it was. I had driven him away from me in the cruelest, most callous way imaginable. I had proven myself unworthy of the love of a good man. Everyone in the village made sure I was aware of that fact. Even my best friends hurled reproach at me. Not that I could blame them, of course. There was nothing they could say that I had not cried out in my own mind a thousand times over."

Gillian twisted to face Cord directly.

"Now you know why I chose to come here—to live in relative obscurity. Now you know why I never married."

"I beg your pardon?" Cord asked blankly. "Your story is tragic, but I heard nothing to explain your decision to run away from the world."

Gillian hardly knew what reaction she had expected from Cord—anything from the coldest contempt to a blazing anger. However, his matter-of-fact puzzlement was completely unexpected.

"But—" Gillian sputtered.

"It sounds to me very much as though, despite your efforts to the contrary, you did not love Kenneth. You wisely declined to marry him—even if it was at the last minute. You could hardly know that he would take such a foolish, drastic step in what anyone of sense would have known was a futile effort to generate love where there was none. You loved him as a dear friend, Gillian, and you could do no more."

If Cord had dashed a cup of ice water in her face, Gillian could not have been taken more aback. "What a cold, unfeeling thing to say!" she cried. "You're right. I could do no more—and that was my sin. I was unable to love him, but I made him feel that my lack of response was somehow his fault. I drove him into a course of action completely unsuited to one of his gentle temperament, with, as you say, a tragic result."

Cord took both her hands in his own. "My dear, very dear Gillian," he said gently. "I cannot believe you are serious about all this."

Gillian gasped, but replied shortly, "Dear God, Cord, Kenneth rode off to his death because of me. Don't you see? I proved that I am completely unworthy of his love—or that of any man!" Gillian was dry-eyed now, but her voice was low and hard and desolate as she spoke again. "In addition, I proved that inside I am cold and dead, for, as so many people told me—" She laughed shortly. "Even the vicar strongly implied that since I could not love someone like Kenneth, I must be incapable of love."

Her mouth twisted into a bitter caricature of a smile. "And now, Cord, I trust I have explained to your satisfaction why I do not wish to hear your candy-box words of love or your proposal of marriage. I'm sure it is your earnest wish at this moment to leave me to my tedious reflections, and you have my leave to do so."

For a long moment, Cord stared at Gillian. Pain fairly radiated from her, flaying him with her anguish. She really believed everything she had told him! She thought herself a monster, unloving and unlovable.

Once more, Cord gripped Gillian's shoulders. He forced himself to harden the gaze that bored into hers.

"Gillian, you've just spouted the most arrant nonsense I've ever heard."

In response to her shocked gasp, he slid his hands down her arms to her hands.

"For God's sake, Gillian, one cannot force oneself to love where one's heart is not enjoined. You could no more help *not* returning Kenneth's love than you could help being born with gray eyes. In addition," he continued in a milder tone, "though I must say I feel a sincere pity for Kenneth, for unrequited love is painful in the extreme, it is—well, one might almost say, ludicrous—for a man to attempt to change his character—his personality—even his life—to suit the expectations of another. Gillian, my dearest girl, you must put aside your guilt, for, if there is blame to be laid in Kenneth's tragedy, it must be at his own door."

She merely stared at him as though he were speaking in a foreign language. He tried again.

"You know," he said slowly, "Kenneth's situation was not unique. In the Peninsula, I knew many a fine young lad who had joined up to impress a young lady. Sometimes the stratagem worked beautifully, but in most cases it turned out to be a bad idea. Young Monkton, for example, cut quite a dash, and served honorably, all for the girl he left behind. He used to read parts of her letters aloud. She was most impressed with his shiny brass buttons and his shako and all the rest. However, four months after he arrived in Spain, he received a letter saying she was betrothed to the son of a neighboring squire. Apparently, a swain in hand was better than another fighting in a distant land. Poor Monkton moped about the camp like a miser bereft of his hoard. For some time we feared he might put a period to his existence. It was not long, however, before a pretty young senorita caught his eye—and a few weeks after that, he had difficulty recalling the name of the girl back home."

"Oh, for heaven's sake, Cord," snapped Gillian, "I appreciate what you're trying to do, but Kenneth was not like that. He wasn't a shallow young chub—he was wise and good and steadfast."

"So are many dogs, but one does not fall in love with one's St. Bernard."

Gillian jumped up from her seat on the boulder. "I thank you for your assessment of my behavior—and of Kenneth's character. I cannot believe you would be so unfeeling. I had hoped you would understand, but you persist in applying your arrogant, masculine standards to a situation you obviously cannot understand." She whirled and strode to where Falstaff munched placidly. "If you will excuse me, I have duties that require my attention."

She awaited with obvious anger his necessary assistance in remounting. Cursing himself, Cord hastened to her side.

"Gillian, listen to me," he growled. "I am truly sorry for what happened—to Kenneth, of course, but mostly to you. You have flayed yourself raw, blaming yourself for something that simply was not your fault. You have withdrawn yourself from life. You have no doubt proved yourself invaluable to your aunt and uncle, but in living with them here in the back of beyond, you have dug yourself a hole into which you plunged yourself and pulled it in after you. I cannot help but find your situation a tragic waste."

He gazed at her, creating an anger in his own eyes to match her own. He knew that were he to reveal the pity that roiled within him, her attitude would soften. He realized, however, that this would allow her to fall back into her slough of self-inflicted despair.

"You are still a young woman, Gillian—young and beautiful and vibrant. You deserve a better fate than entombment with a man whose love you could not return." His voice softened. "You deserve to live, my love. You deserve happiness and the right to forge your own path. Perhaps I was wrong in my perception of your feeling for me. I will not importune you to marry me, for I cannot make you love me—any more than Kenneth could. I can only urge you—with all the love I bear for you—to throw off the chains you have worn for so long. Come out of the long winter of your isolation from the world. It is spring, Gillian! A time for hope and renewal. You must—"

He stopped abruptly, aware that he was beginning to sound like a religious tract. He glanced at Gillian. She was not so much as looking at him. She had lifted her hands to the pommel of her saddle, and one knee was raised expectantly. It was as though she had not heard him. Resigned, he cupped his hand for her foot.

Once in the saddle, she wheeled about and cantered off. Cord, atop Zeus, followed. They did not speak on the journey back to the cottage.

By the time they arrived at their destination, Gillian was as exhausted as though she had spent two days on a forced march. She held herself rigid in her saddle, for she felt that at the slightest jar she might simply fly apart in great, jagged shards. Inside, she was a mass of whirling, conflicting emotions. Uppermost in her mind was Cord's astonishing, appalling response to the words she had spoken. She had revealed a secret she had kept buried for four years. She had opened herself to him as she had not done to another living soul. She supposed that it was too much to expect any degree of understanding from him. In fact, she had expected anger—perhaps even denunciation—but his matter-of-fact attitude to what she had done was incomprehensible.

He thought her anguish absurd—unnecessary! He even put the blame on Kenneth! Impossible as it seemed, Cord was angry, not at her indefensible behavior, but at her attempts to deal with the responsibility for destroying another human being. True, Cord had made a career out of avoiding his own responsibilities, but she had thought him changed. Even so, her sin far outweighed a life spent in the pursuit of pleasure. Why could he not understand her anguish? Why could he not understand her reasons for rebuffing his declaration of love?

His declaration of love!

Gillian became abruptly aware that through her private hell, sizzling spurts of happiness had been surfacing for some moments—like bubbles through a stew from a fire beneath. She drew a long, shaking breath, and sent Cord a sidelong glance.

He loved her! He really loved her! He had offered her not the tawdry ribbons of a brief liaison, but the silken ties of a lifelong commitment. He wanted to marry her! She should be displeased that her efforts to dissuade him had been for naught, for she did not want him to love her, after all. He deserved a woman who could love him fully in return, and she was so terribly flawed that . . .

For a moment, she allowed herself to envision marriage to Cord. She imagined the children they could make together—the years spent in maturing together, sharing life's joys and sorrows.

No. It could not be, and she might as well—

Her thoughts were abruptly shattered as she became aware they were approaching the cottage.

"What the devil—?" blurted Cord abruptly, and she followed his gaze to observe a large carriage pulled up before the front door. Even from this distance she could make out the crest emblazoned on its door.

"Oh, my God!" groaned Cord in increasing discomfiture. "They found me."

Gillian whirled to face him. "Who? Who is it, Cord? What are—" She stopped abruptly as comprehension dawned. "Oh, no—don't tell me. Is it—?"

"Yes," replied Cord in a voice of deepest doom. "It's my Aunt Binsted."

Chapter Twenty

Cord swore at some length. At least Gillian assumed that's what he was doing, for he kept the main theme of his remarks under his breath.

"How do you suppose she found you?" she breathed.

Cord sighed gustily. "One would gather the gods are mightily peeved with me."

"But what is she doing here? At the cottage?"

"I suppose—" began Cord, only to interrupt himself with an infuriated, "Oh, my God!"

The object of this new burst of fury became apparent as the front door was flung open and a small, but vocal group of persons catapulted themselves onto the drive.

"Cord!" cried the first of these, Cord's Aunt Binsted, Gillian presumed.

Following her was a stout gentleman of florid complexion and behind him, a tall, slender young man whose raiment proclaimed him a Tulip of the first stare. Accompanying him was a willowy female, fluttering her hands in some distress. Bringing up the rear was a short, stocky man, dressed in a voluminous frieze coat, beneath which peeped a waistcoat of a rather virulent red.

Good God, thought Cord in growing fury. A Bow Street Runner?

The marchioness, appearing to have recovered her dignity, halted. Drawing herself up, she waited for her nephew to dismount and approach her.

It needed only this, thought Cord, to set the seal on one of the most wretched afternoons of his life. He had feared his aunt would catch up to him eventually, but why now? He desperately needed to continue his conversation with Gillian. He could not let her turn away from him in such anger. Now, with his family massing on the horizon, he would not likely get a moment alone with her for hours—if at all.

Wearily, Cord strode toward the little group. Lady Binsted, abandoning her temporary reticence, surged forward. "Cord!" she exclaimed again. "Your people at the manor told us you were here. You wretch! How could you do this? We feared you dead! You left us all in the most appalling bumble broth! And poor Corisande! And all the while you've been here in this snug little bolt-hole, whiling away your time with—" Here she sent a disdainful glance to Gillian, who had accepted Cord's assistance in dismounting and now approached Lady Binsted with a friendly smile.

At this, however, she halted, dropping her outstretched hand. Cord knew an urge to grasp his relative and shake her till her elegant coiffure tumbled across

that patrician nose. "Aunt," he said frigidly, "allow me
to present Miss Gillian Tate. She is—"

"Yes, I know." The marchioness waved a petulant
hand. "I have already met—Oh, here they are."

She turned to acknowledge the presence of Sir Henry
and Mrs. Ferris, who had by now come out to join the
group in front of the house. Sir Henry stepped up to
stand nose to nose with Cord.

"Cord, who the devil are these people? They claim to
be related to you, but I never saw such a gaggle of
bacon-brained jaw-me-deads. If you—"

At this point, Aunt Louisa intruded. "Yes, yes, we
must sort this out, but may I suggest we return to the
parlor? We can't stand out her brangling like village
wives at market."

Wheeling about, she herded her recalcitrant guests
back into the house, and, once having settled them in
the parlor, she rang for tea, her panacea for any ill—
physical, emotional, or social.

"Now then," she continued when order was restored.
She spoke to Cord. "Lady, er, Binsted and her husband—and the rest—appeared here about half an hour
ago, demanding to know—if you would believe—where
we were hiding you!"

This statement brought a fresh outburst from the marchioness, her husband, Wilfred and the Runner. Corisande, as she had since the beginning of this imbroglio,
remained silent.

Cord raised a hand. "Will you all please be still for a
moment?" He spoke quietly, but in a tone Gillian had
never heard him use. Neither, apparently, had Lady
Binsted, for she turned to her nephew with a look of
surprise.

"Yes, of course, Cord," responded Aunt Louisa. "You
will wish to speak with your family in private." She
nudged her brother. "Henry and I will just—"

At her words, Gillian, too, made as though to leave
the room, but Cord interrupted. "No, please. Stay here,
if you would—Sir Henry and Aunt Louisa—and most
especially, Gillian. You are almost my second family,
and I would have you hear what I have to say. Now
then," he continued, his gaze encompassing the intrud-

ers, "first of all, I am aware I owe you"—he looked at Corisande—"all of you—an apology."

"Apology!" snarled Wilfred. "You ought to be horsewhipped."

Cord sent him a startled glance, but made no response. Instead, he turned again to Corisande, who flushed and dropped her gaze. He said then to Lady Binsted, "I am sorry you were put to the trouble of tracking me down here—or rather," he said, staring for a moment at the Bow Street Runner, "hiring someone else to do so."

"Hamish McSorley at yer service, yer lordship," declared the Runner, stepping forward officiously.

"For," said Cord, continuing as though the man had not spoken, "I plan to return to London within the next day or two."

" 'The next day or two!' " screeched the marchioness. "Cord, you will pack your bags and come with us this instant. Your behavior has been intolerable, and I will not—"

She halted abruptly as her nephew bent on her a look of such chill virulence that she quailed.

"As I said," he continued quietly after a moment, "I shall be returning to London, but merely long enough to close Cordray House."

" 'Close Cordray House!' " echoed Lady Binsted again, this time in a faint voice.

"Yes, for I plan to take up residence at The Park for the foreseeable future. There is much to be done there—matters I have neglected for too long."

For once, his aunt was silenced, but Wilfred spoke up again.

"And you have nothing to say to Corisande?" he asked, his face pale.

Cord drew a deep breath. "Yes, I do." He moved to Corisande, who stood to one side, pale but composed. "If I might have a word with you alone, my dear?"

He turned to lead her out of the parlor, but to his astonishment, she resisted his gesture.

"No," she said calmly, adding a moment later in an apparent non sequitur, "there has been a change in your brother's status."

"What?" asked Cord blankly, echoed by Lady Binsted and the marquess.

"Yes," declared Wilfred, smirking slightly. "You shall find my name on the next honors list."

"What?" The question echoed around the room again, this time shaded with a marked astonishment.

"Yes, due to certain, er, delicate favors I have performed for the Regent, His Highness has seen fit to recommend me for a barony. In the future," he added, the smirk more pronounced, "you may address me as Lord Culver. And," he continued, his face becoming quite pink with satisfaction, "very soon, you may address Corisande as Lady Culver."

As one, the group swiveled to face Corisande. They did not say, "What?" again, but the word swirled almost visibly in the air like a startled bird.

Corisande did not take her eyes from Cord's face.

"That's right," she said, adding waspishly, "I apprehend that you wish to take me aside for the proposal you delayed for so long. As you can see, however, you delayed a trifle too long."

For a moment, Cord found it impossible to take in her words. Wilfred? Lord Culver? Corisande—his lady? A wave of relief swept over him, so powerful that he was forced to grip a nearby table in order to prevent himself from falling to the floor in mindless gratitude to whatever gods had taken a hand in his affairs. A small sound caught his ear, and he turned to watch Gillian put her fingertips to her mouth to cover the gasp she had just uttered.

Cord moved to Corisande. He took her hand and covered it with his own. "I wish you happy, my dear." To Wilfred, he said, "And I congratulate you, brother mine, on your new bride—and your new title. I wish you the greatest happiness in both." With which graceful speech, he swiveled to face his aunt once more.

This lady, however, ashen-faced and trembling, had sunk into a settee. Her husband sat beside her, patting her hand in a futile gesture.

"Title?" she quavered. "Married? *Corisande?* B-but, Cord, she was for *you*! All these years . . . the planning . . ." She trailed off dismally.

"Now, now, Bessie," murmured George consolingly. "It's all for the best, I've no doubt."

"Yes, but—"

"Yes," echoed Cord firmly. "Absolutely all for the best." He rubbed his hands together briskly. "And now, may I suggest you all repair to Wildehaven? You are welcome to stay as long as you please, of course, and—"

"No," said Corisande again, with great firmness. To the marquess and marchioness, she declared. "Please do what you wish, my lady—my lord, but as for me—" She turned to grasp the hand of her betrothed. "Oh, Wilfred, take me home, please. Now."

Wilfred, not surprisingly, drew her to him. "Of course, my dearest girl. Only, we have no transportation. Cord?"

Cord opened his mouth to offer a carriage, horses and whatever else might be required to see the new peer and his betrothed on their way. He was forestalled by a now-recovered Lady Binsted.

"Nonsense," she said briskly. "Since you two"—she glared briefly at both the Culver brothers—"are apparently completely lost to your family obligations, I see no point in remaining here any longer. Come, George, we will go home now." To Cord she said, "I shall, of course, begin anew to find a bride for you, Cordray. The Duke of Grantchester's daughter was presented last month. She's a lovely little thing. And then there's Frances Morecombe. She—"

Cord rather regretted throwing a spanner into his aunt's plans, for she had brightened markedly at the prospect of sifting through the marriage mart once more. However, he realized that now was the time for the nipping of buds and halting in tracks.

"That won't be necessary, Aunt. You will be pleased to hear that I plan to marry soon, but I shall choose my own bride."

"Oh, but—" began Lady Binsted, but at the sound of that particular note in his voice, she was silenced. With one last speculative glance at Gillian, she swept from the room with a crackle of silken skirts. The marquess followed in some relief, and Corisande and Wilfred trailed behind them, Corisande's hand resting sedately on Wilfred's arm. Mr. McSorley brought up the rear, displaying the demeanor of a large dog, knowing he is unwelcome but determined to squeeze his way into the proceedings.

Cord and the Folsome family saw them out of the house and into their carriage with appropriate expressions of good will. They watched and waved as the ponderous vehicle lumbered down the drive and onto the road, after which, with relieved sighs, they returned to the house.

"I do apologize," were Cord's first words on re-entering the parlor. He laughed ruefully. "I seem to be doing a lot of that this morning. I rather suspected my family would appear at some time to rein me in, but I had no idea they would pursue me to your front door."

He shot a glance at Gillian, but that lady was busy removing a piece of lint from the sleeve of her riding habit. Aunt Louisa chuckled.

"Think nothing of it, dear boy. We were pleased to make their acquaintance—and their arrival enlivened our morning. Not that we needed enlivening after Henry's discovery."

She shot a look at her brother, who had sunk into a wing chair and was now staring ahead of him in a fit of distraction. "Henry?"

Sir Henry jerked to attention. "I have been thinking," he said without preamble, "about the diary. As I said, I must go into Cambridge—to speak with Mr. Neville." He paused for a moment. "On consideration, I have decided not to attempt the translation of the diary myself."

"Henry!" gasped Aunt Louisa, echoed by Cord and Gillian.

"But, after all your work! Your study! You have earned—"

"Yes, my dear. I have earned the right. However, young John Smith has also worked very hard. If it were he who had stumbled on to the *Tachygraphy,* I'm sure he would have made the connection.

"I have enjoyed a long and productive career. John is just starting on his. In addition," he said with a small smile, "the translation itself will no doubt prove tedious. I enjoyed the challenge, but now I'm ready to move on to something else. In fact," Sir Henry continued, steepling his fingers before him, "I've been hearing a great deal lately about the stone found several years ago in Egypt—near Rashid, or as they're calling it now, Rosetta. I am no expert in the field of Egyptian study, of course, but I am, I think I may say in all modesty, skilled in letters. Perhaps I could aid—Thomas Young, I think his name is—in the translation of what will no doubt become a cornerstone in our understanding of that ancient land."

Ignoring the faint moans issuing from his nearest and dearest, he added, "I'm afraid I have not quite the nobility of spirit to let John take all the credit. I shall inform Neville that I have hit on the method of translating the diary, after which—again with your permission, Cord— I'll hand over the *Tachygraphy* to him, to be passed on to John. I shall, of course, be happy to lend my assistance, but I'll stay in the background."

"Oh, Uncle," breathed Gillian, moving to embrace Sir Henry. "How very good you are. This will mean so much to John."

"Well," added Aunt Louisa with a sniff, "I suppose it will be all right—as long as you get the credit for discovering the translation, Henry," she concluded severely.

Sir Henry laughed. "I'll get it in writing, m'dear. If you will excuse me for a moment—"

He left the room to return a moment later, a single sheet of paper in his hand.

"I worked for a little while this morning on the first page of the first volume, which I transcribed some time ago." Reverently, he lifted the paper in his hands like an acolyte making an offering. "Would you like to hear it?"

In response to their unanimous assent, Sir Henry read:

January 1. 1659/60 Lords=day
　　This morning (we lying lately in the garret) I rose, put on my suit with great skirts, having not lately worn any other clothes but them.
　　Went to Mr. Gunnings church at Exeter-house, where he made a very good sermon upon these words: That in the fullness of time God sent his son, made of a woman, &c. shewing that by "made under the law," is meant his circumcision, which is solemnised this day.
　　Dined at home in the garret, where my wife dressed

> *the remains of a turkey, and in the doing of it she*
> *burned her hand.*
>
> *I stayed at home all the afternoon, looking over my*
> *accounts.*
>
> *Then went with my wife to my father's; and in going,*
> *observed the great posts which the City hath set up at*
> *the Conduit in fleet-street.*

Sir Henry let out a long breath, like a great "Amen,"
and glanced about.

"Not quite what you would call an earthshaking insight into the Restoration," he said huskily after a moment, "but, behold Mr. Sam Pepys discoursing on life in
London almost two hundred years ago."

Mrs. Ferris said nothing, but reached to touch her
brother's hand, her eyes bright with happy tears. Gillian,
watching, felt her own throat tighten. She was so very
happy for her uncle, she reflected, and to think that the
realization of his dreams had come about because of . . .
She glanced at Cord. This proved to be a strategic error,
for at the same moment he was looking at her. She felt
his gaze as though she were being washed in a tropical
sea, and she looked away, flushing.

Dear Lord what was she to do about him? About the
treacherous weakness he had created in her defenses?
She was honest enough to admit that she wanted nothing
more than to acquiesce in his declared desire for her.
The idea of spending the rest of her life with him was
like looking through the gates of Heaven into an impossible vision of bliss. Conversely, she thought dismally,
the concept of life without him was almost too painful
to contemplate.

She reminded herself that she had lived for six-and-
twenty years without the exhilarating pleasure of Cord's
company. She could exist without him for the years remaining to her. What she could not do was ruin both
their lives by marrying him.

For she knew that what she felt for Cord was not love.
It was an infatuation, and as sure as apple blossoms in
May, the "fine madness" that Cord had spoken of earlier
would dissipate. She knew with perfect clarity that Cord
was not the pattern of virtue that Kenneth had been. If

she could not love Kenneth, how could she possibly expect to love Cord, with all his imperfections? She, too, was flawed, of course, and Cord would soon tire of seeking love where there was none to find.

She jerked to attention, aware that Uncle Henry had donned his coat, preparatory to his trip into Cambridge. Clutching the *Tachygraphy* in his hand, the elderly academic accepted the further congratulations of his little family and his good friend. In a moment he had left the cottage and clambered aboard his gig, waving jubilantly as he clattered off down the drive.

Waving in response through the window, Aunt Louisa extended an invitation to Cord for luncheon.

"No, I cannot stay, Mrs. Ferris, thank you," he replied courteously. "I must return to Wildehaven, for I have an appointment with Mr. Jilbert. I shall return tomorrow, however. Would you see me out, Gillian?" he asked after a moment.

Inwardly, Gillian flinched, but she replied coolly, "Of course, Cord."

She led the way from the parlor to the hall and out the door. Once outside, Cord laid his hand on her arm. Why, she wondered absently, when his touch warmed her down to her fingertips, did the contact make her shiver?

"Gillian," began Cord, "I cannot leave with matters in such chaos between us."

"Please, Cord." Gillian strove to keep her voice from trembling. "Don't say any more. There is nothing between us—nor can there ever be."

For several moments, Cord stared down at her in silence. When he spoke at last, his voice was ragged. "Just let me say one more thing. Even if I subscribed to the absurd notion that you were somehow responsible for Kenneth's death, it all happened four years ago. You are not the same person you were then. Just because you attempted love once and failed does not mean you must live without love forever. Gillian, I believe there is something—something precious between us. You say you do not love me, but I'm not sure I believe you—or that you believe it yourself. I know that I love you, and

I believe there is a chance for us to build a life together. I beg you not to throw it away."

Gillian struggled for the words to disabuse Cord of his tragic fallacy. "Cord, I am honored—more than I can say—by your words, but . . . don't you see? There is something lacking in me—something basic. Whatever I feel for you—and, oh yes, I do feel something—it is not love. It's . . . oh, I don't know . . . a temporary infatuation or possibly pure lust." A twisted grimace curved her lips. "I suppose the male sex is not the only one to be afflicted with that malady. "In any event—"

"For God's sake, Gillian. Are you going to let one incident color your whole outlook on life—and love?"

"Believe me, Cord," replied Gillian in a low voice. "Once was enough to convince me of the truth of my words."

She backed away from him. "We have spoken enough, I think. I know I am right, and I will not embark on the ruination of your life and mine."

Cord stared at her, and Gillian felt flayed by the pain and yearning she saw in his eyes. He spoke at last in a voice she barely recognized as his.

"Then you are right. There is no more to say. I bid you good day, Miss Tate."

He started to turn away, but halted abruptly, and now his changeable eyes glittered like sea-washed pebbles. "In fact, since there seems to be little point in my remaining in the vicinity, I might as well bid you goodbye. I shall return to London tomorrow."

He stood for a moment, as though waiting, but Gillian summoning all the will power at her disposal, merely nodded.

"I'll leave at daybreak," Cord said. He turned again, and this time moved straightaway to mount Zeus. With a slight lift of his hand, he wheeled about and galloped down the drive.

In a few moments, he was gone from sight, but for many moments, Gillian stood in the sunshine, alone, staring at the path he had just taken.

Chapter Twenty-one

Cord did not return immediately to Wildehaven. Instead, he rode, directionless, for some time before halting abruptly. Looking around blankly, he realized that he had come to the hilltop to which he had brought Gillian this morning. It seemed like a hundred years ago. He dismounted and walked a few paces along the rise, staring unseeing at the beauty of the Cambridgeshire landscape.

How could he have been so stupid? The hedonistic Earl of Cordray, known throughout the realm for his conquests, had fallen victim to a pair of laughing gray eyes and a beguiling smile—whose owner had turned him down cold. The situation would be laughable, if it didn't hurt so much. He had been so sure she returned his love. Even when she spoke of her fatal flaws and cruel betrayals, he had felt that deep down she knew she was talking nonsense. That she would, in the end, nestle into his arms to stay forever.

Should he have taken hope from her declaration that he had stirred something within her? Perhaps he should not have left so abruptly. Perhaps—

No. If Gillian really loved him, she would not have let the ghost of a dead lover and an imagined transgression bind her in its unhealthy fetters. He saw no alternative than to take her at her word. She felt something for him—but it wasn't love.

He would leave Wildehaven tomorrow.

Would he ever see her again? Possibly, for he would visit Wildehaven again. Would she still be at Rose Cottage? Would she want to see him? Was there a hope that in some distant future Gillian's perceived guilt might fade? That she would let him into her heart?

He rather thought not. She was honored, she had said. Perhaps, but it was apparent she was not moved. Gillian Tate did not now and would never love him.

The words seemed to echo within the great emptiness that filled him, tolling like a death knell. He had never felt so lonely—or so desolate. He had become revitalized during his stay at Wildehaven, having come to the realization that he must repair his life. He had been exhilarated at the idea of sharing that life with Gillian. Now, he merely wondered how he was to get through it at all. Unutterably weary, he remounted Zeus and moved off toward the manor house and his unappealing future.

At Rose Cottage, Gillian returned to the parlor, where she sank into a settee and remained motionless, unable to think or feel beyond the desolation that filled her. Aunt Louisa found her here at length.

"Why, Gillian! Whatever are you doing? I thought you with Cord. Has he left? It is too bad he could not stay—but, we will see him tomorrow."

"No," said Gillian quietly.

"I beg your pardon, dear?"

"No," said Gillian again, speaking with great effort. "Cord will not come here tomorrow. He will be leaving in the morning—at first light."

"What? But I don't understand. He said—"

"I know what he said, Aunt," Gillian said tightly, "but he will not be returning here."

The tears that had welled in her eyes could no longer be contained. Gillian rose hastily and turned toward the door, but she was stayed by her aunt's hand on hers.

"Gillian," she said in a firm voice. "Sit down. Now."

Gillian attempted to free her hand, but Aunt Louisa was not to be denied. Slowly, Gillian sank back in her chair, passing her arm swiftly over her eyes.

"And you let him leave?" It was not really a question, but Gillian nodded wordlessly.

"Oh, my dearest child," sighed Aunt Louisa. "How could you have done yourself such an ill?"

"Aunt!" exclaimed Gillian through her tears, "you don't understand."

"Perhaps I don't, dear," the old lady replied gently. "But do you mind if I hazard a guess?"

Searching in her pocket for a clean handkerchief, Gillian did not answer. Aunt Louisa produced one and handed it to her. "Cord asked you to marry him, I take it—and you refused."

"Yes, but—oh, Aunt, I cannot marry a man I do not love, after all." Gillian's cheeks were wet with tears now, and she dabbed at them futilely.

Aunt Louisa's brows lifted. "But of course you love him," she said with a smile. "And he loves you. The two of you have been smelling of April and May since— oh, I don't know—shortly after he arrived her. Even Henry noticed."

"You are mistaken, Aunt. I cannot speak for Cord, but—oh, very well, I admit I am st-strongly attracted to him, but—and this I know only too well—I do not love him. The tender emotion, you see, is not for me," she added bitterly.

The old woman said nothing for a moment, but at last said vehemently, "What nonsense!"

Her words so closely mirrored what Cord had said earlier, that Gillian could only stare.

"Gillian, listen to me." Aunt Louisa, grasped both of her niece's hands in her own. "I have never spoken of this because, well, I felt it was not my place, but—I could not help grieve at the way you have hidden yourself from the world since Kenneth's death."

Gillian gasped, but Aunt Louisa continued hurriedly. "Yes, I know I have spoken of *that* before. But as to the reason for your flight from reality . . ." She paused again for a moment before continuing. "I never knew Kenneth well. I met him only on the few occasions when I visited my sister—your mother—at your home. I must say he seemed a wonderful young man, and it was obvious he was besotted with you. It was equally obvious," she added tartly, "at least to me, that you did not return his affection."

Gillian eyed her aunt in growing concern, but still said nothing.

"I think if Annabelle and your papa had not been so ecstatic at the prospect of your marrying such a fine young man, with such excellent prospects, they would have noticed, too. Although, I must say, you made a supremely successful effort to give the impression to those around you—including Kenneth—and, I think, yourself, that you reciprocated Kenneth's feeling for you, although perhaps that latter effort was *not* so successful."

At this, Gillian grew rigid. She withdrew her hands from her aunt's grasp, but did not move as the old lady continued.

"I'll never forget one afternoon, when you scoffed at Kenneth for refusing to join in a wager—something about jumping across some river on horseback. The project was obviously impossible, and Kenneth refused to endanger either his horse or himself in such a foolhardy exercise. You seemed to feel only contempt at what to most of the rest of us seemed like his sensible behavior. Instead of telling you not to be such an idiot, however, Kenneth merely accepted your taunts in silence—with a sort of sad smile that, frankly, made me want to hit him."

"Dear Lord," murmured Gillian. "I remember that. I knew at the time I was being completely unreasonable, but I was driven by a mindless desire for Kenneth to show some spirit. How I berated myself afterward."

"At any rate, I never once saw you look at Kenneth the way I've seen you look at Cord." Aunt Louisa smiled at Gillian, her wrinkles deepening in understanding.

"I was disappointed, though not altogether surprised, when word came to us just before the wedding that it would not take place after all. And when, a few weeks later, Kenneth hared off to the Peninsula, I could not believe he would be such a looby as to think he must somehow prove himself to you."

"Aunt!" cried Gillian. She could not believe the casual cruelty of one she knew to be the kindest of creatures.

"Gillian, Kenneth was very dear to you. You loved him as a friend—everyone did. I certainly did. But how could any woman love a man who would try to change everything that made him who he was, simply to mold himself to the expectations of another?"

Again, Aunt Louisa's words so closely echoed those of Cord's that Gillian could only stare.

"I speak too intemperately. Many women could have loved Kenneth for what he was. You could not. Nor, I must say, could I. You never knew your Uncle Ferris, my dear, but he was a fine figure of a man. He knew his own mind and followed his own path—and sometimes left me to scramble after him as best I could. Let me tell you, though, Gillian, I reveled in the chase!"

Aunt Louisa's gaze had taken on a faraway look, but now, with a blush, she faced Gillian once more.

"All I am saying, dearest, is that you must not feel guilty about Kenneth's shortcomings. He made his own decision in the end—and, who knows? If the Lord had stayed His hand, he might have come home a hero, and perhaps you would have committed the even greater error of marrying the poor devil, thus ruining the lives of two good people.

Her features grew stern in the face of Gillian's shocked expression.

"The point here, is that, while you did not love Kenneth, it is my belief that you do love Cord. Gillian, real love is God's greatest gift to us foolish humans, and it is not given to us so often that we can afford to toss it aside like an unacceptable piece of cloth at market. My dear, *dear* Gillian, do not allow this opportunity to slip through your fingers. If you have an ounce of good sense—and I know that you do—you will run after Cord and grab him with both hands and never let go."

Gillian made no response, but gazed blindly into the increasing darkness of late afternoon. Aunt Louisa said nothing more, but at last rose from the seat she had taken next to Gillian.

"I shall leave you now, my dear child, but do think about what I have said."

At this, Gillian lifted her head. "Thank you, Aunt," she murmured brokenly. "You are very good. It's just that I . . ." She lifted a hand, unable to complete her thought.

Aunt Louisa nodded and whisked herself from the room with a rustle of her voluminous skirts. Gillian remained motionless for many minutes, until at last the serving girl came in to light the candles against the thickening darkness.

Knowing that Uncle Henry would be returning soon, Gillian rose. She wished to welcome him, of course, after what had no doubt been a triumph for the old gentleman, but she simply could not participate in an evening of celebration. Sending her aunt a message via the serving girl, she climbed the stairs slowly, determined to spend the rest of the evening in her chamber.

At Wildehaven, Cord had finished his instructions to Moresby and Hopkins regarding his imminent departure.

"Very good, my lord," Hopkins had replied imperturbably to the intelligence that his master wished to be packed and ready to leave early the following morning. He shot a sidelong glance at Moresby.

The two had established a certain camaraderie during his lordship's visit to the manor, though, of course it was beneath Hopkins's dignity to declare an actual friendship with one so far beneath him.

"Hunh," mused Moresby later, when the two sat at Mrs. Moresby's scrubbed kitchen table to indulge in a convivial tankard. "What bug do ye suppose his lordship got up his arse to lope off to London so sudden?"

"Well," responded Hopkins in the tone of one who knew very well the workings of his master's mind, "I can only say this. I've rarely seen his lordship in such a taking—and all over a lady!" He shook his head in disbelief.

"A lady? Miss Tate? Sits the wind in that quarter, eh? Me and the missus was wondering about that just the other day. She said she hadn't never seen Miss Tate in such a frustration over a gentleman. 'You mark my words, Moresby,' she said. 'We'll have a wedding hereabouts before the cat can lick her ear.'"

Hopkins snorted. "Doesn't look much like it now, does it?"

Moresby drained a healthy measure of ale. "Ah, well then." He sighed gustily. "The course of true love don't ever run smooth, does it?"

To this, Hopkins deigned to nod in agreement.

Upstairs, Cord readied himself for bed. All evening he had been trying to work up in himself an anticipation of the plans he would set in motion when he returned to London. He could not, however, escape the depression that had seeped into his very bones.

He was sure he would not be able to sleep, but such was his weariness, that he fell into a deep slumber almost the moment after he blew out his bedside candle. He woke early, however, and knew he would not be able to recapture his repose. After a few moments spent in unpleasant reflections, he slid from his bed and donned the garments Hopkins had laid out for him the night before.

Unwilling to wake his man or the other servants betimes, he scribbled a note instructing Hopkins to drive the curricle to London later in the day with his luggage. Cord left his chamber quietly. He would travel to London the way he had come, on horseback. He moved to the stable, saddled Zeus and cantered from the stable yard.

The sky was barely tinged with gray in the east when he crested the rise from which he had first seen Wildehaven those three or so weeks ago. He drew on Zeus's reins and turned to look back at the manor house. Dear God, he hated to go. For he was leaving some critical part of himself behind. His heart, he supposed he would say if he were one of those maundering poets who spoke of love as though they had the slightest notion of what they were talking about.

"Good-bye, Gillian," her whispered.

He upbraided himself harshly. He'd be sobbing like a girl in a moment. He grasped the reins once more, but before he could wheel Zeus about, his attention was caught by a flash of movement beyond the house and somewhat to the west. He observed a horse and rider emerge from a small spinney crowning a nearby hill. Silently, they slid through the shadows into the faint early light of day before disappearing into a winding dale. The rider was slender, seeming too small for her mount, a huge, long-tailed gray.

Cord's breath caught, and his heart leapt into his throat. Was it . . . ? No—he must be—Yes, by God, it was—! Spurring Zeus, he galloped toward the small fig-

ure, still some distance from the house, but headed unerringly in that direction.

The sound of her own hoofbeats masked his until he
was within a hundred yards of her, but when she lifted
her head at last, she swung her horse about and raced
toward him, halting to dismount only when Zeus and
Falstaff were nearly nose to nose. Cord, too, leaped from
the saddle and, running to her, caught Gillian in his
arms.

"Cord!" She was half laughing, half sobbing. "I did
not know you would be leaving so early! Thank God, I
caught you. Oh, Cord! Don't go! Don't go away from
me!"

His only answer was to crush her mouth beneath his
in a kiss that held all the anguished yearning of the night
he had just spent. Nothing in all his experience had ever
felt so good as the curve of Gillian's back against is hand
or the satin slide of her hair through his fingers. He
could say nothing. He could only pour out his feelings
against her lips. At last, he lifted his head to gaze at her.

"I am taking your appearance here at this moment,"
he said gravely, "as an indication that your sentiments
have undergone a change since yesterday."

In answer, she reached up to take his face in her two
hands and pull him to her. This time it was she who
initiated a kiss that sent any doubts he might have had
scurrying to the stars that still twinkled palely above
them.

"To reply to your question, sir," she breathed at last,
"my sentiments have undergone no change at all. It is
simply that yesterday I was too stupid to realize what
they were. It wasn't until the clock struck four a little
while ago that this epiphany finally struck. Remembering
your stated intention of leaving at the crack of dawn
today, I leapt out of bed immediately in hopes that I
could intercept you." Her eyes, smoky and mysterious,
smiled up at him. "Cord, can you forgive me for my
buffle-headedness? I do love you so," she concluded
simply.

At her words, Cord felt his breath leave him; which
fortunately did not preclude his kissing her once more,
tenderly and with great thoroughness.

"My dearest—my only love," he murmured into the scented silk of her hair, "you have just returned my life to me." He pulled back a little to look at her. "Just to make certain that I truly understand you, are you saying that you will marry me?"

"Yes. When?"

Cord gave a shout of laughter, and grasping her about the waist, swung her feet off the ground in great circles.

"As soon as it can be arranged, my darling." He set her upright once more. They began to move toward the manor house, leading their mounts. "You do not have to tell me anything you don't wish to," he said hesitantly. "But, what changed . . . er, what brought you to the realization of your deathless passion."

Gillian sighed. "I'm not sure. A combination of things, I guess. My first reaction to all that you said yesterday was to reject it out of hand. But I thought long and hard about everything. Then, later, Aunt Louisa gave me a piece of her mind."

"Aunt Louisa!"

"Yes, I never realized what a cunning old file she is. I had never disclosed to her my . . . feelings for Kenneth, but she had, unbeknownst to me come to a close summary of what I was going through. A great deal of what she said was a repetition of your opinions."

"My harshly stated opinions. I'm sorry to have grieved you so, Gillian."

She smiled tremulously. "No, my love. It was exactly what I needed to hear. I pondered your words—and Aunt Louisa's—and at last I looked into my heart. I realized finally—in the wee hours of the morning—that I'd been a complete fool. Kenneth was a good man—a sweet, kind, gentle man—but he wasn't the man for me. If I'd been honest, with him as well as myself, I would have never agreed to marry him, let alone led him such a dance. On the other hand, if he'd been honest, too, he would have told me to go find some other man to bedevil.

"His death was a tragic, useless sacrifice, for which the expectations of a number of persons were to blame—mine, Kenneth's, our parents and even our friends. I am desperately sorry Kenneth is dead, but, as Aunt Louisa said, if he had returned, I might have compounded the tragedy by marrying him."

Gillian sighed and turned again to Cord. "In short, I arrived—at last—at a point where I can put the whole sad episode behind me."

Cord blew out a sigh that seem to expel all his doubts and disappointments. "May the poor fellow rest in peace," he declared solemnly and in all sincerity. He bent to kiss Gillian once more, an activity that proved so pleasant that he was compelled to repeat it.

Gillian pulled away from him at last.

"Cord, instead of continuing on to Wildehaven, would you mind if we returned to the cottage? Aunt and uncle will still be in their beds, but I don't think they'd mind being roused for a bit of good news."

"If I know Sir Henry, he's probably been up this hour and more, working on the diary a bit more before he turns it over to John."

Gillian chucked. "I'm sure you're right. In fact, he will no doubt be highly incensed at our interrupting him with such a triviality as a betrothal announcement."

"For which Aunt Louisa will put him firmly in his place."

"Lord, yes. Our news will take first priority with her. You know," she added mischievously, "she had you staked out for me almost the moment you walked in the front door of Rose Cottage."

Cord clapped a hand to his forehead. "I knew it! Another scheming female!"

"Yes, indeed. Ah, the curse of being wealthy and titled—and absolutely lovable," she finished softly.

"How I've suffered all my life," murmured Cord, bending to affirm this assessment by his beloved.

"I am so very glad we have no more secrets buried between us," Gillian declared rather breathlessly at last. "No more revelations of a misspent past. And," she added with a chuckle, "most important of all—at least to one member of my family—no more codes to be discovered."

"Ah, the diary. I wondered when we would come to that. Let me tell you, my love, that in the event your uncle—fine fellow though he is—decides to dip his scholarly fingers into the Egyptian stone translation he will have to look elsewhere for help. For I shall be much too busy to involve myself."

Gillian sent him a sidelong glance. "You mean setting about all the tasks you've neglected for so long."

"Yes, of course. That and starting in on those off-spring I spoke to you about awhile back."

At this, Gillian sent him another glance, this one filled with such warmth and promise that Cord was obliged to kiss her again—several times. At length, Gillian withdrew, flushed and laughing.

"I think we'd best be on our way, love. Enticing as the idea sounds, I think we should not start on that particular project right this minute."

"No," sighed Cord regretfully. "But I suggest an early wedding."

They remounted their horses at last, and turning, trotted toward Rose Cottage, into the dawn.

Author's Note

History credits young John Smith of St. John's College, Cambridge University (afterwards Rector of Baldock in Hertfordshire) with the translation of Pepys's diary, which was published in 1825. Although Lord Grenville seems to have been involved with breaking the code, it is not clear who made the actual connection between Mr. Pepys's shorthand and the Shelton system of tachygraphy. Therefore, the author feels no qualms in creating a story of it-might-have-happened-like-this.